PENGUIN BOOKS

SATURDAY NIGHT AT THE
LAKESIDE SUPPER CLUB

J. Ryan Stradal is the author of *New York Times* bestseller *Kitchens of the Great Midwest* and national bestsellers *The Lager Queen of Minnesota* and *Saturday Night at the Lakeside Supper Club*. His writing has appeared in *The New York Times*, *The Wall Street Journal*, *The Guardian*, *Granta*, *The Rumpus*, and the *Los Angeles Review of Books*. His debut, *Kitchens of the Great Midwest*, won the American Booksellers Association Indies Choice Award for Adult Debut Book of the Year. Born and raised in Minnesota, he now lives in California with his family.

Praise for *Saturday Night at the Lakeside Supper Club*

"Stradal serves up another saga of food and family, hurt and healing, pitched between cliff-hanger moments . . . that make the pages fly." —*People*

"In his previous two novels . . . J. Ryan Stradal writes fetchingly of three lovely things: inventive food, craft beer, and Minnesota. [*Saturday Night at the Lakeside Supper Club*] possesses these same ingredients with added dashes of grief, estrangement, resignation, and love. In other words, it's everything on the menu." —*Star Tribune*

"Stradal . . . displays his gift for writing female characters who are fully realized, sometimes unlikable, but always as flawed and compelling as real people. . . . A loving ode to supper clubs, the Midwest, and the people there who try their best to make life worth living." —*Kirkus Reviews* (starred review)

"Stradal's novels . . . always resonate. . . . He explores universal themes: love, loss, regrets for one's past mistakes, and longings for what might have been—plus, of course, the importance of family." —*Publishers Weekly*

"An interwoven narrative that feels heartfelt and true, suffused with affection for this place and its people past and present. I can't wait for my next trip back home to Stradal's Minnesota." —Bookreporter.com

Praise for *The Lager Queen of Minnesota*

"This charmer of a tale is a loving ode to the Midwest. . . . Warm, witty, and . . . complex, the saga delivers a subtly feminist and wholly life-affirming message." —*People*

"In Stradal's follow-up to his bestselling debut, *Kitchens of the Great Midwest*, the Minnesota native's energetic prose once again captures the optimism of the heartland." —*Time*

"A pleasure to read and the perfect pick-me-up on a hot summer day." —*The Washington Post*

"Delightfully intoxicating . . . will make you smile with its droll humor." —*USA Today*

"This [book] could cement J. Ryan Stradal as the King of Midwestern novels." —*Entertainment Weekly*

Praise for *Kitchens of the Great Midwest*

"An impressive feat of narrative jujitsu . . . that keeps readers turning the pages too fast to realize just how ingenious they are."

—*The New York Times Book Review* (Editor's Pick)

"A sweet and savory treat." —*People*

"The blend of humor, warmth, and longing that [Stradal] uses to portray family relationships makes the book insightful and endearing. Savor it page by page."

—Oprah.com

"A terrific reminder of what can be wrested from suffering and struggle—not only success, but also considerable irony, a fair amount of wisdom, and a decent meal."

—Jane Smiley, *The Guardian*

"A tender coming-of-age story with a mix of finely rendered pathos and humor."

—*The Washington Post*

Saturday Night

≈ at the ≈

Lakeside
Supper Club

J. Ryan Stradal

PENGUIN BOOKS

PENGUIN BOOKS
An imprint of Penguin Random House LLC
penguinrandomhouse.com

First published in the United States of America by Pamela Dorman Books/Viking,
an imprint of Penguin Random House LLC, 2023
Published in Penguin Books 2024

A Pamela Dorman/Penguin Book

ISBN 9781984881090 (paperback)

THE LIBRARY OF CONGRESS HAS CATALOGED THE HARDCOVER EDITION AS FOLLOWS:

Names: Stradal, J. Ryan, author.
Title: Saturday night at the Lakeside Supper club : a novel / J. Ryan Stradal.
Description: New York : Pamela Dorman Books/Viking, [2023]
Identifiers: LCCN 2022039043 (print) | LCCN 2022039044 (ebook) |
ISBN 9781984881076 (hardcover) | ISBN 9781984881083 (ebook)
Subjects: LCGFT: Novels.
Classification: LCC PS3619.T7224 S28 2023 (print) | LCC PS3619.T7224 (ebook) |
DDC 813/.6—dc23/eng/20220829
LC record available at https://lccn.loc.gov/2022039043
LC ebook record available at https://lccn.loc.gov/2022039044

Printed in the United States of America
1st Printing

DESIGNED BY MEIGHAN CAVANAUGH

For Auden,

if he so chooses

Saturday Night
≈ at the ≈
Lakeside Supper Club

One

Mariel, 1996

Mariel Prager believed in heaven, because she'd been there once, so far. She'd like to report that it looks an awful lot like Minnesota. The next best place to heaven, in her experience, was a type of restaurant found in the upper Midwest called a supper club. When she walked into a good one, she felt both welcome and somewhere out of time. The decor would be old-fashioned, the drinks would be strong, and the dining experience would evoke beloved memories, all for a pretty decent price.

SINCE SHE WAS A KID, Mariel had spent countless days at Floyd and Betty's Lakeside Supper Club on scenic Bear Jaw Lake, Minnesota. The place wasn't particularly scenic itself, just a one-story brown wooden building with bright red front doors and tall windows on the side facing the lake. The sign outside read FINE DINING AT A FINE VALUE SINCE 1919, and because everyone trusts neon, fulfilling that promise was the duty of the owner, which, for the past two weeks, had been Mariel. On her watch, a proper supper club meal began with a free relish tray and basket of bread, followed by a round of brandy old-fashioneds, and then a lavish amount of hearty cuisine, with fish on Fridays, prime rib on Saturdays, and grasshoppers for dessert.

BEFORE HE DIED, Mariel's grandpa Floyd had told her that she was ready to take over sole ownership, but this morning, she wished that someone else—*anyone* else—were in charge instead. After locking the front door of her house, Mariel wanted to hurl her body into the lake and float away.

For a long time, she'd simply managed the Lakeside's bar. It was a job she'd kept since becoming the owner, because it was the greatest watering hole in the north. It was loud and smoky, her hands were never dry, she never sat down, and she loved it. Every summer weekend, the horseshoe-shaped bar and its wood-paneled lounge were packed with people fresh from fishing boats and softball games and cars that had driven up from the Cities. It was a place where people chose to be on the most memorable nights of their lives, and it was a pleasure to be at the center of it all.

After what happened last night, though, she wasn't up for any of it, but that didn't matter. If she wasn't standing behind the bar when it opened at 5:00 p.m., people would talk.

. . .

MARIEL'S QUIET, PEACEFUL COMMUTE to work had always been her favorite part of the day. From door to door, it took exactly fifty-four seconds—the time it takes to make a perfect old-fashioned—to walk at an ordinary pace down her driveway, across a county road, up the gravel shoulder, and into the paved parking lot. It had her two favorite smells, the sharp, earthy tang of pine trees on one end, and the stubborn mix of stale cigarette smoke and fry grease on the other, smells she'd always associated with belonging and pleasure. If she spotted an animal en route, she'd give it a name, like that day, when she saw a squirrel she named Pronto. Most important, if she could make it from home to the supper club without any interruption, it'd be a good day, guaranteed. The day before, her husband, Ned, stopped her in the driveway to kiss her before he left for the weekend, and it had been the worst day in a long time.

That morning, Mariel almost made it. She was a few steps into the Lakeside's parking lot when someone ruined her day.

"Mariel!" a woman's voice bellowed from a white station wagon. It was Hazel, the oldest of her regulars from the bar.

Mariel sighed, and turned to face her. "How ya doing, Hazel?"

"Better than I deserve," Hazel replied. "So, where'd you go last night? You just up and vanished on us."

"I was feeling sick, so I went home early." That's all Hazel needed to know.

"Oh, jeez. Food poisoning?"

Mariel just decided to nod.

Hazel responded with a brief, exaggerated grimace. "Well, you look all right today. By the way, nice T-shirt."

Mariel had to look down to remember what she was wearing. It was a Bruce Springsteen concert shirt from sixteen years ago. Maybe the last time she'd been to a concert.

"Thanks. Well, I should get to work."

"One more thing. Your mother called me. She needs a ride home from church, and wants to know if you can do it."

Mariel hadn't seen her mother for more than a decade, until two weeks before at Floyd's burial and wake. They'd made eye contact, briefly, but still hadn't spoken to each other.

"Why didn't she just call me?" Mariel asked.

"She said she tried three times, and it rang and rang."

Mariel had been to see her doctor that morning, so it's possible her mother's claim was true, but when she'd been at home, no one had called.

"Why can't whatever friend she's staying with just drive her?" The last Mariel heard, her mother had been hopping around the guest rooms of various childhood friends since Floyd's funeral. The fact that Florence hadn't gone back home to Winona by now was unsettling. Something was up.

"She specifically wanted you." Hazel looked pleased, which was a bad sign. "I've known your mom for sixty years. It's time, Mariel. At our age, none of us knows how much time we have."

Mariel hated it when older people played that card, especially on behalf of other older people. In her experience, it was true of everyone, at every age.

"I'll think about it."

Was she really going to do this today? She noticed a yellow-bellied sapsucker in the tree above, its red-capped head darting around, no doubt planning even further destruction of her trees in its godless little mind. Then she noticed another, one branch above. Maybe they were gathering their forces, and would soon descend in a cute fog of pestilence, and wipe out the forests, the buildings, the people, everything. Then it would be a lot quieter around here, and she could finally have a relaxing Saturday.

"Don't think too long," Hazel laughed. "Can't keep Florence Stenerud waiting."

Despite not living anywhere near Bear Jaw for fifty years, Mariel's mother was still widely known, somehow loved, and often feared there. It was well known that anyone who disappointed Florence in the slightest, anyone who inconvenienced her or failed to meet her expectations, would have a swarm of baseless rumors unleashed after them in retaliation. Consequently, Mariel was certain that not collecting her mother in a timely fashion from the Our Savior's Lutheran Church pancake breakfast would mean half the town would soon hear that Mariel had been badly injured in a car accident, or was trapped beneath a fallen tree, or had caught a rare, incurable illness, or was getting a divorce, or some heady cocktail of the above.

Mariel checked her watch. It was ten o'clock. "How long do I have, Hazel?"

"The pancake breakfast goes until eleven, but she'd like to be picked up by ten thirty."

"Okay, I'll do it," Mariel said, surprising even herself.

When thinking of how she'd eventually speak with her mother, Mariel had long imagined a tear-streaked deathbed reconciliation, followed by a few decades of regret, and that sounded fine. But maybe it was time, as Hazel said. Mariel was bound for a bad day anyway.

THE ACTUAL TOWN OF Bear Jaw was seven miles from Bear Jaw Lake, in a move the region's invasive Europeans clearly did to confuse future tourists, of which there were now many. At this hour, at least most tourists and lake people were at their cabins, so traffic into town wouldn't be unbearable. Besides a green Borglund Services septic truck up ahead of her, the only other person Mariel had seen going her way was a fiftyish woman with bright silver-streaked hair on a silver bicycle.

Mariel's car radio was playing an interesting song about a guy who wanted to be killed because he was a loser. She flipped through the stations until she landed on a song by Mariah Carey, which was fine, or at least better.

Mariel had actually braced herself to speak with her mom at the funeral. There was just never a moment when Florence was standing alone without people around. Over the years, there were times she'd felt an urge to call, when a normal, well-adjusted person would've called a normal, well-adjusted mother. But Mariel could never bring herself to do it. Two weeks ago, Mariel had important news, news she didn't want her mother receiving from another source. She was pregnant. Or had been, until last night.

SHE HADN'T TOLD HER husband yet. Ned was still down in the Cities, watching ball games with his college buddies through the weekend. She would wait. Ned saw Tim, Erick, and Doug only once or twice a year, and she didn't want to ruin his good time with them.

Her doctor, Theresa Eaton, had said if a miscarriage happened, it would likely occur in the first twelve weeks. Hers happened at six weeks and two days, at work, right after the kitchen closed. She'd seen spotting earlier that day, and called Theresa, who said it was normal.

"See you in a few days," Theresa had said. "To check for the heartbeat."

But that night, as Mariel was making a Midori sour for a customer, she started feeling a sudden, stabbing pain. She ran to the bathroom, locked the stall door and sat down, her head spinning. It felt like her insides fell out. She knew before she could bring herself to look. Her entire body wanted to scream. She put her fist in her mouth, and cried as quietly as possible, to not bother anyone.

ONCE SHE CLEANED UP, Mariel snuck out the back, without telling anybody. She'd apologize later and tell everyone she got sick, she told herself. Mariel thought of her two seasonal bar employees and hoped they wouldn't think poorly of her. As she pushed the rear door open, she'd never felt colder or lonelier.

Outside, she smelled fresh cigarette smoke. She was relieved to see it was Big Al, who'd been a chef at the Lakeside since before Mariel was born. Once, she'd wanted to be a chef herself, and Floyd and Big Al had taught her how to cook everything that kitchen served. He was probably the closest thing she had to family, apart from Ned.

"Leaving early?" Big Al asked, surprised.

"Stomach bug," she told him, intentionally looking away. If he saw her face, he'd know she was lying. Why had she told him about the pregnancy so early? She knew better. But she'd been so happy, and that was impossible to hide from him too.

"Need me to close up?"

"Yeah," she said, but couldn't keep the sadness from her voice.

"Oh no," he said, as if he knew.

She almost broke down and told him everything. Instead, she apologized, and walked home in the dark.

Maybe she wouldn't tell anyone. She'd lost a baby, but that's not the way most people would see it. They'd respond in ways that would be crushing. They'd hug her and say *It just wasn't meant to be.* They'd say *It happens all the time.* They'd say *You can try again!* They'd say that her friend Cathy's mom had nine miscarriages over twenty-five years. But they didn't know all that Mariel and Ned had been through just to have this single brief pregnancy. And Cathy's mom had seven kids. Mariel had none.

What was most devastating was that Mariel had been fine without a child. And she would've been, indefinitely, she knew it. For years, it was just Ned and her, and everything was good. Once they decided to have a baby, it was all Mariel could think about— even after learning about each of their fertility issues and how difficult it would be. After all the time and money spent, and procedures they endured, here she was. Not back to where she started, because there's no such thing. Her body would either bear a child or bear a loss. Either way, the space was made.

Unspoken, then, the loss burned through her memories, desperate for blame. She'd found one culprit. Mariel never touched the bar garnishes other than to serve them, but Friday night, two hours before the miscarriage, she felt suddenly hungry, and with her usual healthy snacks twenty feet away in her office, she lazily ate three green Maraschino cherries. For months, she'd ingested only things that were specifically good for fertility, and never touched anything artificial. Much later, she'd find out that they wouldn't have made a difference, but that didn't matter then. It was her single break from a routine. Now all the green cherries were in the trash, and would never appear in her bar again.

It was all because of those cherries, she'd told herself. It wasn't that Ned's sperm had almost no motility or that she had a vanishing number of follicles. It wasn't the extra pounds they carried or the excessive alcohol they'd once drunk or the fact that she was almost thirty-nine. She could forgive her faulty, mutinous body and move on, because she must. But until then, she'd tell no one.

Mariel was sure that if her mother ever found out that she'd miscarried, Florence would subject her to a blizzard of reasons why it was Mariel's fault, and that was the last thing she needed. For the first time since she'd agreed to pick up her mother, Mariel wondered why she was in such a hurry.

On the radio, Mariah Carey was singing about how a baby will always be a part of her, and the love between her and the baby will never die. Mariel had heard this song a thousand times, but now it was obvious: the person who wrote this song had lost a child. And oh boy, she could hear in Mariah's voice that she wanted a baby again.

Mariel glanced down to change the station, and when she looked back up, she saw the most beautiful deer running across the road, a flawless Terry Redlin ten-point buck. The instant she pressed the brake, she heard and felt a loud thump, and saw that perfect deer flip in the air and vanish. Then everything went black.

WHERE WAS SHE? Mariel unclenched her hands from the steering wheel and opened her eyes. Her car was idling and on the shoulder, but she didn't remember pulling over. Was she dead? Someone else would have to pick up Florence. What an inane first thought as a dead person. Maybe this was hell. Or, less intriguingly, maybe she wasn't dead after all.

Mariel looked in the mirrors; no vehicles were coming from either direction. She didn't notice her neck was sore until she bent over while exiting her car. When she surveyed the front of her little blue Dodge, she saw the passenger-side headlight and turn signal were smashed, there were scrapes on the front of the wheel well, and part of the radiator grille was busted, but then something else seized her attention.

The handsome deer was in a ditch at the roadside, twitching, bleeding, two of its legs snapped like candy canes broken in their wrappers. It was clear he wasn't going to bolt out of there. Looking in his dark eyes, she could tell he knew that he was going to die. Someone needed to kill him and ease that awful pain. If no one else came by anytime soon, it looked like that was going to have to be Mariel.

In northern Minnesota, a lot of people had something in their vehicle capable of executing a large mammal. She and Ned were not those kinds of people. Riffling through the trunk, she found only a plastic gallon jug of water, a quilt, jumper cables, a jerry can of gasoline, an unopened box of Thin Mints, and a bottle of anti-freeze. Not even a knife.

She looked at the deer, and thought about taking the jumper cables and whipping it in the head until it died, but that seemed difficult and gross. Instead, she lifted the old red jerry can by the handle. It was mostly full, so it was heavy enough.

Mariel watched the deer's twitching face and wondered if she could bludgeon its skull with this can. For what felt like a long time, she stood there, holding the can of gasoline, apologizing to the deer, as the lovely, broken creature struggled to breathe.

Then she heard a woman's voice behind her.

"What are you going to do, light it on fire? Jesus H. Christ!"

Mariel turned, and saw a middle-aged woman hop off a silver bicycle. Mariel recognized her, she was certain, but couldn't place her name. Up close, the woman's face was wrinkled, gorgeous, and unapologetic, and the silver in her long brown hair glinted in the sun like Christmas tree garland.

The woman took a deep breath as she stared at the deer, and then looked at Mariel. "There's a fair amount of decent meat on that idiot."

"Yeah, that's what I was thinking." Mariel nodded, even though it was definitely not what she was thinking. She'd never thought of deer as idiots before, and playing the sentence again in her head made her laugh.

The woman seemed to be amused too. "Where'd you hit him?"

"I don't know. I think the legs."

The woman unzipped her light jacket, revealing a gray tank top and a tool belt, and unsheathed a black-handled guthook Buck knife. She approached the deer from behind its back and cut its throat in one quick motion.

"A quality tool saves you time and money," the woman said, as if that should be the obvious moral of this entire scene. She wiped the blade off on the back of the dead animal, and right then, Mariel decided she wanted to be friends with this woman.

HER NAME WAS Brenda Kowalsky, and it turned out that she lived just a mile away.

"I'll get my son to come help me field dress this thing," she said, meaning the deer. "I'm gonna go home and call him. You stay here to tell people you got dibs."

Mariel waited there about fifteen minutes for Brenda or her son to show up, while Florence Jean Stenerud continued waiting in the sun-dappled lobby of Our Savior's for her ride. At best, Mariel wouldn't get to the church until around ten forty-five, at this point. She reminded herself that either way, she wasn't responsible for her mom's dissatisfaction. It wasn't like the woman was abandoned in the Gobi Desert. She was surrounded by her oldest friends, in an air-conditioned building full of strong coffee and breakfast food. Her mother could certainly stand to wait another thirty minutes in that environment.

Mariel checked to see if her car was okay to drive, and it seemed to be, so long as she wouldn't need both headlights. She'd just killed the engine when a shiny Ram pickup truck stopped beside her. The driver was a clean-cut young man whose chiseled face she recognized. He worked at the town's funeral home. Brenda waved from the passenger seat.

"Kyle wants to know if you want the heart."

It took Mariel a second to wrap her head around that sentence. She hadn't even considered that she'd get any of the venison, and she told them so. "I figure, you're doing all the work," she explained.

"You're the one who hit it," Brenda said. "By rights, the meat's yours. My son will even butcher it for you right now, if you want to come over. You're not in a hurry, are you?"

Seeing this loving mother and her grown, helpful son, Mariel thought of Florence.

"Nope," Mariel said.

She followed Brenda and Kyle down a long dirt road, farther and farther from the town, the church, and her mother, toward a vast green farm she'd never seen before. Immediately, something about this place whispered to her, and she knew she wouldn't be leaving anytime soon.

Two

Nothing good ever happens between midnight and five in the morning. This isn't just what Florence believed; it'd been proven. Nobody who wakes you up at that hour is going to have anything decent to offer, or any good news to share. The middle of the night is when things get taken away.

"Florence, Florence," her mother, Betty, whispered in her ear, jostling her.

Florence awoke but didn't open her eyes.

"Are you up?" her mother asked. "I'm sick of this place, let's go find another one."

"Again?" Florence asked. Her mother had grown sick of places lately, usually between midnight and five in the morning. "I kind of like this one."

She honestly did too. Plus, she'd wanted a garden her entire life, and this place had a little plot of dirt out back where she'd planted a single rhubarb plant. It wasn't much, but it was hers.

"No you don't," her mother told her. "Here, put your jacket on."

"Can't I get changed?"

"I packed your clothes already. You can change when we get somewhere."

"Where are we going?"

"Let's find out," her mother said, and smiled.

THESE EARLY-MORNING ESCAPES used to scare Florence. As she got older, though, she realized that being scared did no one any good—it didn't affect her mother's decisions—and it was tougher and more sophisticated to be annoyed. This time, Florence was especially annoyed that her mother chose to leave on such a cold night. There were, after all, such things as weather forecasts, and people could make plans based on them, but her mother sometimes seemed immune to plain common sense. Two days ago, on her twelfth birthday, it was fifteen degrees warmer, and even if it would've been a crummy birthday present to be out on the road with nowhere to sleep, she'd have preferred it to being frozen.

As if Florence weren't perturbed enough, she had to hear one of Betty Miller's favorite sayings, "You can always turn down a ride," again that morning. Since her mother had sold their car years ago, she'd turned down quite a few. At three thirty in the morning, though, it didn't seem like there were enough cars and trucks on the streets of Lake City, Minnesota, to be all that picky. Her mother was, though, and even refused drivers to their faces in a way that made them feel complimented.

"Oh, we can't ride with you," she told one clearly drunk man driving a Studebaker full of cigar smoke. "You're too handsome. We need to wait for someone uglier."

When the man drove off, confused, Florence glared at her mom. "That man wasn't handsome at all. Why do you lie to them like that?"

"Men are fragile, honey," Betty said. "If I told that man he had too much to drink and was liable to kill himself, he might regard it as an insult. And men often lose grace and composure when they feel insulted."

"Why do we have to leave right now? What was wrong with that place?" There were, of course, a lot of things wrong with where they'd been living. That's why her mother had been, out of principle, withholding rent from the landlord, a man named Maylone. He was greasy and mean, had a thin little mustache, and looked at her mom in a disturbing way. Still, it was better than most of the places they'd slept in. They almost never stayed anywhere with indoor toilets or hot running water. Only occasionally did they have electricity. Florence had once actually told her mom she'd help her clean an entire house for free if they didn't have to spend another night in a Hooverville again. Even if they ended up somewhere decent, Betty always found a reason to leave.

"It's an insult to your grandmother Julia to further compromise our standard of living," Betty said. Julia was a Winthrop, her mother liked to remind her.

Florence used to eagerly collaborate with her mother in fantasies about where they'd be now if Henry Winthrop's fortune hadn't been spread only among his four sons, neglecting Florence's grandmother Julia. By now, whatever had trickled to Julia had long since left this earth, along with Julia herself. That Betty and Florence owned nothing tangible from that vanished Winthrop world of spring galas, captains of industry, and private chefs, maids, and butlers didn't make the dream any less intoxicating. For more than a year, Florence even told acquaintances her name was Florence Winthrop, until she'd overheard someone remark, *Look, even the Winthrops hit the skids.*

"Julia Winthrop would be on the streets with us, probably," Florence said.

"She most certainly would not be. And we're not on the streets, we're deciding where to live next. Come on, let's walk to that service station."

Florence didn't want to lug her two suitcases any farther that night—they'd already walked half a mile just to get to the highway— but once her mother started walking, there was no choice but to follow. Closer up, the place didn't look like a nice service station; it looked like a shoddy little house with a couple of fuel pumps plopped in the front yard. It was also clearly not open for business yet. In other words, as far as Betty Miller was concerned, it looked perfect.

"Before long, our prince or princess will come by, and until then, no one will hassle us," Betty said, sitting on a faded white bench between her suitcases, her thin neck raising her alert eyes to the quiet and the darkness.

Florence curled toward her mother for warmth, and collapsed back into sleep.

· · ·

THE NEXT TIME FLORENCE opened her eyes, it was morning, and she was surprised to be leaning fully against her mother, as if the suitcase between them had been moved. She gasped and sat up, looking under the bench, behind it, on each side. All four suitcases, containing their clothes, books, and accessories, everything they owned and had accumulated for years, were gone. Florence didn't know whether to cry or faint.

"Mother," Florence said, in tears, jostling her mom awake. "Where's all of our stuff?"

Betty's eyes snapped open, and as she heard her daughter's words and looked around, she did seem, for two seconds, to be as panicked as a normal person who lost everything should be. Then the moment passed as Betty took a deep breath, smiled, and nodded. "Somebody robbed us," she said. "Good. Now we'll move faster."

"No! No!" Florence screamed in her mom's face, exhausted and livid. "All of my clothes were in there!"

"Well, they were a bunch of old rags anyway. Half of them hardly fit you anymore. Now we'll get you some new things."

"You always say that! Now I don't have anything else to wear besides what I have on!"

"Well, that's a decent place to start. Better than being naked. We'll get new clothes when they come to us. That will happen when it happens, and not one second later." Her mother then glanced away, and bolted to her feet. "Oh, look, I can't believe our luck."

A shiny black Oldsmobile driven by a young woman, traveling alone, pulled into the service station. Florence's mother was much more at ease riding with women. Women drivers did ask more personal questions, and Betty responded by conjuring elaborate fabrications about their circumstances, especially when asked about her husband. Over the years, Florence had heard her mother describe over thirty different husbands, who'd been carpenters, masons, mechanics, salesmen, and had been in every branch of the military. These men had been Catholic and Protestant, Democrat, Republican, and Socialist, city boys and farmer's sons. But not once did she precisely describe Florence's actual father.

Florence didn't overhear what her mother told this woman about their present dilemma, but it was effective. They were getting in a warm, clean car, bound for Red Wing.

"She's visiting her sister," Betty whispered to her daughter. "And her sister might have some extra clothes for us. But she can't just bring us straight there, in case her sister's husband is home. So we'll wait somewhere, and she'll come get us when it's all clear."

The interior of the car was clean, except for a book in the back seat, titled *A Room of One's Own*, by Virginia Woolf.

"I still need to stop at a service station, as this one wasn't open," the driver said to them. "Are you two running from someone?"

Florence's eyes locked onto her mother.

"I prefer to think of us as hopeful and not fearful," her mother said.

"You don't have to prevaricate with me," the woman said, using an impressive word that sounded serious and intimidating. "Is there a man after you?"

"Yes, his name's Mr. Maylone," her mother replied after a moment, giving the name of their most recent landlord. "And if he's not already, he will be soon."

"Please tell me if you see this Mr. Maylone, and I'll put a stop to him."

Florence liked this woman. "He has greasy brown hair and a svelte little mustache," she said, hoping the woman would be impressed by her vocabulary.

"Svelte. Nice word," the woman said, and glanced behind herself to nod at Florence.

"What's your name?" Florence asked.

"Marielle," the woman replied.

There are only a handful of times in life when chance plays an honest part in improving a girl's fortunes. Looking back, Florence could see that this woman Marielle simply bestowed a bit of kindness on two strangers whom she likely soon forgot. Given all that resulted, however, Florence would spend the rest of her life on the lookout for Marielle again, hoping to properly pay her back in a way she'd been unable to as a child.

ONCE IN RED WING, Marielle dropped them off at Jorby's, a local diner. Betty chose seats at the counter next to a pudgy, soft-faced gentleman in a green jacket with thinning hair combed over his pink scalp. Since they'd sat, he'd been lecturing the bespectacled boy pouring coffee behind the counter, who couldn't have been much older than Florence. He was telling the boy to get out of the restaurant business and get a law degree.

Their waitress smiled at the kid. "You won't get anywhere with Nathan," she told the man. "He's one of the owner's sons."

Florence stared at the unhappy-looking boy and thought at least she wasn't him. Imagine, being forced into a lifetime of restaurant drudgery because of who your parents were. She and her mother had options.

The man in the green suit smiled at Nathan. "There's no destiny like the one you make for yourself."

The waitress laughed, and finally turned to Florence and her mother. She regarded them with unmistakable pity. They must've looked as tired and dirty as they felt. "So, rough morning?"

"Not at all. We're doing just grand," Betty said. "We're meeting a friend here, and I just thought we'd get a little refreshment while we wait."

"Okay, then. So what can I get you two?"

"Just coffee for me, I'm not hungry," Betty said. "And whatever my daughter would like."

Florence hadn't even had time to peruse the menu, but she was starving, so she said the first thing that came to mind. "Do you have pancakes?"

"Sure do. How many would you like?"

To Florence, this depended on how much money her mom had. Florence hated it when her mother snuck them out of a restaurant without paying the bill. It always made the food give her a stomachache. "Mother? How many may I get?"

"As many as you want, dear," Betty replied, smiling.

Uh-oh, Florence thought. She knew right then, when she was a grown-up, she would never do this; she would be honest, no matter how others felt about it. Maybe she'd start right now. She was tired and mad and it just came out of her. "No, Mother, I mean how many can we afford?"

Betty still wouldn't wipe the smile from her dang face. "What did I just tell you?"

"I'll take *one*," Florence told the waitress.

"One pancake," the waitress said. "Coming right up."

While she waited, Florence set down the copy of *A Room of One's Own* on the counter and began to read.

"Where'd you get that book?" her mother asked.

Florence didn't look up. "That lady who drove us gave it to me."

"I do not recall any such thing. Did you just steal that nice woman's book?"

"I didn't. I do not steal, Mother. Not like some people."

"Well," her mother said, eyeing the book. "It's in good shape, anyway. We might be able to sell it when you're finished with it."

FIVE MINUTES LATER, the waitress slid a steaming plate of four pancakes between Florence's elbows, pushing the book aside. They smelled like somewhere else, somewhere she deeply missed.

She remembered, long ago, waking up in the big yellow house, in a bed she had to herself in a room she had to herself, hearing adult voices talking somewhere in the house, and smelling this exact same scent coming from downstairs. In a word, they smelled like heaven.

The last time Florence truly felt safe and happy was that morning years ago, so perhaps that was what heaven looked like. A big yellow house on Grand Avenue in St. Paul, with parents making pancakes, yelling upstairs to come down before they get cold.

"Compliments of your neighbor," the waitress said.

The kind-faced man smiled at Florence. "You looked like you needed more than one."

Florence hadn't even finished her own "thank you, sir," before her mother drowned her out with an emotional deluge of gratitude.

"Oh, you incredibly generous man," Betty proclaimed. "You. Are. A. Saint. You are a saint walking among us on earth. How can we ever, ever, ever repay you?"

The man appeared to be a little surprised. "It's nothing. Would you also like some pie? Jorby's has the best in the state, and I've had them all."

Florence knew what her mother was going to say next. "We can clean your house this afternoon. We can do your dishes. Launder your clothes. Anything." Florence hated doing this kind of work. She also hated how her mom would tell her, throughout a day of sweeping someone's floors and scrubbing their toilets, how she should be grateful for this honest labor, and if she disliked it so much, she had better marry someone rich.

"No, seriously, it's nothing," the man said, and smiled at Florence. Nice men weren't always good news. She'd noticed how some otherwise polite and generous men looked at her mom, and Florence was old enough to understand what they meant by certain compliments or gestures. But the more she looked at him, this man didn't seem like those men.

"Go on," he said. "Eat them before they get cold."

While Florence ate, they learned the man's name, Floyd Muller, and that he intended to go all the way up north to Bear Jaw that night, where he owned a business.

"The Majestic Lodge?" Betty asked. Everyone had heard of the Majestic Lodge, but Florence and Betty had never known anyone who could afford to stay there.

"No, but close," Floyd said. "Just up the road a quarter mile."

"Can we go with you?" Florence blurted out. With the benefit of a little premeditation, she decided to use a word she hoped would impress him. "I hear there's a lot of pulchritude up there."

"There may be." Floyd smiled.

Her mother frowned. "Bear Jaw is way up north, in the middle of the woods."

"I want to see it," Florence said.

"Well, you don't get to decide. If I can find work and get us a place to stay in Red Wing, I'd like to stay here. Plus we know that nice lady here, Marielle."

Floyd looked at them, a little astonished. "You came here without even a place to stay?"

"We'll find a place," her mother told him. "Marielle will help us out. Any minute now, she'll be here."

Florence sat up and stared around the diner, checking if maybe that woman was here already and they'd missed each other somehow. Then, she saw him. A man with greasy brown hair, and a svelte little mustache.

For a moment, she couldn't move. Florence nudged her mom. How did he find them? It didn't matter. All Florence could think about was what someone like him could do to people like them.

Florence glanced again at the man. It might not have been Mr. Maylone. But it might have been. It might have been any of the men her mother had ripped off over the years. What did it matter whether this was the most recent one?

"Don't look in his direction," Florence whispered. "He'll recognize you."

"Oh no," her mother said, and turned her back to where the man was sitting. "I'm very sorry, Mr. Muller, but we have to leave."

"Are you in trouble?"

Florence's mother nodded.

"Where are you going? I thought you had to stay and wait for your friend."

"I don't know," Betty said. "But we have to get out of here, right now."

"Let's ride with him, Mom," Florence said.

"We can't just ride with him. It's too far. Besides, he didn't offer. It's rude to invite yourself along. We'll find someone."

"I'm offering," Floyd said. "If you need to go right now, I'm offering."

"He'll never find us up there, Mother," Florence told her mother, hoping it was a convincing argument. "Nobody will."

THE JOURNEY UP Highway 61 seemed to last forever, driving first in and out of the clamor and grime of St. Paul, and into the calming farms and forests of the north. Florence read signs for towns called White Bear Lake, North Branch, Beroun, Hinckley, and Sandstone. Florence was born in St. Paul, in the house on Grand Avenue that was once home to her grandmother, Julia Winthrop Miller. Before the end of today, she would be as far from where she'd been born as she'd ever been.

Florence stared out the back seat window at the endless trees, the strange marshlands and wide lakes, and the smaller and smaller towns hidden like secrets among the tireless, sprawling wilderness. The adults up front, of course, were missing everything. They were talking and joking about things that seemed too sad to be jokes, but her mother was really laughing deeply. It was good to hear.

Her mother seemed to be comfortable in Floyd's company in a way that Florence hadn't witnessed in years. Unlike most men, Floyd was neither smarmy nor nervous around Betty. He never touched Betty, commented on her appearance, or seemed to say anything specifically to impress her. Florence supposed this is what the term "gentleman" meant. Before long, her mother was asking Floyd if he knew whether the Majestic Lodge was hiring. She described it as a dream job for a girl like herself. That's when Florence first suspected her mother liked him. Betty called herself a girl only at times when youth was a useful accessory.

"Dream job?" Floyd asked. "I'm not going to knock anyone's dream job, but I know a place that pays better. A dollar fifty more a week."

"A dollar fifty?" Florence wasn't just pretending to be impressed. "Where?"

Florence hoped that the place he named would be somewhere quiet and clean, like a library or a little roadside museum. She just prayed it wouldn't be some dingy restaurant. The only restaurant work she qualified for at her age was busing tables and dishwashing, and even if it included some free food on the side, it also meant dealing with the endless parade of half-eaten or hardly eaten plates that other people threw away. The amount of food people saw fit to waste was so depressing, it bordered on unbearable.

"My restaurant," he said. "I could use another pair of hands. Maybe two pairs of hands."

Floyd glanced back at Florence, who made sure she wasn't smiling.

"Maybe one pair of hands," Floyd said. "I apologize, Florence. I shouldn't be speaking for other people."

"Well, count me in," Betty said. "For whatever you need. No job is beneath me."

"So, where are we going to stay?" Florence asked. She knew it was presumptuous, but one of the few advantages to being a child was the freedom to ask direct questions, and that was a privilege she fully intended to abuse for as long as possible.

Betty's head snapped around and fired a glare at her daughter. "Florence Jean!" she barked, and then turned to Floyd, all smiles. "I apologize for my daughter. You can just drop us off at whatever motel is convenient to you."

Florence didn't let herself get excited by the mention of the word "motel." It was only for appearances. In all likelihood, once Floyd had dropped them off, they'd walk away and find a cheap campsite or go sleep at a bus stop.

"It's all right," Floyd said. "We got a few guest cabins on our property, and if one's open, you can stay there for free for a few days, if you want, until you find something better."

Her mother seemed equally delighted and confused. Nothing this good ever came so easy, and it was unnerving for both of them. Betty thanked Floyd, and then turned to face her daughter. "Say thank you, Florence."

Florence knew better than to preemptively thank anyone for anything. She stared out the window, at all the tall trees she'd never seen before, the endless, beautiful trees, as her mother's repeated request rose in volume, then in pitch, and then surrendered.

Three

When he was a child, Ned Prager's favorite restaurant was Jorby's. It had all-day breakfasts, a rotating pie tower, bottomless beverages, and a menu so big and awesome, Ned would never grow tired of eating there. Which he did, at least five times a week, for the first twenty-four years of his life. For free.

In 1921, Ned's grandparents, Eddie and Norma Prager—with four bags of Gold Medal flour, a rolling pin, and a dream—opened the original Jorby's Bakery and Café in Red Wing, Minnesota, on an unpaved road called Constitutional Route 3. Within a decade, CR 3 had become part of interstate Highway 61, and Jorby's was its most popular stop for motorists in southern Minnesota.

It was a classic American family restaurant, where everyone could come as they were, the staff knew the regulars, and the generous portions would make the final check feel like a value. When Ned's father, Edward Prager, inherited Jorby's from Eddie and Norma in 1965, he'd watched out-of-state franchises like McDonald's and Howard Johnson's spread across Minnesota, and believed that Jorby's needed to claim the Midwest for family diners before some outsider did.

Within a decade, Jorby's was everywhere, up and down both sides of the Mississippi River, in hardy farmland cities and blossoming suburbs. Some called it homogenization. Some called it good neoliberal economics. It could never be directly voted for or against, either way. No matter whether you liked it or not, Jorby's came to your town and drove hundreds of family-owned restaurants out of business, whether they were crappy or wonderful. Some former mom-and-pop joints became a Jorby's, and they were the lucky ones. In the end, countless restaurant families went broke, and one man accumulated wealth and power on an unprecedented scale.

Ned could never figure out if this was due to luck, or planning, or just the fact that his father was a rich, charismatic misanthrope who never took no for an answer. Ned was not such a man himself, but he didn't believe that was important. With such immense profits, the future could be fairer to everyone, he felt, especially the employees. It just had to be. Ned's mother, Ellen, who was an assistant manager at a Jorby's when she met Edward, agreed with him. They'd both disliked the compromises in Edward's strategy. The pies were no longer made fresh on the premises. The coffee was more watery. The portions became smaller. The wages stagnated. The morale, competence, and loyalty of their cooks and servers diminished. It couldn't keep going like this.

In the meantime, it did. By 1980, there were ninety-one Jorby's restaurants spread across ten states, with plans for two dozen more. One day, they would all be Ned's, and perhaps by then, this avalanche of heedless change and growth could be stopped, or at least thoughtfully reconsidered. Until then, all he had to do was put in his time.

FOR NED, THAT WAS the easy part. There was still nowhere else in the world he'd rather be. His actual responsibilities as the general manager of the new branch in Minneapolis were the hard part. His father promised him if he could make that location profitable for three straight months, or put in a full year—whichever came first—he'd be promoted to executive vice president at Jorby's HQ. Ned was grateful, because no one else he knew who'd graduated in his class from the University of Minnesota would be an executive by twenty-four.

Ned also understood, of course, that along the way, he must also find someone to share this future. Over the years, he'd dated some wonderful, intelligent young women, but each of them seemed to be missing something important. He didn't know exactly what that was, until he observed it while eating a Farmer's Bounty breakfast one cold Minnesota morning in December 1980.

HE WAS AT THE Jorby's he managed, sitting in the huge corner booth with his younger sister, Carla. Ned had dreamed of her being his right-hand woman someday when he ran the family business, and while she was home from college on Christmas break, he informed her of the path she should take.

"Here's what Dad and I think," he said. "You should go to law school, and then work your way up to being company counsel. You'd be my consigliere, like Tom Hagen in *The Godfather.* Wouldn't that be cool?"

"Yeah, no," Carla said. "If I'm going to be a lawyer, I want to be the kind that wanders the streets at night, shooting rapists in the face."

God, he loved her. She was the fiercest person he'd ever met, even more than their father, and she'd be incredible at dispensing vigilante justice, but then he'd hardly get to see her. "I was thinking of something more along the lines of corporate finance."

Carla leaned back in the booth, crossed her arms, and blew a raspberry at her brother. "No fun. How about running a Jorby's, like you are? I want to do that."

Carla might've been the one person on earth who loved Jorby's even more than he did. She was also smarter than him, was better organized, and had a superior head for business. But she was born second, and their father was an old-fashioned misogynist. The family business would be in Ned's hands one day. No other future was possible. When Ned had a son, his son would inherit it too. What to do with Carla had been the family dilemma since she was born.

"Running a Jorby's is not fun, by the way. It's really hard."

Carla sized up the dining room. It was peak breakfast hour and the place was dead. "Can't be that difficult with only one, two, three whole customers," she said, pointing at each of them. "Are you doing anything in the community, any outreach or promotion, to get more butts through the door?"

"Not yet." The truth was, the community saw Jorby's as a hostile invader, and they weren't wrong.

A few days before, a tall, wide man in a brown suit had walked in the door, sized Ned up, shook his head, and said, "Gentrifying motherfucker."

"I guess so," Ned had replied. "And I'm also averse to conflict."

"Rich white nerd," he overheard a woman say the following day.

"Wow, no one's ever called me a nerd before," he replied, which was true. He was a baseball player in high school, and a good one, but a mediocre student. He probably would've had better grades if he ever did homework, like his sister did. "I think you have to be smart to be a nerd."

The woman laughed. "You oughta be smart enough to get the hell outta here."

"I don't think I am," he'd said. "You're stuck looking at me until July." That's when his year was up, and he'd be promoted to the corporate HQ in Red Wing.

Ned had expected his sister to be sympathetic, but she wasn't. When he related these encounters to her just now, she frowned at him, like he'd done something wrong.

"Well, when you invade a neighborhood like we did here, there's a lot of work to do," she said, and then something at the entrance caught her attention. "Oh, look at that woman."

Ned turned. A bundled-up old lady in a wheelchair was outside, visible through the glass doors, struggling to reach the handle.

"Be right back," Carla said, and was on her feet to the doorway before the thought even entered Ned's mind. They both had their mother's heart, Ned was sure, but Carla was as decisive as their father.

By the time Carla reached the doorway, a young woman in white had beaten her there, opening both that door and the lobby door for the older woman in the wheelchair. This woman didn't merely hold the doors, either, she was talking to the lady in the wheelchair, and making her laugh.

Carla shook her head as she sat down. "Wow, that never happens," she said, and laughed to herself. "Maybe when Mom was alive. She used to elbow me out of the way to help people cross the street."

All families have mythic exaggerations, especially about their dead, but that story was absolutely true. Their mother was usually calm and passive, but if someone needed help, she'd set a land-speed record. Their father said she helped random people so often because of her guilt over becoming wealthy, but Ned disagreed. It came too naturally to her.

Ned looked around, and saw that the young woman was seated again, with her back to Ned. Her white clothes were mottled with little stains, and her shiny brown hair was pinned down tight. Something about her seemed familiar. Either way, he knew right then, she was the person he'd always been looking for.

"I think I just fell in love," Ned said, which sounded ridiculous, but didn't feel like it.

"With her?" Carla glanced at the woman again. "Why not. Go for it."

"Wonder what her story is?"

"Why don't you ask her?" Carla said, then laughed. "Too late, there she goes."

Ned turned around just in time to see the young woman leave the restaurant, the glass lobby door swinging shut behind her.

Carla looked at Ned, surprised. "I thought you were going to ask her out."

"I was about to," he said.

No, he was not. Ned Prager did not know how to approach women, perhaps because he never had. He was embarrassed to say that they always just came to him, as easily as everything else in life seemed to. So, he remained seated, and cursed his own cowardice, then and for a long time afterward.

FOR THE NEXT FEW MONTHS, Ned was front of house way more often than usual, looking for a woman in white clothes, with shiny brown hair held in place by hairpins. Some of his customers confused his public presence for interest in engaging with them and their opinions, and several times he was given the evil eye. It wasn't personal, he reminded himself, as he responded with a smile and a hello. One day, Jorby's would grow to become the most popular family restaurant chain not just in the Midwest, but in all of America. By then, these same folks would tell people that they met Ned Prager once, and he was actually kind of a nice guy.

Ned was only here because his father, Edward, was one of those family business owners who wanted his children to do every job from the ground up, to better appreciate the big picture. Ned and Carla were put to work busing tables when they were in junior high, and later were sent around as needed, filling in for servers or cooks or managers. Ned had loved being a waiter, because of the customer interaction. But that same customer interaction as a general manager was a lot less pleasant.

In the meantime, his employees, who liked him, offered to walk him to his car after close, so he wouldn't get beat up in his own parking lot. Even if he had been, he believed it would've been the cost of doing business, and the cost of looking for the woman with white clothes and hairpins. He wandered the floor of his restaurant every day, withstanding muttered insults and outright verbal assaults from people who came in just to tell him he didn't belong here.

"Who are you always looking for?" people sometimes asked him.

"The love of my life," he always replied. Even then, he believed that. He hadn't seen her face clearly; what he had witnessed had been enough.

BY THE TIME HIS YEAR in Minneapolis was over, Ned still hadn't found her. He couldn't stay at that job for one more day, so his six-month search was over. It wasn't for nothing, though, he told himself, because it proved to him that such people existed. His family's annual Fourth of July vacation to Bear Jaw Lake was just around the corner, and that would help clear his head.

He loved it up there. The cabin they'd built on the lake was his family's first vacation property, and still his favorite. There were no electric security fences or chefs or drivers, just a lake house with a private dock, perfect for watching the fireworks. The best feature was the new four-season porch that he and Carla and their dad had built themselves two summers ago, with help from his cousin Eli. He'd discovered he loved that kind of work, building something with his hands. The July trip was always comforting, perhaps because it was the only property they still owned that his mother had slept in, and her presence sang to him from the walls and cupboards.

. . .

It was a few minutes before six o'clock on the final night of their five days up north when Ned and his entire family—Carla, their father, and their stepmother—parked in the lot at Floyd and Betty's Lakeside Supper Club. Other men like his father would never go out to a restaurant like this, but Edward Prager insisted on being a man of the people.

"I need to use the restroom," Ned said, walking ahead. "I'll meet you at the table."

"You don't know where our table's going to be, you dork," his sister yelled.

Ned opened the heavy front door and stumbled into the violent sensory haze of cigarette smoke, the smell of sixty prime rib platters, and tinny piped-in polka music. It took him a few seconds to get his bearings. As a kid, he'd loved all this clamor and kitsch, but now, compared with the tasteful comfort of Jorby's, the Lakeside felt like a county fair.

A waitress grinned at him as she passed. "Boys' room is to the left, hon."

"Thanks," Ned replied. *Boys' room*, he laughed to himself, and that's when he glanced toward the bar, and saw the white shirt, and the shiny brown hair held in place by hairpins.

He'd replayed this moment so many times in his idle hours that it now seemed like a mirage. He saw as she got closer that she was a little heavier than he'd remembered and had a burn scar on her hand and all kinds of moles and freckles that had been disguised by his own revisionism. In other words, she was normal, and she was perfect.

She must've felt him staring, because she glanced over toward him, and when she saw him, she appeared, for the briefest moment, as if she were pleasantly surprised. She looked at him again, and he didn't know whether it was just good customer service, but she seemed happy to see him.

"Hello, I'm Ned," he told her, and extended his hand, which he hoped wasn't sweaty. As she took it, people at the bar seemed to be sizing him up. "It's nice to finally meet you." He hoped that didn't sound weird.

"I'm Mariel," she said, and smiled. "Nice to meet you too."

Months ago, while sitting in his office at the Jorby's in Minneapolis, he prepared an impassioned speech for when he first saw her, but none of it came back to him now, which was probably for the best. "How are you?" he asked instead.

"I'm good. What can I get you?"

A beautiful woman behind the bar who was probably in her late seventies smiled at him. "Hold on, let's send Ned's table over some old-fashioneds," the woman said, and set down four rocks glasses. How did she know how many people were in his party?

"That's okay," Ned said, surprised by the swiftness of the hard sell. "My dad doesn't order alcohol in restaurants. The markup."

"Of course. Your dad's in the restaurant business." The woman laughed as she continued mixing the drinks. "These are on the house."

How did she know what his father did? He wondered, for the first time, how much the staff here knew about his family, and about him. He didn't think of himself as famous outside of his hometown, but maybe he was, and it dismayed him. What nominal fame he had was exhausting. The best part about vacations was feeling like a normal person whom nobody knew.

He also wondered for just a moment if this young woman here was indeed the one he'd seen half a year ago. Then she looked cheerfully at him to say she'd be right over with the drinks, and when her smile lingered, he decided yes.

NED ARRIVED AT HIS family's table just as their waitress, Lois, was asking if they'd like anything to drink.

"Nope," Ned's dad was saying. "That's how they get ya."

Lois watched Mariel approach with the cocktails, and grinned. "Looks like we got ya."

"They're free, Dad," Ned said as he helped pass them out. "Everyone, this is my friend Mariel. Mariel, this is my sister, Carla, my dad, Edward, and my stepmom, Peg."

Lois politely stepped aside as everyone else exchanged variations of "nice to meet you."

"You seem familiar," Peg said to Mariel. "Have you worked here long?"

"Yeah, it's my grandpa and grandma's place, so they put me wherever they need me. This summer, I'm bartending again."

Ned was delighted at hearing this succinct version of his own life. Here was another person whose restaurant family put them through the paces. In addition to being kind and beautiful, she was a woman he could relate to.

"Well, good for you," Peg replied.

Ned thought it was classless of his stepmom to be so patronizing. Ned wanted to announce that Peg had been a Jorby's waitress when she met his father, but thanks to his mother's upbringing, he had the decorum not to do so. "It's awesome how you support your family business," he said instead, as a slight dig at Peg. She didn't do any kind of work anymore, and probably never would.

"I should get back," Mariel said. "It was nice to meet everyone."

"I'll walk with you," Ned said. He could not let her out of his sight without making a plan.

"We're about to order," Ned's dad protested.

Ned turned to look at Lois. "I'll have the fish and chips, please. With torsk," he added, anticipating the question about which kind of fish.

He expected an appreciative glance in response for saving her a bit of time, but instead she squinted and shook her head. "Shoulda been here last night, cutie. It's Saturday, so it's prime rib tonight."

Ned remembered the prime rib platters here. They were less like a meal and more like a friendly opponent. Each plate contained enough food for a sane, healthy adult to have leftovers twice. He ordered his prime rib medium rare, then told his family he'd be right back.

Carla commented that he could take all the time he wanted, and put her feet up on her brother's chair immediately after he stood.

"You get to pick two sides!" Lois called after him. "And unlimited salad bar!"

. . .

"MY FAMILY'S LEAVING TOMORROW," Ned told Mariel at the bar. "But I'd love to take you out for coffee. Or maybe a beer. Or something else? Are you free tonight?"

The two seconds awaiting her response became the most fertile pasture of possibilities he'd ever imagined.

"Well, some friends and I are going to watch the fireworks by the lake," she replied. "Would you like to come with?"

Sadly, this was not a response he'd anticipated. If he had, he would've specified *after the fireworks* to Mariel, but now it was too late. The word "yes" rose from his heart, and was so big and meaningful it got jammed in his throat against what he was supposed to say.

He was supposed to say he had plans with his family. They'd watched the fireworks out on their private dock together every year of his life. It was tradition, and there was no changing it.

"Yes," he said aloud, and he felt for the first time, in that moment, like a decisive man, capable of navigating an unpredictable future.

Four

~~~

Florence, 1934

The Lakeside Inn turned out to be an impressive place, at least for a restaurant. It was decorated like a fancy hunting lodge, with white tablecloths, ornate stemmed glasses, and heavy, gleaming silverware. Its bar glistened with more colorful liquor bottles than Florence had ever seen, and its menu featured food she'd never eaten before, like grilled walleye and steak. The only detail she wasn't so sure about was the mounted fish and giant deer heads on the walls.

"That's not a deer head, that's a ten-point trophy rack," Floyd told her. "Archie Eastman shot that one about a mile from where you're standing."

It was the first time she'd heard the name, of course, and it meant nothing to her, but it was spoken with such reverence, she assumed it must belong to someone important.

"Who's he, the mayor?"

"No, no," he told her, laughing as if that were impossible. "Archie's the fella who lives in that house across the street. He's from out west. Pierre, South Dakota."

"Sir, they pronounce it *peer*, not pee-*air*," she told him. "Peer, South Dakota."

"Oh, that's neat. I wonder why Archie never corrected me. Probably having a good laugh at me." He seemed completely unfazed by this likelihood.

"Did Mr. Eastman have to shoot this one?" Florence asked. "Was he dying, or something?"

"He was going to wander into the road and get hit by a car," Floyd told her. "This way, he hardly suffered. Besides, he looks good up there, don't he? He'd rather be here where people can admire him, right?"

Florence wasn't convinced.

BY THE THIRD MORNING Florence and Betty awoke in that guest cabin, it almost began to seem real. The elusive good fortune Betty Miller claimed would always be around the next corner, and then the next, seemed to have been waiting for them up in Bear Jaw. Betty called the entire situation "a bouquet of miracles," including her new job as an apprentice bartender.

Neither the existence nor the repeal of Prohibition had affected Florence's life much until now. Her mother didn't drink, so it was jarring to see her behind the bar, holding brightly labeled bottles of vodka and gin, learning to mix cocktails.

"It's the best employment opportunity of the decade," Betty said, as if reading it aloud from a newspaper column. "Our country lost a whole generation of bartenders, and now there's a huge need for them."

Her mother was always calculating like this. Betty had been in survival mode for so long, perhaps she couldn't feel safe even amid a bouquet of miracles.

"But you don't even drink alcohol! Do you even want to be a bartender?"

"That doesn't matter." Her mother laughed, and Florence wondered which part didn't matter, or if neither did. "If it means I don't have to work with those catty waitresses. Or get my hands scarred up in the kitchen. It pays very well, with all of the tips. Plus, you know, the one full-time bartender they have, Elisha, is very old."

"So you're thinking he's going to die soon, and you'll take his job?"

"Florence Jean!" Betty gasped. "It's a bad omen to speak of such things. Let's not get ahead of ourselves, please."

Somebody sure was, though. "So, how long, then? A year?"

Betty crossed herself. "I refuse to discuss such a morbid topic."

"But we're going to stay here, no matter what?" Florence was nervous to ask. To spend more than a few months in one place would make her happy enough, but this living situation was the best she'd experienced in years.

There were three cabins on the restaurant property that Floyd rented out to tourists in the summer, and all of them, including theirs, had indoor plumbing and electricity and a woodstove. For once, Florence didn't have to sleep in the same room as her mother. The only thing Florence didn't like was that the cabins were set between the parking lot and the woods, with nowhere good to put a garden. Betty considered that a trifling complaint. Floyd leased the cabin to Betty at one-quarter the weekly off-season rate, permanently, with the rent coming out of Betty's pay.

"I don't know about you, but I can't imagine a place that's better."

As relieved as she was, Florence was surprised by her mother's response. "I can," Florence told her mother, almost involuntarily. "The big yellow house."

Her mother frowned. "That's gone. And it wasn't better. You're fortunate I protected you from how awful it was there."

Her father had indeed become someone it was best never to speak to, but that wasn't the whole truth. Nothing could ever replace that home in Florence's memory, and nothing could make her forget the man her father could sometimes be.

She remembered sitting in her father's lap by a window, watching lazy snowflakes fall against the glass, feeling effortlessly loved. Her mother chose to believe those days were gone, and that the future held more promise, but Florence wanted nothing more than to go back.

"It wasn't only bad times," Florence said.

"It doesn't matter. We're here now," her mother replied. "And I think you're going to love it."

FLORENCE HATED TO ADMIT IT, but her mother wasn't wrong. For starters, Florence was able to go to school again, which she'd missed. Walking there that first day almost made her want to cry, just thinking about simple, luxurious problems like homework and mean girls and making friends. She'd had to make new friends so often it had become a talent of hers. She'd quickly figured out who the cleverest girls were, and within a week, Lois Strunk, Mildred Ducker, and Hazel Seaborg had become her best friends ever.

Florence had forgotten how easy schoolwork was. She wanted to have enough homework so she wouldn't be forced to get a job after school, and found that she had to ask for it. After being in class for only three days, she impressed the teacher, Miss Greer, by electively memorizing the poem "Ozymandias." Miss Greer let her take home an old dictionary, and the following week Florence finished second in the class spelling bee. She had been positive that the word "ingress" had an "e" at the end. It sure seemed like something that word would do, she explained.

"Perhaps you'll be a teacher yourself one day," Miss Greer replied.

Hearing someone believe that she had a future in something besides cleaning houses or cleaning dishes made her want to cry, and she didn't want the other kids to see that. She left the room so quickly she forgot to even say thank you, and sat in the outhouse, and wept.

On the last day of school, Florence saw Archie Eastman for the first time. She and her new friends Lois and Mildred were playing by the lake when they saw him in his backyard, in a dirty T-shirt and black pants, smoking a cigarette and cleaning a shotgun. He was younger than she'd imagined. His shiny black hair fell over his face in long strands, but he didn't seem to notice. He was handsome, like Clark Gable, but intense and brooding, which made him even more interesting. He glanced up once, and when he saw Florence and the girls running and screaming, he looked at them as if they were raccoons going through his trash.

Florence had found out from Lois and Mildred that Archie's lakeside cabin was famous because its previous owner had shot himself in the face in the dining room. She'd also noticed that most nights, Floyd Muller would walk across the street to Archie's place to bring dinner, and quite often stay to visit for a while.

"We mix obscure cocktails and play cribbage," Floyd said, when Florence asked him what they did after dinner. It was clear he was trying to make it sound boring, and it wasn't working.

"Can I come sometime?"

Floyd seemed surprised. "Archie doesn't like kids."

"I can hardly blame him," she said, and Floyd laughed. "What if my mom comes?"

"You know, he doesn't really like people in general. I'll ask him, though."

FLORENCE DECIDED HER MISSION that summer was to get invited to these little private cribbage parties. She'd never known an adult as happy and as in love with his job as Floyd, and in all her years, she'd never had a neighbor as mysterious and intriguing as Archie Eastman.

Still just a bartender's apprentice, her mom didn't have a lot of spending money. They mostly ate food brought home from the Lakeside, and had gone out only twice to buy anything besides basic groceries. Once she had a few changes of clothes, Florence was fine. The library, the woods, and the lake provided free entertainment. The little cabin was furnished, friends were plentiful, and nice, courteous tourists flowed past their little cabin every day.

THEY WERE MOSTLY NICE, anyway. Once, a boy who'd wandered up from the Majestic Lodge with his little brother stopped and asked Florence if she had any cigarettes. He seemed around her age, and his hair was slicked back with Brylcreem.

"No," Florence laughed. "I'm not old enough to smoke and neither are you."

"I know *you're* not old enough," the boy said, shaking his head. "I asked if you know where to get some. I'll pay you a dime apiece."

She knew her mom smoked, sometimes, when she could afford it. Betty would definitely notice a missing cigarette, but a dime for one seemed like a ludicrously good deal, and she'd just hand it over to her mom, if discovered. "There might be one back at home," she said, glancing back at her little cabin.

"*That's* where you live? In that dinky shack?"

It might have been dinky to some, but it was her home now, the best house she'd known in a long time, and she wasn't about to let this little toad insult it.

"It's not a shack. It's a house. It has electricity, and plumbing, and a telephone."

"What house doesn't?" The kid laughed again. "Your dad probably can't afford anything better, can he?"

Considering that she was only slightly irritated by this awful boy until that comment, Florence reacted in a way she did not expect. She shoved the kid hard, with both hands, and he stumbled backward into the road, falling flat on his back, just before a Nils Borglund & Sons Cesspool truck turned the corner. The green vehicle slammed on its brakes and skidded to a hard stop barely three feet from his head. The kid hardly seemed to notice he was nearly killed. He was lying on the ground, clutching his ear, bawling.

Florence's first thought wasn't remorse for almost murdering another child, but fear, at the feral quickness with which she'd let her anger consume her.

The bully's brother was enraged. "I'm getting my dad! He's a lawyer and he'll take you to court!" While he yelled this in a squeaky voice that sounded like a wet hand grabbing a balloon, the words still put fear in her heart. She ran, and not home to hide, or to the restaurant where her mom was working, but up to Archie Eastman's front door.

She knocked and rang and knocked until the door opened. She'd expected him to look annoyed, and he did.

"What is it?" She tried to tell him right then what happened, but embarrassingly, she just started crying.

"Come in, I guess," he said, exasperated, and closed the door behind her.

FLOYD MULLER WAS RIGHT. The walls of Archie Eastman's place were filled with trophy racks, taxidermy, and various skulls and antlers. Beyond that, the place seemed typical, just a spotless home with ordinary furniture, except for the bay window, which had a view of the lake that looked like a movie screen.

While standing with her back to this beautiful view, she told Archie Eastman the true, whole story, not diminishing her blame.

"That kid's dad is going to take me to court!" she cried. "They're going to send me to jail for attempted murder."

"No one's going to jail," he said, with reassuring, dismissive confidence.

"How do you know that? I almost killed him!"

Archie took a deep breath and shook his head. He cracked open his front door, and when he looked back at her, Florence was sure that he was about to tell her to get lost. "Go sit on the davenport," he said instead. "And stay there. I'll deal with it."

SHE DIDN'T THINK IT was polite to sneak around Archie's house while he was gone, but she *had* to. First, she went to the dining room, where the previous occupant had shot himself, and tried to look for a bullet hole in the wall, or even a bloodstain, but found nothing. She did spot the cribbage board and the alcohol bottles Floyd had mentioned. He had almost as many as the Lakeside. Besides that stuff, the entire house was orderly and shockingly sparse with personal effects, except for the main bedroom, which was a complete pigsty.

The house also had a small second bedroom, just like hers. This one was empty of everything but dust. It was the first time she'd been in a house where one whole room wasn't used at all, and it wasn't because there was something wrong with the room, like a leak in the ceiling or a hole in the floor. It was a perfectly sunny, comfortable, beautiful room, for no one.

What surprised her most was that there was little evidence of a life spent with others; no photos of relatives in the hallways, and little personality beyond the animal heads. Archie's weapons, which she assumed existed, given the decor, were all out of sight, but she was willing to wager he had more than that one shotgun she'd seen earlier. By now, he'd been gone for over five minutes, so she supposed she didn't have time to look. She thought she could more politely pass the time by reading something, but the only book she'd seen was the tome on the coffee table, titled *Records of North American Big Game*, which didn't tempt her in the slightest.

Poking into his kitchen, she saw flies dancing around a tower of filthy dishes in his sink. Under most circumstances, she despised doing dishes, but today, she was driven to do it out of both gratitude and pity. It was clear that he had no one to look after him and he could barely look after himself, with this sink, that bedroom, and those filthy T-shirts. For the record, it was her decision. *It feels better when it is*, she thought as she reached for the soap.

"Hey," Archie said, loud enough to startle her. "What are you doing in here?"

"Your dishes." She was almost finished, and it was the best job she'd ever done.

"I didn't ask you to touch my stuff," he said.

"That's why I did it. If you'd asked me, I would've been insulted."

"All right," he said, and nodded like he understood. "So, it's all taken care of. You'll never see that boy or his family again."

"What? They're not taking me to court?"

He winced and shook his head. A few strands of his long, shiny black hair fell onto his forehead. "Everything's going to be okay," he told her.

Without thinking, she threw her arms around him. He didn't hug her back, but it didn't matter. She hugged Archie as tight as she could.

It was hard to imagine that, in time, she would ruin this man, and everything he loved.

Five

Ned, 1981–1982

The Fourth of July crowd had thinned out from the Lakeside, and Ned was happy that Mariel was able to get off work a little early. The folks who remained seemed like older locals who'd seen Bear Jaw Lake's display of patriotism enough times to know it wasn't worth surrendering a prime barstool.

"I have one more thing to do," she told him, leaving him alone at the bar with her grandma Betty.

"Don't worry." Betty grinned at him. "She likes you."

Hearing that made him smile. "Thanks," he replied.

"So, do you work for your dad at Jorby's, then?"

"Yeah," he replied. "He just promoted me to executive vice president."

"Whoa. How old are you?"

"Twenty-four."

"I bet all the girls are nuts about you." Betty shook her head. "Who's your girlfriend back in Minneapolis?"

"I don't have one. And I live in Hastings."

"Hastings? Why?" She asked that as if something terrible had happened to her there.

"Well, I always wanted to live halfway between an oil refinery and a nuclear power plant." That was his go-to joke about the place, but she didn't laugh, so he figured he owed her a straight answer. "My family's company HQ is in Red Wing, but I wanted to be a little closer to the Cities."

"Well, that's a schlep to come up here."

"I don't mind driving."

"You got some snazzy car, I s'pose, then?"

"Just my dad's old Mercedes." He could've had one of his dad's Porsches, and he enjoyed driving them, but they were too showy and impractical. He almost mentioned this, because he thought it would score points. Maybe he should've, because Betty was biting her lip and shaking her head like he'd just cursed in church. It seemed like all of his answers irritated this woman.

She crossed her arms and leaned forward. "So, you like my granddaughter?"

"Yeah," he said, taken aback by the directness.

"What do you like about her, then?"

"A lot of things. She's kind."

"She's kind?" Betty looked surprised.

"You don't think she's one of the kindest people you've ever met?"

"Well, I'm unfamiliar with your type of upbringing, but it's certainly possible she could be that for you." Betty put her hands down on the bar. "So, tell me. What does a handsome rich kid like you, who lives four and a half hours away, want with Mariel?"

It finally dawned on him: Betty wasn't afraid that he was going to sleep with Mariel and then ditch her. She was afraid that Mariel would fall for Ned and move far away. Which he hoped would happen, without question, if everything worked out.

Just then, Mariel appeared, and said they had to hurry, or all the good spots would be gone. She said good night to her grandmother, who shouted to be careful. "Always," she replied, without looking back.

MARIEL GUIDED THEM TO where her friends were, in the patch of open, undeveloped earth across the road from the supper club, which went right up to the water. The trees were far enough away on either side to not block the view, but close enough to lend an impression of privacy. It was as perfect a fireworks-watching spot as there ever existed. It was a miracle that no one had put a house or a cabin here, he remarked, as he slapped a mosquito on his neck.

"There used to be one, I heard," Mariel said, and took in the crowded shoreline scene. "There they are."

Ned introduced himself to Mariel's friends, a couple named Zach and Alli, as they cleared space for Mariel's blanket. Then Ned heard the pleasing snap of aluminum cans around them, and his heart sank. He was about to admit his habit of poor planning when Mariel pulled two cans of Hamm's from her purse, and handed him one.

As they waited for the fireworks, he talked about how long he'd been coming up to Bear Jaw, how beautiful it was, and how great it would be to just live up here someday. At one point, he shifted on the blanket, and his bare arm touched her bare arm. She didn't move hers, and he didn't move his either, and lying there, talking, with their arms touching, was so unbearably sexy, he'd think of it for years.

He was about to tell her how nice this all was, as the first rocket of the evening broke the darkness, and lit up their faces.

THEY'D BEEN THE LAST people left on the shoreline for a while before he worked up the nerve to kiss her. One of the things he discovered about making out on a scrubby patch of wet ground near a lake is that he didn't like making out on a scrubby patch of wet ground near a lake, besides the company. There were bugs everywhere, their heads and elbows kept hitting rocks, and he accidentally knocked over their cans and rolled her into the spilled beer. When she suggested they go back to her cabin for more beer, he was just as relieved as excited.

WHEN SHE LED HIM to one of the little rustic shacks on the supper club property, he tried his best to hide his surprise. Earlier he had told her that his family had a "little cabin" across the lake. Her place was what most people meant by the word "cabin," a cozy, tiny wooden structure. It reminded him of college life, how you could see most of someone's possessions all at once in a single room, defiantly asserting a personality. In Mariel's case, there was a Bruce Springsteen poster, stacks of books, an old Hamm's beer sign, a lot of candles, and a couple dozen albums, which Ned instinctively began riffling through. Nothing told you more about a person, in his opinion, and this collection put her over the top. Bob Dylan, Stevie Wonder, Nina Simone, Leonard Cohen, Roberta Flack, Patti Smith, John Prine, and of course, Bruce Springsteen.

He would never tell Mariel this, at least not for a while, but his mom had enjoyed a lot of these musicians too. And she also would've dug the beer sign and the cribbage board. His mom may have married a guy with a lot of money, but Ellen Prager only truly loved simple pleasures until the day she died. She preferred beer to Pomerol, popcorn shrimp to caviar, and after all of the family trips to Switzerland, India, Italy, and Kenya, her favorite vacation destination was the Sands casino in Las Vegas. Seeing the way Mariel lived made him think of his mom, once and always a farm girl from New Prague, and how much she would've liked Mariel, right away.

"Your place is awesome," he told her.

"Thanks. It'll do."

It'll do will never do, his father would say. *People have the lives they settle for.* But most people weren't as insulated against events outside their control as his father was. "I think it's perfect," said Ned.

"There's the kitchenette. And the bedroom," she said, indicating the door, but not opening it.

"Can we go in?" he asked, realizing too late that this may have come out more forward than he'd intended.

"We're not going to have sex," she said. "At least not right now."

"Oh, okay." He was relieved to hear that it remained a possibility, and might've said so like a total nimrod, had she let him keep talking. Instead, she kissed him.

In his life, he'd experienced some kisses that felt like drowning in honey, some kisses that felt like getting fed by a large flightless bird, and a few that felt like budget dentistry. Mariel's kisses erased all thoughts and sensations except kissing and being kissed. He'd never taken drugs, but if this is what they were like, he saw the point. He'd forgotten about everything else in the world, until they somehow agreed to stop, and after a last kiss in the doorway, he walked home in the dark, with a numb, tired mouth and a different future.

By THE TIME NED awoke at eleven the next morning, breakfast had long since been cooked and served. His father and stepmom were out on the pontoon boat, which was Ned's favorite of their boats, and also the oldest. He'd have gone with them if he were awake, but here he was, watching them from a distance.

Carla was out back in the hammock, reading a Jon Hassler novel that belonged to Ned, drinking a Bloody Mary. Ned made himself some of his mom's favorite coffee, instant Suisse Mocha, in her old Sands mug, and stirred it as he meandered outside.

Carla dog-eared the page she was on. "So, stud-boy, how was your night?"

Ned smiled involuntarily. "Pretty good."

"Pretty good?" Carla laughed. "So, what, did you bone her?"

"No, we didn't want to rush into things."

"Why not? Equipment failure?"

"You don't have to have go all the way to have a good time." He took a sip of coffee, and watched his father's boat approach their dock. "How was it here last night after I left?"

She shrugged. "A little weird."

While Ned was off having the most memorable July Fourth of his life, Ned had totally forgotten to consider what it might've felt like from his sister's perspective. Just because he could easily imagine her being fine without him doesn't mean that she was. "I'm sorry," he said.

"It's okay. You gotta live your life. Is that what you came out here to say?"

"No, there's something I wanted to ask you. I don't think I'm gonna ride back home with everyone today. Mariel has tomorrow off. So I want to stay up here an extra night."

"Cool. So you can finally bone her?"

"No, I just want to spend more time with her." Ned sighed. "So, can you drive back up here tomorrow and pick me up? Please?"

"Nope." Carla laughed. "Get her to drive you."

"But I don't even think she has a car." He actually knew that Mariel did, but a nine-hour round trip seemed like a lot to ask so soon.

"If I gotta burn a sick day to drive back up here and drag your ass home, you're gonna owe me a favor. A huge one."

A hundred feet away, Edward and Peg stepped onto the dock. "Dad's coming up."

"Here, hold this." Carla passed him the Bloody Mary. He wondered if it was because she was leaving the hammock, but she didn't budge. "Dad reams me out when he catches me drinking."

"Is this the favor?"

"Nope," Carla said, and went back to her book.

"A little hair of the dog?" his dad asked, pointing at the drink in Ned's hand. "Hey, put down the booze for a second, and help me put the cover on the boat."

"Dad?" he asked in a higher, nervous register. "I'd like to stay up here another night."

"So would I, but we've got a shitload of work this week."

"Well, I have three weeks of paid vacation time, right? I want to use some of it now."

"You're serious? You've been the executive VP for two days, and you want to take a vacation?" His father shook his head. "I knew I promoted you too early. Shoulda waited until you were married."

Peg, who'd stood there with the piqued focus of a cat watching a can of wet food being opened, released a long sigh. She'd long ago given up on trying to get Ned and Carla to like her, and was now gloriously blunt. "He just wants to spend more time with that girl from the restaurant."

Ned nodded. "Yeah, pretty much."

Edward shook his head. "And how the hell do you think you're going to get home?"

"Me. I'm driving back to get him," Carla said from the hammock.

Ned glanced over at his sister, who winked at him. *Siblings united*, he thought.

Ned's father pursed his lips, looked over his insolent brood, and turned back toward the pier. "Help me with the pontoon cover," he said in Ned's direction, and once that job was finished, he didn't speak to Ned again all day, until he requested an extra pair of hands to help load up the car. Carla was the only one who told him goodbye.

THAT NIGHT, NED WALKED Mariel back to his family's place after work. She'd never been inside a house on this side of the lake before, she'd said, but once she was inside, she took it all in quietly.

"I know some of the furniture is really garish," he told her. You can say whatever's on your mind, I won't be offended."

What she said surprised him. She asked, "Would you call your dad a happy person?"

"I don't know," he said, which was the truth. "He loves his job, which I guess is a good thing, because he didn't really have a choice. Are you the only heir to the Lakeside, or do you have siblings and cousins to deal with?"

"Just me," she said, as if it was something she was afraid to say aloud. "Not taking over anytime soon, though, I hope."

He'd never dated someone before who'd also inherit a restaurant. He was momentarily transfixed by what he confused for fate. "Me too," he told her. "One day I'll own my family's entire restaurant chain." This was something he usually never discussed unless he was asked. He tried not to be too proud of it.

"Oh, which chain?" He didn't believe that she didn't know, because most locals up here seemed to know everything, but it was still polite of her to feign ignorance.

"Jorby's," he said. He knew she must like it, because she'd been there.

"Oh," she said. "Neat."

"You know, it's the second fastest-growing family restaurant chain in the Midwest," he said, only because he sensed her intrigue evaporating.

"I'm not surprised." She opened one of the kitchen cabinets, and then paused. "May I have a glass of water?"

"Sure, help yourself." A moment later, he realized he should've gotten it for her, but he supposed he was still stunned by her apparent nonchalance. Maybe she was actually impressed, and just trying to play it cool. Everybody liked Jorby's. Every town wanted one. When he looked at her again, she was drinking out of his mom's Sands mug. No one ever used that mug besides him and his sister. It was so bizarre to see it in the hands of someone else, someone outside the family.

"Oh hey—" Ned said, with a suddenness that startled Mariel, and the mug fell from her hands onto the hard Mexican ceramic tile.

As Ned took in the mug, now broken into five pieces on the floor, he felt his blood turn to lava. If anyone else had done this, he would've been furious and upset. Instead, he restrained himself, remained quiet, and told himself to breathe.

Mariel fell to her knees to clean up the pieces. "I'm so sorry!"

"It's okay," Ned told her, and meant it, kneeling next to her to wipe up the spilled water with a decorative towel ineffective for the task. "This mug was . . . you know, it's all right."

"Do you have Krazy Glue? Maybe we can fix it," she said, holding the shards of the old mug in her hands, like they were newborn mice. She didn't even know what this object had meant to him, and the care she showed toward it was heartwarming.

The mug was indeed fixable, but that was not how he wanted to spend his limited time with her. "It's okay. I can do it later."

Then, kneeling on the floor next to her, wiping the tile, she apologized again, and to let her know it was okay, he kissed her. She kissed back with an intensity he did not expect. Soon, they were doing something that had probably never been done before in that kitchen, and it was indescribably awesome.

. . .

AFTERWARD, THEY EMBRACED for what seemed like a record time, nude on the cold, uncomfortable kitchen floor. When they finally separated, he turned away, out of some illogical but hardwired modesty, and she laughed at the tile marks on his butt cheeks, and he laughed, too, at his ability to surprise himself.

THE FOLLOWING DAY, they were still in bed when he heard a car horn honk, and Ned knew it was Carla's grimy yellow Le Car idling in the driveway.

"That's your sister's car?" Mariel asked. She seemed amused.

Carla had plenty of money from their father, too, probably far more than he did by now, because she never spent it. Even the Le Car was bought used.

"Yep, that's her, all right," Ned replied. "Need a ride?"

TEN MINUTES LATER, Ned left Mariel with a kiss in the parking lot of the Lakeside.

Once they were back on the road, Carla grinned at her brother. "Well?" she asked.

"No comment."

"Great. Now what are we gonna talk about?" Carla sighed. "She is cute, though."

"She's not cute. She's incredibly beautiful."

"I wouldn't go that far. The Taj Mahal is incredibly beautiful.

But she's cute. So, you're gonna throw your whole summer away driving up here and back, aren't you?"

"Hell yeah. You should find someone up here, and we can carpool."

"I'm gonna be busy. Dad just made me general manager of the Jorby's in Minneapolis."

He'd heard this might happen. "If you tell him you'll go to law school, he might at least give you a better franchise."

"Nope." Carla laughed. "I told him I want the job."

Ned felt bad for the Minneapolis Jorby's, how it was evidently being treated as some kind of proving ground for Edward Prager's children. He hoped, though, that his sister would wise up and get that JD. What good is a family business if it doesn't keep the family together?

THE NEXT DAY WAS Ned's first board meeting with the executive leadership, and Ned was pumped. He'd looked forward to this day since he was a little boy.

His dad called these meetings "Tuesday coffee," and served a giant spread of Jorby's breakfast food. Ned made sure that he was the first to arrive, not only to impress his father but also to grab some food while it was still hot. He didn't know where to sit, if people had usual seats, so he just sat in the middle, facing the doors, so he could greet everyone who entered.

The first person to arrive after Ned was the general counsel, Charles Webb-Ford. Ned had read in a company newsletter that Charles was forty-six, happily divorced, and enjoyed golf and single malt Scotch. He'd attended the University of Pennsylvania, which Ned didn't know was an Ivy League school until he read that in Charles's profile.

"Hi, Charles," Ned said, extending his hand. "I'm Ned Prager. Good to finally meet you."

Charles winced as he shook Ned's hand. "You're eating the food?"

Ned felt like he'd breached some unspoken protocol, and felt terrible. "Should I have waited until everyone was here?"

Charles shook his head. "Nobody eats the food."

Ned did, because he loved it. But Charles was right. None of the next nine people who came in touched the spread.

The last of the nine was his dad's old high school buddy Fritz Lauder. "Uncle Fritzie" was a gregarious, childless souse who'd treated Ned with the deference due a future boss since Ned was a toddler. Ned had liked Fritz when he was a kid, but as a colleague, it was more complicated. It took less than a day to figure out that Fritz wasn't the most popular person in the office, especially with the female employees. Ned's secretary also reported that while Fritz enjoyed his salary and title as chief marketing officer, he delegated all of his tasks to his overworked staff. Even so, Fritz was untouchable while Edward was in charge.

Fritz slapped Ned on the back, congratulated him, and then grabbed a sausage that he held in his mouth like a cigar. That was the only food anyone else touched.

"Executive vice president," Fritz said. "You deserve it."

Ned shrugged. "Well, right now, I'm the least qualified person here to have any executive responsibility. I really don't know anything about what I'm supposed to be doing."

Everyone went quiet and stared at him.

Finally, Fritz burst out laughing, and was really guffawing loudly, like this was the funniest thing he'd ever heard. It was disconcerting, but also infectious. Pretty soon everyone in the room, except Charles, was laughing too. Fritz slapped Ned on the back again. "Good one, kid. You really had us there for a second."

Ned's father, the last person to arrive, pointed at Ned as he entered. "That's my boy. He appreciates a value-priced breakfast," Edward said, and everyone laughed again.

"THAT WAS FUN," Ned told his father afterward.

"What are you, nuts?" Edward Prager laughed bitterly. "I hate these meetings. You want fun? We've got an eight a.m. tee time at Minikahda on Saturday. You, me, Fritzie, and, guess who? Uncle Nathan. He's coming because I said you'll be there."

Ned's uncle Nathan was a judge in Bloomington whose ideas of a good time were reading tomes on medieval history, reciting baseball statistics, and criticizing people for making insufficient retirement plans. He viewed the entire outside world as people who needed to know things that he alone could inform them about. Golfing with him was brutal. If anyone was within earshot, it took him five minutes to sink a two-foot putt. And this Saturday, Ned intended to be on the road to Bear Jaw by one so he could get there in time for supper. With this lot, he'd also be forced into a cocktail lunch afterward. It'd be pushing it.

"Dad, I have plans."

"Change your plans. You should spend more time with Uncle Nathan. It's extremely handy to be on good terms with a judge, you know."

Ned didn't intend to end up in any situation where it'd be handy to be on good terms with a judge, but there was no use arguing this with his father. The larger point, about being in charge of his free time, he did briefly weigh whether to argue.

He'd been waiting for this job for so long, and he was thrilled to finally have it, even if it meant intimidating meetings and enforced camaraderie with lecherous rich alcoholics. But now that he was falling in love with someone, his heart and mind had no greater priority. He'd have to figure out a way to do everything.

His father, meanwhile, was still talking. "You should take Nathan out to the Lincoln Del some night. Or to a Twins game. He's got season tickets on the first-base side."

"That's a great idea," he told his dad. And it was, but with somebody else.

NED SAW MARIEL seven more times between early July and late September, and while each hour with her felt more wonderful than the last, none of them would be spent at a baseball game. Sadly, work and baseball schedules didn't permit them to visit Ned's favorite place on earth together until it was almost too late. While golfing one Saturday morning, Uncle Nathan mentioned that the final Wednesday of September would be the last Twins game ever at the Met. As soon as Ned could, he bought the best two seats available. He planned for that afternoon to be a memorable one, either way, despite the rain in the forecast.

Ned and Mariel arrived at the stadium early, so he had time to relax amid the best artificial environment ever invented, and take in the aura. He knew people who felt that way about places like theaters and church, but to him, those settings were compromised by time and certainty. A play was never going to remove its most prominent actor halfway through act 1 due to ineffectiveness; a preacher would never crush the hopes of his flock and send them home disappointed a couple of Sundays a month. That's why Ned loved baseball. It might break your heart, but you believed in it anyway. In a life of certainty, he cherished this elective relationship with peril.

"When does the game start?" Mariel asked him.

"In an hour and twenty minutes," Ned said, and leaned back in the best uncomfortable chair in the state.

"Better question, then. When is it over?"

"Maybe never. Once it begins, there's no promise that a baseball game will ever end."

"Oh." Mariel looked down at the field. "What side are we on?"

Wow, she really didn't know baseball. "That's third base, right in front of us."

"Oh," she said. "What happens there?"

"If a batter ends up there, it means he's about to score."

"Is that what the third baseman does?"

"No, the third baseman plays defense," he said. "If you want, I can explain the game as it goes on, but if you'd like me to shut up so you can figure it out yourself, let me know."

"Thanks," she said. "I'm kidding, by the way. I just wanted to see how you'd react."

"Oh." Ned laughed. "How'd I do?"

"You did extremely well. I thought you were going to be way more scandalized when I asked what happens on third base."

"Everyone has a first baseball game sometime."

"By the way, keep your eyes open when a right-hander is up. This is good foul territory for pull hitters."

Ned smiled at her. "How is this your first Twins game?"

"Used to watch them with my dad. And I played softball in high school. And on the college team at UMD."

"Wow, college softball, that's cool," he said, genuinely impressed.

"I actually wasn't planning on it, but my dad was sick by then, and I thought it would cheer him up to come up and watch me. He loved watching my high school games."

Ned was afraid to ask. "Did he make it to one of your college games?"

"Not when he was alive," she said, and looked away.

NED HAD PLANNED every step of what he was going to do next, but now it seemed so much more difficult, and not just because baseball was so personal and emotional for Mariel. For the first time in memory, he was attending a game with someone who was even more obsessed than he was. She was so deeply attentive, he wasn't even sure when to make his big move. She'd been right; their section had been peppered with foul balls, and they'd nearly got their hands on one hit by Mickey Hatcher. Whenever a batter was up, especially a right-hander, she wouldn't even glance at Ned.

Halfway through the game, Ned's heart began to beat like a trapped squirrel's. He and Mariel had been seeing each other long distance for almost three full months, and it was more than enough time for Ned to know what he needed to do. Hell, he could've done it after that first night. But he was glad he waited, so it could be a momentous occasion.

He needed a box of popcorn for his plan. "I'm going to get a snack," he informed her, standing up. Nothing too encouraging was happening on the field; it was the bottom of the sixth inning, the Twins were losing 5 to 2, and a rookie hitting in the eighth spot, Tim Laudner, was at the plate.

"Go between batters. It's rude to block people's view during an at bat."

"Oh, yeah," he replied, sitting down again. He knew that, but had lost his ability to think clearly hours ago. One pitch later, Laudner fouled out to the catcher. "Back in a bit," he said, as casually as he could muster.

"ONE POPCORN," HE TOLD the kid at the register. He heard cheering coming from behind him and glanced back toward his section. "Did they score?"

"Probably not," the kid said.

Ned handed the kid a small box from Gerber Jewelers in St. Paul, where his father and grandfather had each bought their rings, and felt nervous for a moment to be trusting an eight-thousand-dollar engagement ring to a strange teenager. "Can you just put that at the bottom of the popcorn?"

The kid held an empty popcorn box in one hand, the ring box in the other, and winced. "You want this covered in popcorn?"

They'd now attracted the attention of the other employees. "I see what you're doing," a young woman in a visor said to Ned. "Is that an engagement ring?"

This was getting out of hand. Ned glanced around. Now the people behind him in line were smiling at him. He looked back at the young woman and nodded.

"Can I see it?" the young woman asked, already opening the box.

"I guess," Ned said, seeing it was too late to stop her anyway.

"Holy crap!" the young woman yelled. "Is this real?"

"Yeah," Ned said.

Now everyone behind the counter wanted to see it. They talked over themselves about how many carats the diamond was, and how much it must've cost.

"If I had a ring like this, I'd sell it and buy a Corvette," the visor woman said.

"No way, I'd sell it and buy a boat," said a shorter co-worker of hers. "You can live on a boat. You can't live in a Corvette."

The kid who first handled the ring now stepped in. "Come on, we gotta put some popcorn on it," he declared, and took the box back from his co-workers.

The young woman with the visor watched it disappear beneath kernels, and then looked at Ned. "You must loooooove that girl."

The kid handed over the box of popcorn with a weird frown. "You realize that you're getting slightly less popcorn because of the space the ring box takes up."

Ned nodded. "I think I can live with that."

"I'll try to put some more on top to make up for it," the kid said, piling on another scoop of popcorn. "Just want you to get your money's worth."

. . .

THE INNING HAD ENDED before Ned even paid for the popcorn, and he had to wrestle through a crowd to get back to his section. From a distance, he saw Mariel standing up, talking animatedly to the women in the row behind her. She appeared to be holding something. It was a baseball.

"I caught it!" she yelled to him. "I caught a foul ball!"

"Wow, that's amazing."

"I can't believe it! This is the best day of my life!"

Ned was starting to fear that his popcorn surprise was going to be savagely upstaged. "Who hit the ball?"

"Mark Funderburk!"

"Cool." Ned said. Funderburk was another rookie, and the latest guy called "the next Harmon Killebrew." Maybe he would be. But he wasn't yet.

"Mark Funderburk is my new favorite player of all time."

"I'm happy for you. I wish I'd seen it." He held out the popcorn. "Want some?"

"No, I can't stand popcorn. It gets stuck in my teeth."

How did he not know that? God, he was a dolt. "Maybe later," he said.

BY THE BOTTOM OF the ninth inning, even though the Twins were still down 5 to 2 and weren't likely to stage a comeback, Mariel hadn't lessened her attention on the game or her grip on that baseball. Ned had eaten three quarters of the popcorn by himself and was getting sick of the taste. He should've told them to hold the butter. At the time he was a little distracted. The ring box was now just visible.

"Please help me out with this," he said, offering her the popcorn.

She didn't even look at it. "I told you, I don't like popcorn."

"But I don't want it to go to waste."

"Then take the rest home."

Ned waited for the pause between batters, took another fistful of popcorn out, and held out the box again. "Do you want to just look at it? It's really beautifully done popcorn."

She laughed. "What are you talking about?"

He kept the popcorn extended toward her, and she at last set down the baseball and took the box. "There's something in it," she said, and as she recognized the shape, she let out a startled yelp.

"Open it," he said. He still couldn't tell whether she was happy. Her eyes glistened, but when she turned to him, her expression was a blossom of anxiety. He'd screwed up. It was too soon.

"Ned," she said, smiling, and it was the best his name had ever sounded. "Yes, yes, I will, Ned. Can we do this at home, though? This is mortifying."

God, this was crushing. He had imagined her weeping and throwing herself on him and the world melting away. That's what he wanted this moment to be. Still, he'd heard the words he'd hoped for. At least, he was pretty sure he did.

"You know, I think I still need to get down on my knee and officially propose to you."

She looked like he'd just asked her to lick the floor. "No, I'd break up with you and leave you right now if you made a scene like that."

All he could do now was laugh, mostly at himself.

"All right. But you'll marry me?"

"Yes," she said, tears in her eyes. "Yes. Yes."

"Can I kiss you?"

"Not right now in front of everybody. Maybe after the game, when everyone is leaving."

They sat, silent, in the ambience of a disheartening baseball game, until Roy Smalley hit a fly ball to the shortstop and the Twins officially lost.

"I guess that's it," Ned said, and then saw the fans in the rows ahead of him climb down onto the field, followed by a rush of people from behind him. "Wow, nobody's leaving."

Everywhere, fans flooded onto the field, scooped up dirt and grass, and yanked any future memento that would budge. Ned and Mariel sat there, watching as a major league ballpark was looted all around them, until she finally leaned over to kiss him.

IT WAS NOW BEYOND TIME to meet Mariel's mother, but Florence Jean Stenerud wouldn't set foot inside Ned's condo in Hastings until Ned and Mariel were married. Ned suggested meeting at a Jorby's, and Florence wanted to meet at the original one in Red Wing, which was a pleasant surprise. When she arrived, she stood just inside the doorway for a while, and stared around the place, holding up a family behind her.

"It's changed a lot," she said, sounding a little sad.

"The original building was torn down in the seventies," Ned told her, and introduced himself. She looked at him like she'd expected someone more handsome.

"It's just me you have to deal with. Her father's passed on," Florence said.

"She told me. I'm so sorry."

"It's a shame. He would've been excited by this whole shebang," she said, perhaps meaning him and Mariel. "He liked cheap pancakes."

The host seated them and immediately brought them coffee and fresh cream; Mariel reassured Florence that everything she ordered was on the house.

"So when's the date?" Florence asked.

"I don't know yet," Mariel said. "We're working on it. But we'll have everything covered. All you have to do is show up and have a good time."

"That sounds awful," Florence said. "I'm the mother of the bride, I have to help with something. You know, Ned, she's my only daughter and I hardly even see her anymore."

"I didn't know you'd be interested," Mariel replied. "You're so busy."

"Yes, but I just keep thinking about my own wedding. Everything but the groom was a lousy decision. But if you have it all figured out, I don't want to be in the way."

Ned's heart honestly went out to Florence. If what she said about her own wedding was true—and why wouldn't it be?—it was the least they could do to make a lonely woman a little happier. "Florence, we'd be honored to have your input," Ned told her. "We insist."

Mariel sighed.

"What did I say?" Ned asked.

"Nothing, it's fine."

"Well, one thing does come to mind," Florence said, pouring

cream into her coffee. "Maybe it's two things. The invitations and the seating arrangements. I could take those burdens from you."

"Well, I don't know, Mom," Mariel said. "You don't even know who our friends are."

"I do too. Just talked to Cathy Cragg's mother in church. And you know who else I always see is Sarah Ladner's mom. You probably heard, Sarah's going to Carleton."

Mariel vaguely remembered Sarah Ladner. She was a few years younger in school, and always seemed nice, but Mariel didn't recall hanging out with her once, let alone being friends. Would her wedding be full of such people?

"I did not, Mom, because I don't know her."

"Also, I just volunteered at a wedding, and they had a very nice caterer who was reasonable. I asked her if she could do chicken à la king as an entrée, and she said maybe she could."

"Yuck." Mariel shook her head. "And why did you ask that? You didn't even know we were engaged until a couple of days ago. And what if we don't want chicken à la king?"

"It's classy if it's done the right way. And you know, the nice thing about doing it at my church in Winona is that everything is on the premises. You can have the food and dancing right there in the new fellowship hall. There's none of that driving from one place to another. That's how Mary Schiavelli's uncle died, he got into a car accident on the way to his son's reception. They had to have it at a Knights of Columbus because they were Catholic. Their whole entire wedding day became a senseless tragedy."

"Mom, I appreciate the ideas, but since we're paying for the wedding, we're making the final decisions on everything."

"Don't kid yourself. He's the one paying for it." Florence pointed her fork at Ned. "Look at that snazzy ring he got you. You could probably sell that ring and buy a boat. You'd still have money left over for another nice ring."

"Yeah, I don't think I'm going to do that."

"No, you'll probably lose it down the bathroom sink in some dive bar. Don't come crying to me when that happens."

"I won't, I promise you."

Ned was fascinated by how quickly this conversation had spun off the rails. He wondered what Florence would be like when she wasn't meeting her only child's fiancé for the first time. "I think I'll get our waiter," he said, and raised his hand.

Florence's attention hadn't budged from Mariel. "By the way, are you going to get a job? Or are you just going to lollygag around?"

"I'm working, Mom. At a supper club called Wiederholt's. I start tomorrow."

"Well, that's something." Florence sighed. "Probably as good as you'll get, with no other kind of work experience."

"She had other options," Ned said. "You know, I told her she could work with me at Jorby's, and she said no."

"Well, it's not what it once was," Florence said, setting down her cup. "The funeral home has better coffee."

A muscular young man in a Jorby's uniform with a name tag that read DEAN came to their table.

"Hello!" he said. "So how's everybody doing today?"

"I can't imagine a better morning," said Florence.

NED WASN'T AS DISTURBED as Mariel to have their wedding plans colonized—he was too preoccupied with trying to figure out what the hell he was supposed to be doing at work. The executive vice president's responsibilities were intentionally undefined. Find a way to be useful, his father had told him, without further clarity or direction. While he was theoretically linked into the chain of command of several departments, no one really needed him around. He sat in on each department's weekly conferences, where per his father's orders, he was supposed to tweak everyone's plans a little, whether necessary or not. Every time he actively involved himself with a project, he discovered it would've proceeded more efficiently without his involvement. The only thing he did that made him appear busy was to call frequent and arbitrary meetings with middle managers who were helpless to refuse.

"What did you do when you had this job?" he'd asked his father.

"I drove two hundred miles a day, looking for places to buy, or places to build. You'll have to go farther out than I did. Colorado. Kansas. Ohio. I want at least two Jorby's locations in each of those states by 1983. You up for that?"

Ned remembered how often his father was gone, and how long his trips were, and how much it affected his family. He couldn't do that to Mariel. "What about something closer to home?"

His father seemed surprised. "Sure, what's your idea?"

"Dad, I'm asking you. What can I do to help the company here in Red Wing?"

"That's not for me to say. You gotta blaze your own trail. Either bring Jorby's into the unknown, which apparently you don't want to do, or bring the unknown to Jorby's. How you do that is up to you, provided it's legal and makes a profit. And in the meantime, don't smile so much. Makes people think you're not hardworking."

In the weeks that followed, Ned did his best to seem like

someone serious and deserving of the top job. When he saw lower-level employees coming toward him, he tried to look busy. He especially tried to seem industrious in front of his secretary, because the admin staff's lunches were where an executive's internal reputation was cemented.

Mostly, he'd close the door and spend hours staring out his window at the impressive brown river and the old, kind trees waving at him from below. He'd looked forward to working in this exact office for more than a decade, and now it was perhaps the one thing in his life that disappointed him.

Amid it all, Ned also kept trying to convince Carla to work with him. It was obvious she could help him, but once she'd turned a profit in Minneapolis for three straight months, that's where she wanted to stay.

"How'd you do that?" he asked her on Christmas Eve, while on his third cup of glogg.

"It wasn't hard," Carla said. "I moved my office to a corner booth for a few hours a day. I put up with some shit for a while, but now the customers just come and talk with me. I've taken a lot of their suggestions."

"Like what?"

"I lowered prices, hired some old people back, raised wages, reintroduced some old menu items."

"Jeez. Why don't you just leave your checkbook on the counter, and hand out pens?"

"Oh, please. You couldn't get Minneapolis out of the red for a year. I had to try something different."

"Yeah, but how are you even making a profit if you lowered prices and raised wages?"

"Volume."

"All right, but how are you even getting people in the door?"

"Like I said, I'm meeting them. Eating at other places on the block. Shopping at the local stores. I even started going to church up there. Now they come in, they say hi. They know I'm not a bullshitter."

"Pretty soon, profit's not going to be enough. They're gonna need to see growth."

"Let me worry about growth." Carla laughed at him. "You used to be fun when you'd get drunk at Christmas. I'm gonna go drink with your fiancée instead."

"She's not drinking right now."

"What? Why the hell not?" Carla asked, but seemed to realize the answer just as she finished the question, and screamed.

"Carla," Ned said, but there was no reason to restrain her. Everyone may as well find out now.

Maybe the news would be enough to distract everybody from the fact that he had no idea what he was doing at work. Maybe he couldn't do his job, but he could do his duty and produce an heir, who most likely would be a far better person to run Jorby's someday than he'd ever be.

"Everyone!" Carla yelled. She seemed even happier than he was. "Ned and Mariel have some news!"

AFTER A CHRISTMAS EVE split between their families, Ned and Mariel spent Christmas Day together, just the two of them, in the hazy realm of the hesitantly pregnant. They imagined the next December would bring a much larger Christmas tree with many more presents. They imagined having to move from their condo to a place with room for a nursery. Ned openly wondered if it was a boy.

Then, three days later, on a Monday, it was all gone.

She told him in the morning before he left for work. She tried to brush it off, and kept saying it was a surprise anyway, and maybe they weren't ready, which was all true, but it didn't stop them from being heartbroken. Driving to Red Wing, Ned realized that he was too upset to think about anything else, and that Mariel must've been too. He turned around and drove home and they made an impulsive decision. Even if that brief pregnancy was unintentional, he wanted them to try again, even if they weren't married yet, even if they weren't ready. A switch had been flipped, so now for Ned, the opposite—a life together without children—seemed like darkness.

TWO MONTHS TO THE DAY after Christmas Eve, while staring out the living room window at snow falling onto the freshly shoveled sidewalk, Mariel revealed the news: she was pregnant again.

"I've known for two weeks," she said as Ned embraced her. "I just wanted to be more sure. But I'm still scared."

"That we'll lose it again?"

"No, this time, I'm scared it will actually happen."

"I think that's natural. I'm scared too. I think everybody's a little scared."

"I'm a lot scared," she replied, and took a deep breath. She was trembling. "If we really have a kid, I don't want to be like my mom."

"You had an amazing father," he told her, hoping it would help. "He's a part of you too."

"Yeah, my father was great, but he died, so I probably also have abandonment issues."

"Well, then I've got them too." He laughed to himself. "I think our baggage fits in the same overhead compartment."

"God, Ned. Don't joke about this. I'm telling you, I don't know if I can actually do this. I'm just going to mess them up for life."

"We're both definitely going to mess them up for life, but give us some credit. We're at least going to put our own spin on it."

Mariel opened her mouth to respond, but then started weeping. Ned embraced her. He wasn't worried at all. "I know you, and I know you're going to be a fantastic, thoughtful, loving mother."

"You're not listening. I need to think the worst is going to happen so I can be happy if it doesn't happen. You can go ahead and believe we're going to be great parents and that everything is going to be fine, but I'm not there yet. And let's not tell people this time until it's obvious."

"I completely agree."

"Oh, shit," Mariel replied. "Shit, shit, shit. I'm gonna be showing by July. I'm gonna be pregnant in all my wedding pictures."

"Wow," Ned said. "That's awesome."

"That's it. You can be quiet for the rest of the day," she told him.

WITHOUT FLORENCE'S HELP, Ned and Mariel would've had an intimate wedding in the backyard of Ned's parents' house in Red Wing, invited about forty guests, and hired Big Al Norgaard from the Lakeside to come down and cook for everyone. By April, it was clear none of this would happen. Florence lined up her church down in Winona, her pastor, her chicken à la king, and her tables full of distant relatives, school acquaintances, and church friends whom Mariel only vaguely recalled and Ned didn't know at all. Every day, Florence informed them about some new detail that had been resolved. Flowers. Programs. The cake. Even the music. They'd tried to put up a fight, but any time they made a decision of their own, Florence would override it immediately. It didn't matter that Ned's parents were paying for most of it. Florence rolled over them too. If they had opinions, they were wiped away like snowflakes on a windshield.

FREE OF ANY SAY in their wedding planning, Ned and Mariel had time to shop for a house. With a lot of help from Ned's dad, they bought a place on a large wooded lot in the upscale enclave of Sunfish Lake, with a hot tub, a swimming pool, and four more bedrooms than they presently required.

"What are we going to do with all of this space?" Mariel asked him.

"Fill it," he said.

THEY DID, WITH A housewarming party the first weekend after they moved in, and invited most of the people they'd invited to their wedding. Mariel's future maid of honor, Cathy Cragg, was there, along with their best friends from high school, college, and work, and most of their closest relatives, including Ned's future best man and favorite cousin, Eli. Florence, meanwhile, mailed in her regrets, because Sunfish Lake was too far to drive at night, especially with all of the maniacs on the road these days.

Around eight, Carla put on Prince's *Dirty Mind* album, and when people started dancing, it had begun to feel like the best party they'd ever attended, and Mariel turned to Ned and asked if they could just get married right then.

Ned looked across their dazzling new home, took in all the people out by the pool, and felt their warmth and the four cans of Hamm's in his veins. In this moment, he'd never felt better in his life, never felt more confident, or more in love with everything and everyone he saw.

He couldn't imagine that he'd feel the same way at Florence's church in Winona.

"We got the license in a desk upstairs," he said. "And the rings are up there too."

"You're serious," she said, delighted. "I just feel bad that Betty and Floyd aren't here."

Ned and Mariel had thought about inviting them, but it seemed like such a long drive for a party, even if they would've stayed the night. "We'll make it up to them."

"And don't we need a judge?"

"Hey, Eli," Ned called out. "Do you think your dad is still up?"

"JUDGE PRAGER," Uncle Nathan answered the phone.

"Hi, it's Ned."

"Oh, you. Heard you were at the Met, for the last game there."

Oh crap, Ned thought. He'd totally forgotten to look for Uncle Nathan that day. "Oh yeah, last fall. Yeah. Say, are you free tonight?"

"You know, I was there. You couldn't find me, or something?"

"I'm sorry, but we kind of wanted privacy. I proposed to Mariel at that game."

"Yes, I was made aware. You know, that's not very private, doing it at a ballpark. I heard you gave her a ring in a box of Cracker Jacks."

"No, it was just regular popcorn."

"Well, that's dumb. Cracker Jacks would've been better. You know, because they have that free toy inside. Then it could've been a ring instead of the toy."

"Next time, I'll use Cracker Jacks. Say, I have a favor to ask you. I'm calling because we want to get married."

"I know, in July, right?"

"No, we want to get married tonight. Can you please come down and officiate?"

"Oh. Well, that's interesting. What about your big ceremony and all that?"

"We've decided we just want to get married right now."

"You know how your father likes tradition. He'll be pissed to not be there."

"He's here now."

Nathan laughed. "What's your address? I'll do it just to see the look on your dad's face."

Forty minutes later, Ned and Mariel gathered their guests on the back patio by the pool. Uncle Nathan yelled at everyone to be quiet.

"We have gathered here today for the wedding of Edward Jonah

Prager the Third and Mariel Betty Stenerud," he announced, staring right at Ned's dad as he spoke, and then turned to Ned.

Several of their friends gasped.

"What's going on?" Ned's dad shouted.

"Edward, do you take Mariel to be your lawfully wedded wife, to love, to honor, and to cherish, from this day forward?"

"I do," Ned said.

Uncle Nathan grinned and nodded. "Mariel, do you take Edward to be your lawfully wedded husband, to love, to honor, and to cherish, from this day forward?"

"I do," Mariel said.

"You got rings?" Uncle Nathan asked. "Well, now's the time."

Ned slid his ring onto Mariel's finger first, and then she moved a gold ring onto his. He felt her warm hand trembling as she did it.

"What just happened?" Ned's dad asked. "What's going on?"

Uncle Nathan, noticing Edward, couldn't stop smiling. "Then, in front of these assembled witnesses, by the power vested in me by the state of Minnesota, I hereby pronounce you husband and wife."

Ned had tears streaming down his face. He looked at his wife—his wife!—and she was weeping too. He wanted to kiss her so terribly, but he thought he was supposed to wait for an order.

"Is that all?" Ned asked his uncle.

"That's the minimum legal requirement," Uncle Nathan said, and noticed the spread on the outdoor table. "Are those Doritos?"

"Aren't you supposed to say, 'You can kiss the bride'?"

"Sure, do what you want. Kiss the bride. Just keep it decent."

They kissed while their friends cheered and then stopped cheering, and kissed until they began cheering again.

Ned would often think of the joy of this moment in the years to come. Soon, almost everyone around him would change, and the grace and wonder in the world would be beyond his grasp. If it weren't for these memories he could replay in his head like old songs, he wouldn't have believed that his heart had ever been capable of such happiness.

Six

Florence, 1934

Florence felt the most important thing to do when becoming friends with someone was to bring something to the table. Because she wasn't allowed to mix cocktails, obscure or otherwise, she would learn cribbage in hopes of unpacking the mystery of Archie Eastman. The other grown-ups in town who'd heard of him spoke of him with wariness and respect.

"I'd want him on my side in a fight," said the wiry old bartender, Elisha.

"He seems ominous," Miss Greer said.

"I think you should leave him alone," said Floyd. "He needs his quiet."

"My mom always said the exact same thing about my father," Florence had replied. "And he still liked to play games with me."

Since the day Archie Eastman had come to her rescue against that mean boy with the lawyer dad, he'd gone back to avoiding her, which made him all the more intriguing. Florence had come to distrust adults who overtly tried to please children, and gravitated toward the Archie Eastmans of the world, the ones she'd have to win over. He played cribbage, so how ominous could he be? She saw no harm in asking him for a game. She also figured someone like him would consider it no fun to play against a beginner, so she planned to become an expert before challenging him.

She borrowed the cribbage board and deck of cards from one of the other guest cabins, and brought it to the restaurant in the early afternoon before it opened, and played against herself, hoping somebody would notice. Floyd did, right away.

"What ya doing there?" Floyd said, his voice as warm as a borrowed coat.

"Mastering the game of cribbage," she said, trying to sound unimpressed with herself.

"Kind of hard to master a game without an opponent. Reset the pegs. I'll play you."

"I think it's the best game in the world," she told him.

"You and me both," he said, and started to shuffle the deck.

"What do you like about it?"

"I'd say because it's like how life is supposed to be, I suppose," Floyd said, pausing to smooth down his sparse hair. "A mixture of luck and strategy."

"I hear you play it a lot. My mom says you play cribbage with Archie Eastman all the time after work."

"What?" He stopped shuffling the cards, seemed to think about her statement, and then began shuffling again. "Oh, yeah. Sure. Sometimes."

"She said you must have a tournament going, because you're there so late. I just want to know if I can join."

"Maybe," he said, and set down the deck of cards. "Actually, you know, I should probably get to work here. We'll have to take a rain check."

"Of course," she said, trying to keep the dismayed surprise out of her voice. "You know where to find me."

Floyd laughed and smiled at her as he walked away. It reminded her of how grocery clerks smiled at her before they knew that her mother was a thief. "You know, that kid Al Norgaard always comes in early. Why don't you ask him?"

It was cold comfort being stuck with the pimply fourteen-year-old busboy, but he indeed came in early, and he was delighted to play a game of cribbage with her.

"I've heard you're a master," Al said, and she did not disabuse him of the notion.

OVER THE NEXT FEW DAYS, after he'd beaten her four games in a row, Al Norgaard finally quit being pleased with himself and started teaching her the game. Soon, she was playing with the kitchen staff, like Floyd's mom, Jutta, and other people who came by in the afternoons, like Ken Eddy, the liquor sales guy.

By mid-July, she was finally able to beat Al three times in a row for the first time. Now, perhaps, she'd be a worthy opponent for Archie Eastman, she hoped.

"Leave that man be," Floyd told her when she asked. "I earned his trust. It takes a long time with some people."

"You're right, Floyd goes to Archie's to play cribbage *a lot*," Florence told her mother the next morning as she made oatmeal again. For years, when they bought food, it seemed it was only ever oatmeal, canned beans, and her mother's favorite, canned mandarin oranges. They were what Betty ate to comfort herself, but they had the opposite effect on Florence. To her, the sharp, cloying stench of mandarin oranges reminded her of eviction notices and seeing your breath while indoors. Even when she was starving, she hated them.

"Seems like a dull pastime to me," Betty replied. "But frankly, I'm glad he's not out playing the field."

"Why don't you want him out in the fields?"

Her mother shook her head. "Playing the field."

"Why don't you want him playing in the fields?"

"Never mind, honey," her mother said, and blushed.

Now, Florence figured it out. "Are you gonna ask him on a date?" She'd wondered about this since their drive north.

"No," Betty laughed. "As much as I'd like to, I certainly cannot ask my boss out on a date. It's unprofessional. I need to wait for him to ask me, though I doubt he ever will."

"Floyd is very professional, too, isn't he?"

"Yes, from what I hear, he's never gone out with any of his employees, ever. Which is very respectable."

"Well, then what about Archie Eastman?"

"Archie Eastman?" her mother asked. "He's kind of creepy."

"He's not creepy. He saved me from that boy and his dad."

"Yeah, I don't know what he did, but he put the fear of God into those people. But he shouldn't have to deal with our problems. Besides, I thought we agreed that you were done fighting other children."

"I'm not the one who starts it."

"You lose your head, though. Don't you?" Her mother sighed. "I guess we can agree that Archie was helpful, but you shouldn't choose a life where you need that kind of help."

"Mom, I didn't choose that life." Florence looked on as her mother poured bland, unadorned oatmeal unevenly between two chipped bowls. Most of the bowls and plates that came with the cabin had cracks or chips, and her mother never used the unblemished ones unless there were guests. "Anyway, what if Archie asks you?"

"I'll compliment him and politely say no. He doesn't even seem to have a job. I've already dated my lifetime quota of unemployed men. I'm holding out that Floyd comes to his senses someday."

"So, you wanna work as a *barmaid* the rest of your life, is what you're saying." She knew her mother hated the term.

"I love working at the bar. It's the best job I've ever had," her mother snapped, and frowned at Florence. "Which reminds me. Two weeks ago, I told you to stop hanging around playing cribbage, and get a job yourself. Remember our deal? If you didn't have a job by now, Floyd's going to hire you to wash dishes, and you're gonna do it."

"Give me three more days. I'll find some kind of work, I promise."

"Three days," her mom sighed, and gave Florence the bowl with the most oatmeal.

THAT EVENING, while her mom was at work, Florence knocked on Archie Eastman's door. He was wearing a white T-shirt and dirty black slacks, and held a squat glass of bronze-colored liquid. "What now?" he asked.

"I'm ready," she said, and held up her cribbage board. "I'm good enough to join your tournament."

"Tournament," he replied, as if he'd never heard the word before.

"Yeah. I bet I can beat you three out of five."

He pulled a pack of cigarettes out of his pocket, shook one out, and lit it, all without looking, which was something Betty couldn't do. Florence had seen her try.

He exhaled his first drag completely before looking at her again. "What if I beat you?"

She hadn't thought this over. She stood there as dumb as a bag of potatoes.

He spoke again before she could. "What can you wager?"

She had no money, and few possessions, at least any she could gamble with. "I'll do your dishes?" she offered, but as soon as she said it, she knew how pathetic it seemed.

He glanced over toward his kitchen, nodded, and then opened the door all the way.

"What are you going to wager, then?" she asked him.

"I won't lose," he said, and walked ahead of her into his home.

. . .

SHE'D JUST ENDURED HER second loss in two games when she finally built up the nerve to ask him something she'd been thinking about.

"My mom says I need a job," she told him. "But I'm too young to work anywhere."

"You're good at dishes," Archie said, resetting the pegs. "Floyd could hire you."

"You sound like my mom. I don't want to wash dishes over there. How about I work for you?"

"No."

She'd anticipated that reply, and had a convincing response ready. "You clearly need some help here. I can clean your house, I can cook too."

"No. Let's keep it friendly."

"I'd do it for a dollar a week."

"You still gotta drop two." He pointed to her cards. "How about the Majestic Lodge?"

"I told you, I'm too young."

He took a long drag from his seventh cigarette since she'd arrived. "You know that kid, Al Norgaard? He used to work the parking lot over there. Carrying luggage. Freelance. Made a dollar a day some days."

"Hm." She tried not to seem impressed, but that was a lot of money. "Freelance means I'm not actually working there for real, right?"

"That's right. Also means you keep all the money."

"Can I also work for you?"

"You can lose to me," he said, and shook his head. "You still gotta drop two."

"How about, if I win, you have to hire me."

"No," he said. "So, what do you actually want to do?"

"I want to make enough money so I can buy back the big yellow house in St. Paul."

"I meant for work."

"I think I want to be a teacher," she said for the first time. It was scary to hear herself say it. "Do you think I'd be a good teacher?"

He looked at her with a placid, impressed stare. It reminded her of how her father, who didn't enjoy much, used to look at the sunset. "You're the second person I've ever let into my house. I'd say you can do anything you set your mind to."

Florence was washing the dishes when she heard the door open, and thought she heard another voice. She left the kitchen to see that it was Floyd. He reacted as if she'd walked in on him taking a bath.

"What's she doing here?" Floyd asked Archie.

Archie laughed. "We had a tournament. She lost."

"Oh," Floyd said, and then turned to Florence. "I suppose you should be off to bed."

"I know how to play cribbage with three players," she said.

"Come on, Floyd, one game," Archie said, and put his hand on Floyd's shoulder.

"All right, if that's what everyone wants," Floyd replied. "One game."

THEY ENDED UP PLAYING FOUR.

It was the happiest night she'd had in years. Floyd seemed uncomfortable at first, but after a couple of cocktails called Corn 'n' Oil, he lightened up. He belched. He cursed. He laughed, and not just his polite, agreeable laugh. He laughed so hard he spit Corn 'n' Oil all over the cards, and the five of clubs got a stain on the back of it, so now anyone could tell where it was.

At one point, Florence left them to get a glass of water, and after she turned off the spigot, she overheard the men talking.

"She's not going to tell her mom," Floyd was saying. "And if she did, what would she say?"

"There's something you can do to get ahead of it."

"I know what you're thinking. No."

Archie laughed. "That woman hates me. It has to be you."

"We're not talking about this now. She's in the kitchen, she's probably listening to us."

"So what? We're going to be gone in a few months. You think they're not going to talk then?"

"Quiet!"

Florence had spied on enough people by then to give it a few moments before she came out, and to pointedly ask what they were talking about when she was gone.

"Grown-up stuff," Floyd said, and handed her the deck of cards. "One more game?"

. . .

SHE LEFT AFTER THAT fifth game, but only because it was almost midnight and she was tired. She didn't want to go, and they didn't ask her to, either.

The bar at the supper club was closed by then, but she assumed her mother was still there cleaning up. That's why Florence screamed when she opened the door and saw her mother sitting there, in the dark, waiting for her.

"Trying to sneak back home?" Betty shot up from her chair and put her hands on Florence's shoulders. "Where were you?"

"Nowhere," Florence said, because it was the first thing that came to mind. Finally, she thought of something better. "Out with my friends."

"Have you been smoking?"

"No, I haven't!" She could say that with conviction, because it was absolutely true. She did try it once, with Hazel Seaborg, and it was gross.

Betty put her nose to her daughter's sleeve. "Cigarettes."

Because her mother didn't like Archie Eastman, she felt she couldn't say where she'd been, or she'd be forbidden from playing cribbage with him ever again.

"It was Hazel," she said, and because Hazel had snuck cigarettes, Florence wasn't being a liar, just a snitch. "I'm really tired, may I go to bed?"

"Hazel Seaborg? I'm calling her mother tomorrow," Betty said as Florence bolted away and closed her bedroom door. "That's the end of this late-night gallivanting around!" her mother shouted after her.

Florence changed into her nightgown in the dark, shaking off her mother's words, hoping that Hazel could forgive her. As she got under the covers, she comforted herself thinking about the great time she'd just had tonight, and then thought about why. The conclusion she came to confused her. It was because, somehow, it had felt like being part of a family.

THE NEXT DAY, Florence walked down the road to the Majestic Lodge. Outside the grand entrance, amid the exhaust fumes and clatter of luggage carts, she gazed at the guests' long automobiles, giant steamer trunks, and oversized bags and had a better idea. She'd ask people unloading their cars if she could clean their windshield and headlights for two cents a car. She just had to run back up to the Lakeside first and borrow a bucket of water and some rags from Floyd. He was surprised at the request.

"That doesn't sound better than cleaning dishes."

"Trust me, it is," she told him, and returned down the road.

Maybe she should've asked for a higher rate, because the majority of these rich tourists agreed to her offer. She'd expected more of these folks to be mean, but the ones who weren't interested mostly just ignored her. After four hours, she had fifty-eight cents, and she returned home, exhausted.

HER MOTHER CAME HOME on her break that evening with hamburgers from work and in an unusually chipper mood, even for her.

"You will never guess what happened," Betty said, beaming, proud as a pharaoh. "Floyd finally asked me on a date. Can you believe it? He's going to take me to a dance in Bemidji."

"Oh," Florence replied. She'd hoped for this once, but now that it was happening, she felt unprepared. She began to get worried that her mother would screw it up somehow and they'd be forced to leave. "That's nice, I guess."

Betty's smile collapsed. "Oh, Lord," she said. "It just occurred to me. I don't have a thing to wear to a dance." Her mother, so happy when she opened the door, now was as anxious as a bird trapped in church. "And after buying groceries yesterday, I have hardly a cent left over."

Florence knew what she had to say. "I made fifty-eight cents today. Working at the Majestic. You can have it."

"What? You did? You got a job there?"

"Sort of." Florence nodded. "Cleaning windshields and headlamps in the parking lot."

"Oh, my resourceful girl." Florence knew her mother well enough to know what she'd say next. "Can you go back tomorrow and make even more?"

When Floyd came over to collect her mother for the dance that Friday, he smiled and said, "Now there's something beautiful."

"Where?" Florence asked. She wasn't being mean; from his tone, he could have been talking about a sunset or a Chrysler.

"Your mother," he said.

Florence was watching to see how her mother reacted. Betty

could barely contain her delight. Florence had never seen her mother so infatuated, and she decided to do her best to be happy for her.

BETTY MILLER HAD BEEN tolerably upbeat most of Florence's life, but ever since coming home after that date with Floyd, she had become a vessel of ecstatic joy. Watching her mother dancing around the cabin, singing out of tune, Florence felt the concrete of a future life hardening all around her.

Florence knew she should be grateful, because this was a good life here, a life many people would've killed to attain, a life of full stomachs and warm beds. Plus, if her mother continued to date Floyd and they got married, they could have these things and more, for a long time.

But in her heart, she was hesitant to embrace this future, and not just because it would inevitably mean she'd be forced to do restaurant work. She'd seen the real Floyd, the version of himself he was around Archie. Funny, relaxed, even affectionate. He wasn't like that with Betty at all, at least in front of Florence. Maybe he would be—and this was a strange thing to think, but there was no better way to put it—once he loved Betty Miller as much as he loved Archie. She didn't want to see her mother be *settled for*. She was too great a woman, and deserved better.

WHILE HER MOTHER WORKED LATE, Florence spent more and more time with Archie and Floyd. She learned many other card games besides cribbage—she especially loved poker and pinochle—and even beat Archie a few times. Unfortunately, he wouldn't give her anything she actually wanted as a prize, like shooting lessons or an introduction to taxidermy. Instead, he gave her Indian head pennies, spent shell casings, and one time, a pair of loaded dice. They looked and felt just like regular dice, and they instantly became the best thing she'd ever owned.

"You've used these!" Floyd shouted when he saw them.

"Just once," Archie replied. "Maybe twice."

"You're gonna get it, cheater!" Floyd yelled, and pulled Archie out of his chair and tackled him onto the ground. Archie was laughing the whole time, and soon Floyd was laughing. Taking all of this in, Florence started cracking up herself, seeing grown men behaving like boys her age.

The moment Floyd heard Florence's laugh, he stopped, and looked at her as if he'd forgotten she were there, and announced that he was going to the kitchen for some water.

"You use those dice, and I'm going to start charging you rent again!" Floyd shouted as he walked away.

"What did he mean by that?" Florence asked Archie.

"He owns this place. The fella who sold the Lakeside to Floyd's dad used to live here."

"Is he the one who shot himself in the dining room?"

"That's what they say," Archie said, looking away toward the kitchen. "You know, I hope it works out with Floyd and your mom. It'd be the best thing for everybody. Especially you."

"Why?" Florence asked.

"For starters? You'd be the future owner of the Lakeside Inn."

"No," was all she could manage to say in the moment. "I want to be a teacher. Like you said."

Archie looked at her as if she'd just failed a test she was expected to ace. "You could do a lot worse than own a popular restaurant. Coming from your background, that's an incredible stroke of luck."

"I know, but I didn't ask for all that. I just want to do what I want to do."

"That's a selfish attitude."

"I'm not selfish." She tried to return his disappointed glare. "If I know one thing, it's that if I don't get what I want for myself, no one will."

"Floyd told me about how hard your life was before you came here. And if that's the only thing you've learned from it, I feel sorry for you."

At that point, Floyd strolled back into the living room, carrying a tray with three glasses of water, one for everybody. "What'd I miss?" he asked.

"Nothing," Florence said, rising to her feet. "It's just that my whole future has been decided, without my say." Before anyone could calm her down, she bolted out the door, and walked off the road into the woods.

For a while, she didn't go anywhere in particular, just deeper into the moonlit forest, where she couldn't see the lights from the Lakeside Inn anymore, her tears serenaded by crickets, her mind simmering with thoughts that cooled into plans.

A FEW DAYS LATER, Betty came home from her fifth date with Floyd, looking flushed and anxious, like she'd somehow messed something up.

"Mom, what's wrong?" Florence didn't want her mother to be hurt, but if Betty and Floyd broke up, maybe it wouldn't be the worst thing in the world for Florence. Maybe it needed to happen for her to have any chance at all to make her own decisions about her future.

"I don't know if I should tell you," her mother replied.

Florence decided to say nothing, because that was the best way to get people to keep talking.

Betty sighed. "I don't know if he's actually interested in me. I know he's a gentleman, but he still hasn't even kissed me yet. I wonder if he's seeing someone else."

"I know who," Florence blurted out.

Although she had no idea what she was truly talking about, Florence told her mother everything she'd witnessed over at Archie Eastman's, doing her best to make it seem as unusual and improper as possible. With each unnecessary detail, Florence felt her heart twist in her rib cage, but her future was at stake, she reminded herself.

Her mother began to cry, and Florence knew then she'd won, and she'd get what she wanted. Even so, she felt rotten for what she'd just done.

THE NEXT MORNING, Betty Miller seemed as chipper as ever, and told Florence she planned to break up with Floyd before work that day. "This is what I get for dreaming big," Betty said. "Whether or not what you said is true, I suppose it's best that Floyd and I keep it professional anyway."

. . .

THAT AFTERNOON AROUND FOUR, Florence was curled up on the cabin's scratchy yellow davenport, trying to read a giant book called *Les misérables*, when she heard a hard, serious knock on the door. For a moment she thought it was a telegram with the terrible news that an accident had happened and she'd somehow inherited the restaurant anyway.

It was Floyd. She expected him to be angry or upset, but he just seemed tired.

"Hi," he said. "May we please talk for a moment?"

She invited him in, but he kept the door open and remained standing just inside the transom, like a gentleman.

"Your mother came to me today, regarding some rumors she'd heard. We talked, and I want you to know," he said, and wiped his forehead. "I want you to know that I've asked her to marry me."

"Oh," Florence said. She couldn't move or speak further. *This is what happens when you put your wants above other people's needs*, she could hear her mother say.

Floyd tried to smile at her, and although it was a kind smile, it was hard to watch. Florence didn't see a person about to get married to the love of his life. At the time, she couldn't have described what she saw. Many years later she realized she'd seen a person whose boat had sunk and who was holding on to flotsam for survival. And there he was, smiling at the hurricane who'd capsized his happy, calm existence and replaced it with a life of floating, a life of getting by.

"Is that all right with you?" he asked.

"No," she said. "I want you to still be friends with Archie, like how you were."

He laughed. "I'll still be friends with Archie. I'm going to ask him to be the best man."

"When is it going to happen?"

"In October."

"Whoa," Florence said. "This October?"

"Yeah, that's the plan," he said, like someone about to do laundry. "When you know, you know. Why wait?"

"I guess."

"I need to talk to you about something else."

"What?"

"Your father."

This was her least favorite topic in the world, especially from the mouth of someone who didn't know him. "It's all right. You don't have to. My mom divorced him a long time ago," Florence said, her voice trembling over the D-word.

"I know I can't ever take his place," he told her. "Not that I'd even try to fit in the shoes of a war hero. But besides that, you love him, and he loves you. You will always have him. I just want you to know that you will always have me, too, not replacing him, but alongside him."

It was a kind and fair thing to say, she'd realize one day.

"That's nice to hear," she replied. "But you know, he's coming back someday."

She didn't believe that, even then, but for some reason she had to say it. After Florence and her mother left him, her father had sold their big yellow house and, they found out later, had spent most of that money trying to track them down. Before he could find them, he had an altercation in a hotel that landed him in the state hospital in St. Peter.

Her mother had just told her this recently, years after it happened. A kind man went to France to fight in the Great War, and a violent man returned, was how her mother described it. Florence only knew the second man, but that was the only father she'd had.

She hadn't seen him since December 19, 1929, and had lost the one picture she had of him years ago when their original bags were stolen. But he was alive, she was certain. "He's going to get better and he's going to come back," she told Floyd, if only to hear it herself.

"I'd say, if I were him, I'd come and see you as soon as I were able," Floyd said, and nodded. "And I want you to know, if he's better, he's welcome as a friend in our lives."

"All right," Florence said, unnerved by the thought of this situation. Floyd sure wouldn't be saying this if he'd ever met the man he was speaking of. If he were set free today from the place that kept him safe, he'd drive up here just to sock Floyd in the jaw.

"I should go," Floyd said. "I just thought you should be the first person to know."

"What did my mother say?" Florence asked, although she knew the answer.

"She told me I should ask her again, with a ring," he replied, and smiled again as he left.

THAT NIGHT, WHEN HER mother came by on her break with a bowl of plain spaghetti for Florence's dinner, Florence forgot to be excited about her mother's news.

Betty didn't seem to mind. "Doesn't somebody look pensive today?"

"I'm happy for you," Florence replied, trying her best to sound like it.

"You *should* be happy. Can you believe how lucky we are? How blessed we are to have both met Floyd?"

"Yeah, that's true."

"You were quite wrong about him, obviously. The jury is still out on that Archie Eastman, though."

Florence had rarely been more eager to change a subject. "I made forty-two cents today at the Majestic Lodge," she said.

"Oh! I have a great idea!" From her mother, this statement was usually bad news for somebody, often Florence. "I know how you can make a dollar every day."

In a month, at that rate, she'd have more money than she'd ever had in her life. "Doing what?" Florence replied.

"Well, Floyd has done so much for us. And right now, he really needs help in the kitchen."

This is how a future gets derailed, she thought. She'd heard enough regrets in her lifetime to know that dreams don't always die because of something terrible, but more often because of something that's merely acceptable. "For how long?"

"For as long as you can."

"Mom, there's only two weeks before school starts."

"Yes, honey, and that's why he's so desperate. He'll never find anyone for just the next two weeks. You'll be able to keep doing it after school starts too."

"I thought I didn't have to work during school."

"You might want to. It's a different job than you've had before, you might like it. Floyd needs a new salad girl."

"Oh." She didn't feel an incredible hatred toward salad, she supposed, but she never saw herself as a salad *girl*. "What does a salad girl do?"

"What do you think? She makes the salads."

"A person does that?"

"Well, they're not going to hire a dog to do it."

"Yeah, I know, but it's just one person, like, that's all they do?"

"Look, honey, I know you don't like old food and dirty dishes, so here's a job where you're making new food and working with clean dishes. What do you say to that?"

There were a lot of things she would've liked to say to that, some of which would make her mother probably regret ever having a child. Instead, Florence sighed. "So when do I start this salad gig?"

"Right now. Finish your dinner, and come back with me."

"Oh, jeez. Why, did people order salads that aren't being made?"

"Yes, they did. Jutta's trying to make them, but Jutta's supposed to be on the line."

"All right." Florence felt like one of those ancient Greeks she'd read about, doomed to an obscene punishment. Sisyphus had his boulder, Prometheus had an eagle eating his liver, and Florence would have salads.

IN REALITY, it *was* all right. People actually didn't order salads very often besides the Swabian-style Kartoffelsalat, which Jutta made herself from a family recipe. Florence even looked forward to seeing Al Norgaard every day. He was funny, and stood up for her. If someone in the kitchen snapped at her when tickets stacked up and she fell behind, he'd come in as soon as he heard about it, and let them have it.

"I'll look out for you, and you look out for me," Al told her, which didn't just mean that she had a friend, but implied they were, in his eyes, equals.

By October, Florence was perilously close to enjoying one of her duties in particular. Before the meal was served, or even ordered, Floyd had the bizarre idea to set out a free tray of snacks for customers. Every off-season, between October and May, he traveled around the Midwest to see what other restaurants were up to—this is why Florence and Betty had encountered him at Jorby's Bakery and Café in Red Wing—and at some joint in Wisconsin, he'd been served a complimentary array of cold appetizers they called a relish tray.

"I'm borrowing this idea," he told the owner, who said Floyd could go right ahead, provided his restaurant was more than thirty miles away.

"People should leave here happier than when they entered," Floyd told Florence when he made the relish trays her responsibility. "May as well get started on that immediately."

"What should I put on it?" Florence asked.

"Something you'd be impressed to be given for free," Floyd replied.

On Florence's watch, the relish tray was a lazy Susan of black olives, halved radishes, pickled herring, cheese curds, carrot slices, and gherkins, served with crackers. This, to her, was an exotic assortment of luxury cuisine. When she'd been in the grocery store with her mother over the years, most of these items were routinely ignored due to their expense or impracticality. Now she got to handle them every day.

Still, even the relish tray and Al Norgaard weren't enough to make her forget her previous kitchen jobs and how much she'd always despised this environment. She hated being on her feet all night in a close, cramped kitchen, she hated seeing the food people threw away, she hated accidentally cutting her fingers, she hated overhearing ludicrous demands from customers, and most of all, she hated the nickname Al Norgaard called her.

"Hey, future boss," he said one night in October.

"Never," she told him. "I'm going to be a teacher."

"You're gonna own this place one day," he replied, and she thought she detected a hint of jealousy. "No matter what you are."

THAT'S WHY SHE WOKE UP on the morning of the wedding unwilling to move. Today, she'd become the legal heir to a restaurant, and she could not bear thinking that her chance for a legitimately happy life would be crushed by this destiny.

"Up, up, up!" Betty sang, cracking open her daughter's door.

From a young age, stubbornness had been Florence's greatest weapon. When she needed something to happen, her heart and body turned to concrete and no one could move her. She could wait out anyone until they folded. She could wait for months. Years.

"I'm not leaving this bed," she said. "Until you understand something. I'll stay here all week, if I have to."

"I'm listening," Betty replied, smiling.

Florence sighed. "All my life I've been cleaning up after people, making their food, throwing their food away. Maybe that's okay with you, but I don't want to be a servant when I grow up. Not like that."

"Oh, I understand," her mom nodded. "Whatever you want to do in your life instead, I'll support you. Floyd will too."

Florence groaned. It was never fun to argue with her mom, because of her mom's upbeat attitude. "What I'm saying is that I don't want to inherit that restaurant."

Betty shrugged. "Then sell it. You could probably get a lot of money for it."

"What?" The thought had never occurred to her. "Really? How much do restaurants sell for?"

"Well, the guy who opened the Lakeside as a speakeasy sold it to Floyd's dad for six hundred dollars. You'll certainly get a lot more than that."

She couldn't imagine ever having that much money at once. "I'd sell it for six hundred dollars, right now."

"Just maybe not when Floyd's still alive. He might find it disrespectful towards his family. His father and brother built the Lakeside into what it is now."

Florence hadn't heard much about Floyd's father and brother, beyond the circumstances around their deaths. Three years ago, they were killed in a car accident, coming home from a hunting trip. The restaurant was supposed to have gone to the brother someday. It only became Floyd's because he had poor eyesight and was such a lousy shot that he quit hunting.

For the first time, Florence wondered how often she'd walked into a family-owned restaurant or business and entered a circumstance born of a tragedy. For the rest of her life, whenever she walked into any mom-and-pop business, she'd wonder to what extent it was a living tribute to the lost.

"So, Floyd would be mad, if I sold it?"

"I would be, too, honestly, but when we're dead, we're not going to care. Now, up, up, up, it's a big day for us!"

Florence had to lie there for a few minutes anyway, just to feel like she'd put up a fight.

ALTHOUGH SHE'D never attended a wedding before, Floyd and Betty's wasn't nearly as glamorous as she'd imagined them to be. The church still looked like the church, only with more flowers, and the reception was going to be at the Lakeside, not someplace grand like the ballroom at the Majestic Lodge. Her mother's friends and co-workers did look a little better all dressed up, especially Al Norgaard, who looked like an actual adult man in his suit. He was sitting in the back row with Lois, Hazel, and Mildred, with a wide space between him and the girls.

"May I go sit with my friends?" Florence asked. She understood that her mother had to wait in the church office until the ceremony, but there was no reason *she* had to.

"Not until you tell your mother how she looks on her wedding day," Betty replied.

"You are glowing with pulchritude," Florence said. "May I go?"

"Are you sure you don't want sit up front? You're the only family I've got here."

When her mom put it like that, Florence did feel a little bad. "Well, Mother, I have a request, then," she replied.

HER FRIENDS WERE THRILLED to be sitting in the front row of a wedding, especially Mildred, whose two favorite things, after Nancy Drew, were weddings and wedding receptions. No boys had yet shown the slightest interest in her, which was unfortunate because she was absolutely obsessed with almost every boy in school, while Florence, who'd already attracted the attention of a popular jock named Don Kochendorfer, didn't really give a crap.

"Your mother's dress is so beautiful," Mildred said. "Did you help pick it out?"

"It's what she could afford, so it didn't matter what I thought," Florence replied.

"If I had a dress like that, I'd wear it all the time. Like to school, and everything."

While the minister was talking, Florence gave a little wave to Archie Eastman. He responded with a curt nod. He'd never been an ebullient guy, but he'd seemed despondent in the weeks leading up to the wedding. When she went to his place to play cards, which was less often now because of work and school, it didn't even seem like he was trying to win. But today he looked even more handsome than usual, and he seemed happy for his friend, or at least as happy as everyone else. Including the bride's party and the rest of the groom's party, he was the only person up there besides the minister who didn't work at the Lakeside.

When the minister said to kiss, and introduced them as "Mr. and Mrs. Floyd and Betty Muller," everyone cheered.

"Your mom only had to change one letter in her last name," Lois said as they watched the couple walk back down the aisle together. "What a bonus."

AT THE LAKESIDE, half of the dining area was cleared out to make room for a polka band and a dance floor big enough for the thirty or so guests. Some friend of Betty's in a full-sleeve, floor-length dress from the 1890s commented how nice it was to have live music in a place like this, meaning a place not as snooty or expensive as the Majestic Lodge. Before her mother could respond, that same woman asked, now that Betty was married, if another child was in her plans.

"Heavens, no, the Lakeside is our baby," she replied. "And to your earlier observation, we're going to build a giant new room just for music and dancing and wedding receptions."

Florence was wildly relieved by her mother's first reply; the only thing worse than restaurant work was the ceaseless, unpaid childcare inflicted upon an older sister. She'd seen it happen. Even so, Betty Miller would be here the rest of her life, Florence realized then. Her mother had stopped running, and Florence, somehow, found it in her heart to be happy for her, even as she knew she wasn't done running herself.

After dinner, Florence had spotted her mother talking to Archie by the bar. She wasn't sure if she'd ever seen the two of them speaking before, and snuck up behind them to eavesdrop, while pretending to get a glass of water.

"After tonight, you stay away from Floyd, and you stay away from our family," Betty was telling him.

Archie looked back at Betty the way an owl watches a rodent before striking. "I don't know if that's your decision."

"Think about it," she told him. "Only one of us gets Floyd. Only one of us can win. You know who that is."

"I do," Archie said, picked up two cocktails from the bar, and walked back to the reception, where the musicians were warming up. Florence watched him walk all the way to Floyd, hand him a drink, and toast. When Floyd laughed his beautiful, real laugh, Florence looked at her mother, whose hands were balled into fists, her ring gleaming like a knife in an alley.

ONCE THE MUSIC STARTED, Al Norgaard kept asking Florence to dance, and she kept saying yes, but only because he was such a good dancer. Lois thought he was handsome, and maybe he was. Although, like most boys, he was much handsomer when he was quiet.

"Do you want to hear my good news?" he asked between songs.

"No, I want some water."

"I'll tell you first. After I turn fifteen tomorrow, I'm getting promoted to dishwasher! Isn't that great? I'm going to be in the kitchen! One step closer to being a cook!"

She envied him, she really did. Al was on track to do the only thing in life he'd ever set out to do, in the only place he'd ever lived. It was also clear that he was telling her this to impress her, because he liked her, and not in the all-consuming, erratic way that her friends liked boys, but the way a bird likes a tree whether it has leaves or not. *Here he comes again*, she said to herself, watching him return from the bar with two glasses of water.

He had almost made it back to her when Lois stepped into his path. "Free to dance?" she asked him. Lois was assertive like that.

"Sure," Al replied, and handed Florence her glass. "Here you go."

"I'm dancing with him," Florence said. She downed half of her water, set it down, and grabbed his forearm, in a way that seemed to surprise them both. "I hope you're ready," she told him, and pulled him away, toward the music and the lights.

Seven

T he day after their housewarming party, Ned and Mariel informed Florence that the bride and groom for whom she was planning a wedding had just spontaneously been married. To soften the blow, they decided Florence should be the first person to know that Mariel was pregnant.

"That explains the quickie wedding, then," Florence replied.

"No, Mom," Mariel replied. "That wasn't the reason at all."

"That's what everyone's going to say. I don't suppose that occurred to you."

"No, it didn't occur to us, Mom," Mariel said. "Because we don't care."

. . .

NED AND MARIEL ASSUMED Florence would need some time to cool off, so they were shocked to see her car in the driveway the following Tuesday morning.

Ned watched from the kitchen window as Florence retrieved several elaborately wrapped presents from her trunk, all in playful, infantile patterns. These weren't wedding gifts; these were baby gifts.

"Hey," Ned said, calling his wife over. "Guess I was wrong. I thought she'd be upset about the baby being conceived out of wedlock."

"It's her first grandchild," Mariel said, and set down her coffee. "I guess we better go out and help her."

FLORENCE CONTINUED TO SURPRISE Ned and Mariel all morning.

"By the way, it makes perfect sense, what you did," Florence told them. "Your family shouldn't be throwing money away on some lavish wedding with a baby coming."

"Wow, Mom." Mariel said. "I'm glad you see it that way. I thought you'd be disappointed that all those arrangements you made went out the window."

"Oh, I never seriously made any arrangements," Florence said. "Now, I have something important to say. If it's a boy, I have a suggestion for a name. Gustav. Because that's a real man's name."

"That's actually our first choice," Ned said. *Not for that precise rationale*, he thought. "We wanted to honor Mariel's father."

"And Julia, if it's a girl," Mariel said. "After Julia Winthrop."

Florence snorted a little upon hearing the name of her celebrated ancestor. Perhaps Julia Winthrop was too high a bar. Mariel had actually suggested it as a joke, but Ned loved it. His mom's favorite Beatles song was "Julia," so the name itself made him think of her.

"We'll see what happens," Ned said.

Florence smiled, and for just a moment, it seemed like she was satisfied. Then that moment passed. "I'll tell you what's going to happen. You're going to need a lot of help with that baby. You have no idea."

Ned realized one major reason why Florence was keen about becoming a grandparent. This time, Florence's assumed usefulness was unimpeachable. As a mother colonizing every detail of her daughter's wedding, not everyone had perceived her as thoughtful and generous. A baby was another matter. At last, her support and involvement, even if unsolicited and only on her terms, would be regarded by all as helpful and kind.

FOR THE FIRST TIME since she was a child, Mariel wouldn't be going north to work at the Lakeside that summer. It made practical sense, as her OB was down here, and, of course, her husband, plus her new home and all its comforts. But Ned could tell that her choice to spend the summer at home made no emotional sense at all. Mariel deeply missed working at the Lakeside. "We'll visit," Ned promised her, which they did the following weekend. They popped into the Lakeside right after it opened for the evening.

"Heard about your wedding," Betty said immediately when she saw them.

"Yeah, it was a real last-second decision," Ned replied. Betty would never admit as much, but anyone who knew her could tell that she was furious to have missed it. Ned agreed to take the heat. "It was all my idea."

Floyd, meanwhile, was amused. "You eloped at your own house, huh?"

Betty shook her head. "That doesn't sound very official. You know, we haven't just hosted receptions here, but ceremonies too. And very few have ended in divorce."

Ned didn't have living grandparents, and although Betty was still a little wary of him, he loved and admired both Betty and Floyd. They'd put so much of themselves into their supper club— he could see how keenly they wanted it to thrive, to be worth inheriting. He understood that, but it was like watching them build a snowman with the last patchy snow of spring, on a clear day, with the warm sun rising.

THAT AUTUMN, Ned and Mariel were back home in their kitchen playing a game of Trivial Pursuit when she went into labor. "He's coming," she said.

"Are you sure?" Ned asked. Like she wouldn't know.

"Do you remember any of those Lamaze exercises?"

"I thought you'd remember them."

"I don't remember shit." She looked down at her empty pie on the game board. "Clearly."

He rose from his chair, and posed in the middle of the room as if he were seated. "Is this one? Where you sit on me like I'm a chair?"

"I don't know. But I don't want to do that." She sighed and rolled the dice. "Let's just finish this bloodbath, and then see where I'm at."

"But you're in labor."

"Yeah, and I will be for a while. I want to at least get a wedge first."

A COUPLE OF HOURS LATER, they finally left for the hospital. Ned packed the car, and flipped to the bookmarked page in his Hudson's street atlas. Was he ready? It was happening, either way.

"I'm scared," Mariel told him.

"I'll get you there safely, I promise," he told her.

"No," Mariel said. "I'm scared that he won't like us."

GUSTAV EDWARD PRAGER WAS born on October 20, 1982, at five pounds, twelve ounces, and nineteen inches long. He was tiny and pink as an Easter ham, and when he first cried, he was speaking for all of them. Mariel asked Ned to hold the baby, but the moment he had his son in his hands, Ned bawled so hard the nurse had to take Gustav away and give him back to his mom, who was able to keep it together.

While Mariel slept that night, Ned didn't ever leave the baby, even to sleep. He sat watching his son's tummy rise and fall, arrested by the twitching of his tiny fingers.

Who let *him* have a dang baby? He wanted to run out in the hall and ask somebody. He was as ignorant as any new father, and yet here he was, sent a delicate little boy to watch over.

. . .

ONCE THEY WERE HOME, Florence drove the two hours from Winona up to their house every day, and startlingly, Ned's stepmother did the same from Red Wing. Without making a big deal out of it, Peg showed up and appointed herself their night nurse so the new parents could sleep. Peg arrived right before they went to bed and left right after they woke up, so they hardly spoke with her, and could only reckon with her sudden, baffling generosity between themselves.

One night, about a week after the birth, Ned got up to go to the bathroom and saw Peg, holding his son in her arms, softly singing Barry Manilow's "Can't Smile Without You" to Gus.

He hadn't planned to speak with her. He rarely had, even though she'd been spending almost every night at their house. But that night, they talked for over an hour, the longest the two of them had ever spoken. He'd learned, among many other things, that she'd planned to be a pediatric nurse had she not met Ned's dad while she was waitressing at a Jorby's.

"That's why I was always tired and late to my shift," she said. "Nursing school was tough. Had my heart set on it, though. At the time."

"You could still do it," Ned told her.

"I'd been working solid since I was fifteen. Never had a week off in seventeen years. Your dad said that if I married him, I didn't have to work unless I wanted to. I think I needed a break more than I needed to be a nurse." She looked down at the newborn in her arms. "But I want to do this. If it's okay with you."

"Thank you," he told her, a little amazed.

"I always wanted kids," she said. "You know, your dad and I finally tried about five years ago, once you and Carla were both in college. Turns out that I can conceive, but I can't carry."

"I'm sorry," he said. After all the years when Peg had tried to get Ned to like her, through gifts and compliments, it was tonight's experience that did the job. It was never her fault, he realized. He'd never felt compassion for her before because he'd never created the space in his heart for it.

He and his sister had been so hard on Peg. When they found out, nine months after their mom died, that their father was dating a Jorby's waitress who was fourteen years younger, they let her have it, for a long time. He'd hoped to drive her away, which he was now ashamed to admit. Instead, she'd stuck around, and now here she was, an indispensable part of his life.

FLORENCE AND PEG QUIETLY tended to this newly expanded family, alternating their practical omnipresence like the sun and moon. When Mariel was upset about her problems breastfeeding, Florence was actually a comfort. She told Mariel that she also didn't produce enough milk, and it was painful for her too. Only some small minority of women found breastfeeding easy, Florence told her daughter. "Sure, keep trying, but don't kill yourself. Your health and well-being is important too. Don't ever be ashamed to give him formula," she said.

Ned, meanwhile, was back at work full time a week after his son's birth, and as grateful as he was for his stepmother and mother-in-law, he wasn't happy that they saw more of his son than he did.

"What can you do differently?" Mariel asked him.

"I don't know," was all he could say. "My dad used to be gone all the time when I was little, and when I asked him what he was doing, he'd say, 'Something for my family.' But it didn't make sense to me. I never wanted to be like that. But now I feel pressured that I have to be."

"You don't have to be," she replied.

Then we lose everything, he wanted to tell her. He didn't want to say this aloud, because he was afraid that she might decide they should.

His days at work were just becoming more bearable too. While he hadn't yet come up with any profitable innovations or broken into any new markets, he'd discovered a potentially useful pursuit that he actually enjoyed: going out to lunch.

STARTING IN AUGUST, Ned went out for lunch with a different employee every day, just to get to know them. It was always the highlight of his workday. Even if many of them may have said yes because they were afraid to say no, everyone at Jorby's HQ liked free food, especially when it was food from somewhere other than Jorby's. Ned loved asking questions and listening to people talk about whatever they wanted, and the employees seemed to enjoy it too. He learned a lot about day-to-day life at the company, picking up a few suggestions for improvements, and he'd even heard some amusing assessments of his family. The R&D team apparently called Ned and his father "Luke and Darth," which Ned thought was awesome. He promised the person who told him this that no one would get in trouble.

. . .

ONE SNOWY AFTERNOON DOWNTOWN at Bev's Cafe, eating lunch with a security guard named Edgar Caquill, Ned opened up about himself. He usually encouraged his guest to do the talking, but Edgar was such a patient and understanding listener, and that day, Ned had a lot on his mind.

"You should spend more time with your son, absolutely," said Edgar, who'd said he had three kids himself. "This time just flies by, believe me."

"I know, but I already took so much time off last year. I mean, how does it affect your morale if the heir to the company, a guy who's only in that position because of nepotism, is at work half as much as you are?"

"Dude, it's life," Edgar said. "People understand that. You got engaged, got married, and had a kid. You can't do those things on the clock."

"You have three kids, though, and you're there every day."

"Yeah, I suppose I should take my own advice. One of these years, I guess."

"Have you ever taken a family vacation?"

"Vacation?" Edgar laughed. "I can barely afford to take the boys to a Twins game. Not that I'm complaining. I put myself in this financial situation."

"You're a Twins fan? We should all go sometime." He hoped that this didn't seem weird. It wasn't easy to make new friends as an adult, let alone with people he could fire, but Ned really liked this guy. "It'll be my treat."

"Oh no," Edgar replied, looking toward the window, past Ned's shoulder.

"Oh no, what?" Ned turned around and saw that there was a commotion outside, right in front of the window.

A teenager opened the front entrance and yelled, "Somebody, call an ambulance!"

Ned watched Edgar scramble out the door to help, and then, just as quickly, run back inside.

"Ned," Edgar said. "It's your dad."

THERE'S NO REHEARSAL FOR some moments in life, two of which happened to Ned within a month: witnessing his first child come into the world, wailing amid a chorus of jubilant voices, and seeing his father, fallen on the cold sidewalk, silent among a trickle of panicked strangers.

Edgar was already on the ground, administering CPR. Of course he knew it. Ned did not. All he could do was kneel by his father's head, ferociously babbling, "Dad, can you hear me, can you hear me?" at his father's pale, unmoored expression.

Looking back on that moment, Ned felt terrible that his first thought was, *I'm not ready.*

Eight

n the summer of 1940, the entire kitchen staff of the Lakeside Inn was in love. Everyone, all eleven of them, were head over heels at the same time over somebody. Its effect on the food that was served was something that could never be taught or purchased. Florence had never experienced anything like it before, and the rest of her life looked for it everywhere.

There was a young dishwasher, ablaze with the blitz of a new summer romance, who often broke out in song. There was a chef, who'd been ferociously and quietly in love for a decade, who hummed and smiled all day. Then there were two people, a line cook and a salad person, who were just about to celebrate their fifth anniversary as a couple, and still couldn't take their eyes off each other.

There were three things Florence could watch forever. Fire burning, water flowing, and Al Norgaard working. Of course, he'd long been watching her, too, waiting for the right time to ask her out. To Florence, going on an actual date with a boy felt like the official end of childhood, and she wanted to wait until she was thirteen. Even then, she'd made him wait until after the Fourth of July. Now, five years after that walk around the lake when they first held hands, they were going to the Majestic Lodge on a date for the first time, and they both knew they would talk about the future.

SINCE HER BRIEF RUN as a windshield washer in their parking lot, Florence had avoided the Majestic Lodge. She didn't know whether it was a good thing that she recognized the employees at the front desk from church. Maybe she was out of place here years ago, but now she and her mother lived with Floyd, in his handsome Victorian in town. They weren't rich, but they were comfortable, and could afford to eat at the Majestic, although Florence never joined them. Betty and Floyd always went by themselves, for special occasions.

She bet some of the employees thought she and Al didn't belong there, the way they were gaping at the joint like children. It was hard not to stare, even as cynical as she was. The lobby was like an enormous, lavish log cabin, with a ceiling higher than any cathedral she'd ever seen, and vibrant, clean carpeting, wildly ornate lighting fixtures, a shiny grand piano, and thick woodenframed sofas that looked too expensive to sit upon.

"You know who stays at places like this?" Al said. "Famous people. Like Al Capone."

"No, he stayed at the Thunder Lake Lodge in Remer," Florence replied. Her mother had learned this from a customer at the bar. "He's never been here."

"When I was eight, I snuck in here once, just to see what it was like, and they kicked me out. Do you think it's weird that we live right by a place like this and never come here?"

"Not at all," she told him.

THE RESTAURANT WAS ON the side of the hotel that faced the lake, and the best seats were up against the floor-to-ceiling windows, fifty feet from the water. Florence and Al were seated against the wall on the opposite side, in a dim corner, under an oil painting of an obscure bearded voyageur. Florence wanted to complain, but she'd have sat them here too.

Their waiter ended up being Bobby Eaton, who'd been in her grade. Florence had won a unanimous, unopposed victory for class president, but would've lost to Bobby if he'd run. He was a star quarterback, was smart as a whip, and like Florence, was working full time through the summer to pay for college. A year later, he'd drop out over Christmas break and join the Army Air Forces, and three years after that, his bomber would be shot down over Czechoslovakia. But in the summer of 1940, Bobby Eaton was still a sweet young man who'd never left Minnesota, and it was a comfort to see him here, another kid who'd grown up poor, in a place like this.

"See, nice people work here," Al said after Bobby left their table.

"Wonder how he got the job?" Florence mused. "He probably makes serious tips."

"You'd work here?" Al seemed surprised. "Instead of the Lakeside?"

"Maybe I could do both. Pick up a couple shifts here a week."

"Huh, I suppose," Al said, nodding. "You know, I'm glad you like to work. Most fellas don't want their wives to work. I do. Or, I would."

"Are we married? When did that happen?" She smiled to let him know she was joking.

"How about next summer?" Al asked. "You want to get married next July, and have kids?"

"What?" Florence asked, and started laughing, which didn't seem to be the reaction he'd expected. "I want to go to college and be a teacher."

"I know, until you inherit the Lakeside. Gotta have someone to pass it down to, right?"

Florence had ignored Al when he'd brought this up over the years. He'd been obsessed with her status as his future boss since they were kids themselves. But today, with college a little more than a month away, she could not ignore it anymore.

"I don't want to inherit the Lakeside. When Floyd and Betty pass away, I'm going to sell it. And I don't want kids."

Al looked at her as if she were possessed. He opened his mouth to speak twice but couldn't find any words. Finally, when he did, he simply asked her why.

"I actually think I'd be a good mother," she told him. "If I wanted to do it, and I don't. Kids are terrible. They're like a tornado hit your house. I just can't be working all day and then come home and clean up after some child. I've seen it, it just never stops."

"I don't know," Al said. "I think having a kid would be the best thing in the world."

"You put in all that thankless work, and love them to death, and they're just going to leave you someday. I can't bear it; I don't even want to think about it."

"Oh. Well, if you were running the Lakeside, and you were training them to take over someday, they wouldn't leave."

"It's never going to happen," she told him, and in that moment, that was the honest truth.

And he knew it. "Well, then I guess there's no point."

He looked so serious, she laughed again. "To what?"

"To us, I guess. To being together." Two big fat teardrops fell onto his cheeks. What had she done?

"Al, no," she said, taking his hand in hers, which he accepted, without conviction. "Can I just take back everything I just said?"

"Only if you truly didn't mean any of it." He wiped his eyes with his thumbs. "And I know you did mean all of it."

"But I don't want to break up with you. We can figure this out."

"What's there to figure out?" He shook his head and took his hand back. "Why can't you just be a normal woman who wants to be a mom and have kids?"

"That's not normal for me, Al. And why can't you be normal? Why do you have to be the one guy in the world who wants to be a dad at nineteen?"

"My dad was nineteen when he had me and he was the best dad ever." He took a deep breath, wiped his cheeks, and stood up. "I gotta go."

This was all happening too fast. Bobby Eaton hadn't even come back yet to get their order. "What? Hey. Let's talk about this."

"But there's nothing to talk about." He looked her in the face with his big teary eyes, and it ruined her.

She watched Al leave the room, and knew then what she'd lost. The version of her he once saw, the one that was so incorrect and so beautiful and so loved, was gone.

SHE SAT THERE FOR a long time, ordered the cheapest thing on the menu, which was a dismal garden salad, and waited. For the first hour, she was sure he'd come back, and when he didn't, she kept waiting anyway. Bobby Eaton brought her a glass of burgundy, on the house, and she sat there like an adult, drinking alone in public. The magic alchemy of the Lakeside kitchen would now be ruined, and it was all her fault.

Of course, it would've happened eventually. But she never thought it would've been because of her and Al. They were going to stay together while Florence was at Duluth State Teachers College. Then she'd come back and teach in Bear Jaw, or somewhere close by. Neither of them had any money, so she figured they were in no rush to get married. Now, she wasn't sure if she ever would.

She knew that one of them would quit the Lakeside, and it must be her. She'd have to tell her mother and Floyd tomorrow morning. If there was even a chance Al would quit first to avoid seeing her every day, it would break her heart even more. The Lakeside was his whole life, and he was the future of that kitchen. Everyone could see it already.

She dropped her fork onto the remnants of her bleak salad and waved Bobby over.

"Tell me about working here," she said.

. . .

TWENTY MINUTES LATER, she'd spoken to the restaurant manager. She told him she had a high school diploma, five years' restaurant experience, and a willingness to work long hours for low pay. He told her to come in the next day at three.

Leaving the Majestic, she wasn't tired, and didn't feel like being alone, so she walked to Archie's. She still saw him from time to time. Floyd did too. If Betty ever figured it out, she never said anything. The company line was that Floyd never saw Archie again after the wedding.

Sometimes on nights after the kitchen was closed and the bar was slammed, Floyd would tell Betty that he was taking Florence home, and instead they'd both sneak over to Archie's for cribbage and poker. While Floyd and Betty were a machine who ran the Lakeside Inn together with steady harmony and precision, Floyd and Archie were a fireworks display. Florence observed more life in that relationship than she'd ever witnessed before or since. Not that she'd ever explain that to anyone. People wouldn't understand, Archie had told her, and she was certain that was true.

She wished she could. It was real love, unlike her mother's marriage to Floyd. It was real because they were honest with one another, and the core of their bond was so solid they could argue without hurting each other. *Arguments are the leaves, and the relationship is the trunk*, Archie liked to say. *One comes and goes, and the other doesn't change, except to get stronger.*

He would know, because even when Florence was around, there had been a lot of arguments. Archie had openly soured on their covert arrangement, and had been trying to convince Floyd to move with him to Chicago. He claimed he had friends in Old Town who would welcome them, and they could live how they wanted. Floyd never had much to say about it when Florence was present. He was probably hoping it would blow over. Instead, it picked up more force each passing year.

That's why Florence wasn't surprised to hear raised voices before she knocked on Archie's door. She was surprised because as she got closer, it sounded jubilant.

Floyd answered, smiling and holding a champagne flute. "Florence! Just the person we wanted to see!"

"The only person we wanted to see," Archie replied, from somewhere.

Florence was all ready to talk about her breakup and her new job. Instead, she was handed a champagne flute and informed of the big news. Floyd had finally agreed to go to Chicago, and they were packing their essentials tonight and leaving in an hour.

"Oh," Florence replied. "What about the Lakeside?" She supposed that place, in this context, was a proxy for everything, and everyone, in it.

"Your mother can run it with Al," Archie said. "Everyone's a winner."

I wish that were so, Florence almost said. Instead, she finished her champagne and asked for Floyd to take her home.

"I'm way too drunk to drive," Floyd said. "You can get a ride home from your mother. Just tell her you don't know where I am."

Archie hugged her. "You know, I came up here to be alone. I never thought I'd be in love again, and then I fell for Floyd. Thanks for being a friend to us. We're gonna miss you, kid."

"I'm glad I met you," Floyd said, and hugged her too. "I know I'll see you again sometime."

She'd been there only about fifteen minutes before she was back out in the darkness, wandering toward the closest lights as slowly as she could.

FLORENCE SAT AT THE BAR, just so she could revel in Betty's ignorant joy for a while. It felt devastatingly cruel, sitting there, watching her mother laugh with customers. Her mother deeply loved Floyd, and everything about Floyd's secret departure would crush her. She'd be the subject of pity again, and not on her terms. This woman, who'd managed to withstand so much, was about to be dealt an indignity and loss from which she might not recover. The Lakeside Inn wouldn't change a bit—same music, same food, same drinks, same trophy racks—but by this time tomorrow, and for the rest of Florence's years, it would feel like a beached shipwreck in which her mother would remain the captain.

But Betty belonged nowhere else. She was the happiest she'd ever been at any job, especially since the cranky old bartender, Elisha, retired. On her own, Betty had transformed the bar at the Lakeside Inn. For the first time, she was the center of attention for a positive reason, and she reveled in it—even if her mixing skills were, at first, far behind her people skills. Betty started her career by serving a lot of cocktails that were a bit different than customers were used to. Nevertheless, she was so warm, patient, and positive, no one wanted to offend her by telling her she'd screwed up their order, and a few of her lucky concoctions ended up becoming inconceivably popular.

Because Betty loved it, and put in the work, her luck soon evolved into skill. Elisha had left behind a sizable stash of pre-Prohibition Boker's Bitters, and she improved upon the bar's brandy old-fashioned by soaking a sugar cube in Boker's, giving them a flavor that literally couldn't be found anywhere else. Floyd had long been picking the black cherries from the trees in their yard to make his own Maraschinos, and Betty added maple syrup and cognac to the syrup the brined cherries rested in, giving them a richer hue and flavor. Betty's cherries became famous, and hundreds of customers every year would ask to buy them by the jar, but she only ever sold them one at a time, in the heart of a cocktail.

The previous June, she invented her first drink that earned a name. She tried to get people to call it the Winthrop, but everyone called it Betty's Lemonade. Two ounces whiskey, four ounces fresh lemonade, and a splash of Bubble Up, served over ice in a collins glass, topped with one of her cherries. By Labor Day, it's what almost everyone was ordering.

A few times, Florence had tried to help out at the bar, emptying ashtrays and refilling water glasses, but it was only so she could watch her mother in her element. All kids should have the experience of watching a parent be truly great at something. It was a tremendous boost to Florence's own confidence, somehow. Behind that bar, her mother dazzled, even deep into the wee hours, when it was just her and the regulars, and even when her teenage daughter showed up, about to drop a bomb on everything.

"Hey! What brings you here, Florence?"

"I just need a ride home. I can wait."

Just then, a customer requested Betty's Lemonade, and her mother spun on her heels. Florence sat there for a while, taking in the spectacle of a woman in love with everything around her. Betty Miller felt like everyone deserved her best work, all the time, and that's what people needed, to know they were deserving of it, just by being themselves. Because she left every day feeling happier and more full of life, she wanted the same for her customers. *If we can't turn back the clock*, Betty liked to say, *we can at least slow it down a little*. She was the one watching the door to welcome in each weary body, and she was the one who waved luminous souls farewell into the night.

It took Florence a while to figure out why Betty was like this— that it was because her mother was grateful. Everything she touched behind that bar she handled with the deliberate care of someone who'd gone without for so long, someone who never let anything go to waste. As she finished preparing the cocktail, she dropped a cherry into a Betty's Lemonade from just above the surface of the drink so not a single drop would spill.

Florence called her mother over, and kept her voice low.

HER MOTHER told her apprentice, a quiet, bespectacled former classmate of Florence's named Howie Gibson, that she had an errand to run. She asked Florence to wait at the bar.

"Okay," said Florence, who didn't want to go back to Archie's anyway.

"If I'm not back in thirty minutes, tell the sheriff to get me," Betty whispered. Sheriff Latch, sitting six stools away, was a regular and could be trusted to handle any situation with maximum discretion.

One of the other regulars, a tall woman named Ann who wore a wide-brimmed cowboy hat, ordered a beer for Florence. "You look like you need it," Ann said. "How are you doing?"

"I don't know yet," Florence said. "Ask me again tomorrow."

BETTY CALLED THE BAR twenty minutes later and told Howie to close up for the night, and to give Florence a ride home. There was no mention of Archie, or Floyd, and everything about Howie seemed totally normal. It was only once they were alone, walking to his dad's old black DeSoto, that Howie shed his discreet bartender persona and behaved like a friend again.

"I heard about you and Al," Howie said, as he opened the passenger side door for her. "I'm sorry."

Florence was startled to hear his name. That part of the evening seemed like last week already. "How did you know?"

"From some customers tonight who'd been at the Majestic Lodge. Everybody knows."

I'm getting out of this town as soon as I can, she thought. "So, you're up in other people's business and you don't even know what's going on under your own nose, I bet."

"I can't help what I overhear. What do you mean?"

"My friend Lois likes you." Lois had just started working as a waitress at the Lakeside not because Florence worked there, but because Howie did.

"Lois Strunk? Really?" Howie was so taken aback, he almost

drove off the road. All the guys liked Lois. Many had asked her out, but Lois hadn't said yes to any of them, because she'd only had eyes for one person.

"Yeah, and if you don't crash the car and kill us, she'll definitely go out with you."

"Wow, Lois Strunk," Howie said, like her name was a shooting star.

She remembered the simple pleasure of saying someone's name, the mild hallucinogenic thrill of each syllable falling into place. She remembered the tickle at the top of her spine when she spoke Al's name, and felt the kindness in his voice when he spoke hers. It was the sort of kindness a person could live with forever.

THE HOUSE WAS DARK and quiet, but after she'd been in her room only a few minutes, Florence heard her mother and Floyd arrive home. Neither one said a word, nor checked on her. Florence could sense their tension radiating through the house. She turned off her light, and lay on top of the comforter in her clothes, unsure if she'd done the right thing, unsure if she'd ever fall asleep.

THE NEXT MORNING, Florence awoke to hear voices down in the kitchen, and when she opened her bedroom door, the smell of pancakes wafted up to her.

She descended the staircase, and saw the back of Floyd's bald head. This was not the person she wanted to be alone with right now, even for a second. She knew he would turn around, and his face would be livid with rage and sadness.

"Florence?" he said. His eyes were missing a spark, but his face was trying to smile. It was an expression she hadn't seen on him since his wedding to her mother.

"Yes," she said.

"I know what you did."

"Yes, sir."

"When you leave this town for college, stay gone, as long as I'm here." His voice was hushed, but agitated, like a teakettle after the whistle stops.

"I understand," Florence said, and then something occurred to her. "What about Christmas?"

"You can always come visit your mother, anytime," he said, and turned away.

"I'm so sorry," she said, but he didn't reply.

THAT EVENING, SHE STARTED work at the Majestic Lodge. She biked to the lake from town, which meant she'd have to bike home in the dark, but it was worth it for the alone time. There was something she had to see by herself.

Archie Eastman's car was gone, and the cabin's front door was unlocked. She still said hello as she walked in, and felt the echo of her lonely voice. Almost everything of his was still there, the furniture, the trophy racks and taxidermy, but the house was quiet. For a moment she wondered if he'd really left for good, but then she checked his bedroom. It felt as invasive and weird being in there as it always had. She was in there just long enough to check the closets and drawers. All of them were empty.

She'd never see Archie Eastman again.

SHE BIKED DOWN THE ROAD to her new job and, forgetting where the employee entrance was, walked in through the lavish front entrance like a guest. Someone was playing the song "In the Mood" at the grand piano. It wasn't a hired musician, either, it was some arrogant-looking young prep in a short-sleeved shirt and shorts who was preening and swaying as he played. His overwhelming confidence was disconcerting to her. If these were the kinds of customers she'd be dealing with, she despised this job already.

"Hey," she barked at him. "Who do you think you are, Ira Gershwin?"

"No, just a college student," the young man replied, and turned, extending his hand. "Gustav Stenerud."

His handshake was firm, and his teeth and smile were perfect. "Florence Miller," she said. "Which college? Some awful place like Harvard?"

"I like you," he said, and laughed, with genuine good humor. "No, Duluth State Teachers College. I'm going to be a teacher. What about you, where do you go?"

For a moment, she couldn't move or speak.

This stranger didn't look at her and see the person she'd been. He saw another college student like himself. That was all she needed to feel like leaving Bear Jaw wasn't merely an escape, or even an opportunity to thrive, but a chance to be someone else entirely.

She heard the lobby clock chime. In a minute, she'd be late to meet her new boss. While she was in no rush to relinquish this stranger's idea of her, she began to walk away, turning back only to say that she'd see him later.

Nine

≈

Ned, 1982-1986

S o, this ain't good," Ned's father said the following morning
from his hospital bed.

"At least you're going to be okay," Ned told him, even
though that really wasn't the case.

A heart attack, they call these events, but from Ned's perspective, they attacked a great deal more. Although it was supposedly
minor—the term Ned kept hearing was "NSTEMI"—the effects
weren't. One day, Edward Prager was a ruddy, barrel-chested codger, lighting a cigar after a steak, and the next day, he was an old
man in a hospital gown, as pale as uncooked poultry, listening to a
list of things he needed to do and things he could do no longer.

"I was finally getting to a point where I could almost relax and
enjoy the life I earned," he said. "Now, most of it's gone."

. . .

EDWARD DIDN'T MIND giving up smoking or alcohol. He'd have given a lifetime supply of booze and cigars for just one steak and a few strips of bacon, and would no doubt sneak them whenever he could.

Ned could not let this happen. Before their father got home from the hospital, Ned and Carla went to help their stepmother clear the kitchen. Ned felt like a pirate, ransacking his father's happiness. Like Ned, his father hadn't chosen the family restaurant business, but he loved it, and he'd loved its food—its meats and starches, its sweet desserts—and in exchange, this food tried to kill him, as it had killed Edward's father. The red meat, ice cream, candy, ranch dressing, and chips were bagged up and given away, mostly to the housekeeper and the gardener.

"Damn," Carla said, looking into the emptied fridge. "What's even left for him to eat?"

Peg, who'd been wrecked and sleepless since the day of the heart attack, covered her face with her hands. "I don't know. Someone has to go get him healthy food. I can't do it."

"I'll do it," Ned said, before Carla could. It felt all right, taking charge.

NED HAD INTENDED TO go shopping for his father alone, but then Florence offered to help them.

"Mariel should go with," she said. "She needs to get out of the house. I'll watch the baby."

Mariel agreed; she'd felt cooped up, especially with the onset of winter, and was desperate to do anything, even an errand as dull as buying healthy food for her father-in-law. But she'd never gone anywhere without Gus before.

"Your mom is nothing if not overprotective," Ned said. "He'll be fine."

Mariel took a deep breath. "Let's go now, before I change my mind."

NED HAD ALREADY PERUSED and spurned the unappealing produce section at their local grocery store, so that afternoon, Ned and Mariel's mission was to hit two co-ops in Minneapolis. It was the first time she'd been in any kind of store for over two months, and her enthusiasm was delightful and expensive. Frankly, Ned was just glad to be with someone willing to make the decisions. Ned had never been in a co-op before and found them bewildering. He didn't even know that carrots could be other colors besides orange, or that brown rice was healthier, or that rutabagas existed.

"Are you serious?" The woman at the cash register grimaced at Ned through her thick eyeglasses. "How long have you lived in Minnesota?" she asked him.

"All my life," he replied, staring at the oblong softball-sized vegetable in his hand as if it had fallen from space.

"And you've never had a rutabaga? You sad, sheltered young man."

Ned and Mariel joined both co-ops they visited that day, at Mariel's insistence, and also bought a book of recipes, which included one for rutabaga soufflé.

.   .   .

"WHAT THE HELL IS THIS?" Edward Prager asked the hot yellow mass on his plate that night.

"It's dinner, Dad," Ned told him. "Never mind what it is. We didn't know, so you won't know, either."

Their father took a bite, and started to weep, silently, which froze everyone at the table. Edward never wept.

Carla, glassy-eyed now herself, stared at Ned. "You know what? Fuck it. Let's grill him a steak, and if he dies in two months, at least he dies happy."

"But I don't want him to die," Ned replied. "I want Gus to grow up with a grandpa. Mariel's dad died a long time ago. I want him to know our dad."

"But look at him. He's heartbroken. Dad. Don't take another bite."

"I'm fine," their father said, at last, wiping his eyes. "Rutabaga. I haven't had it since I was a kid. My grandma used to make it."

"Wait," Carla said. "So you like it?"

"No," their father replied, and ate it all.

THAT NIGHT, NED WATCHED as his father chose to live, and chose rutabaga. Ned was grateful and relieved to have only been interim boss for two uneventful weeks, and not just because he wasn't ready to take over his dad's job. The months he'd spent as executive vice president, with little to show besides the goodwill and wisdom derived from dozens of expensed lunches, proved it. His father's strength was that he saw people as part of a whole;

every week he made decisions that could hurt individuals for the benefit of a larger purpose. By this point Ned had eaten with over half of the employees at HQ, and he'd have been heartbroken to let go of any one of them. If the company faltered under Ned's softer touch, and it might, Gus would have to be the kind of unsentimental, practical person capable of saving it, for himself, and for his own children.

By the last weeks of spring, Gus was, thankfully, still a sweet, funny, chubby little guy who liked stacking cups, mushy peas, and the book *I Am a Bunny*. Ned wondered many times over the past few months whether his father had been sweet and funny as a baby. Ned had also wondered if it was too late for him to become more like his father. If he could step into Edward's shoes, maybe his son wouldn't ever have to. Maybe his son could always be sweet and funny. He knew for certain what Mariel and her family would prefer.

MARIEL'S SIDE OF THE family had their own plans for Gus, of course. When they brought him up to Bear Jaw the week before Memorial Day, the battle began, as many battles do, with an inaccurate claim.

"There he is!" Betty Miller shouted from the bar, beaming. "There's the future owner of the Lakeside!"

"We'll see," Ned said as he watched Mariel deliver Gus to the clutches of his great-grandmother. "Absentee owner, maybe."

"Supper clubs don't have absentee owners," Betty said, as if relating a strict edict of a higher power. "Look, you can tell he loves it here."

No, you could not. Poor Gus looked confused and overwhelmed inside that supper club, even for a baby. "Who knows what will be on this piece of land in thirty years," Ned said, and then he felt bad, because it made everyone go quiet.

He wasn't wrong, though. The Lakeside probably only still existed at all due to lack of local competition. The Majestic Lodge was going to seed, and there was nothing else around for twenty miles but fast food and bar grub. The first decent chain restaurant to show up in Bear Jaw might just wipe the Lakeside out.

"We should talk about something more cheerful," Betty said. "Like where Gus is going to be spending his first birthday."

"That's five months away," Mariel said. "I can't plan that far ahead. I don't even know what we're doing tomorrow."

Ned knew they'd discussed this. "He's having it at the Jorby's in Red Wing."

Mariel glared at him. "Really? When was this decided?"

"I know we talked about it," Ned said. "It's important to my dad. With his health, it might be the only time."

"Well, that makes sense," Betty said. "Next year he'll be up here, then."

"Sure, we'll see," Ned replied. "But either way, Gus should come up here more often before it's gone. Maybe next summer."

Betty glared at him. "The Lakeside's been around for sixty years because it's a part of a community. Maybe not everyone appreciates that, but Gus will."

So this is how it is, Ned thought. Betty must've viewed each of Gus's legacies as mutually exclusive, just like he did. Gus would either own and operate a single backwoods supper club in the middle of nowhere, and live a modest life until inevitable failure struck, or oversee a vast empire of popular family restaurants as it spread wider across America, and make tens of millions, or more.

"Next time, we'll have it somewhere besides Jorby's," Mariel said. "We can plan on that."

WITH THE EXPENSE AND attention Ned's father rolled out for Gus that October, it was impossible to think of a better setting than Jorby's. Everybody in Ned's world reveled in seeing Gus, the future of the franchise, celebrate his first year on earth at the flagship location. Virtually everyone who worked anywhere at the company headquarters showed up, from Fritz Lauder to Ned's favorite security guard Edgar, pushing the attendance well past the fire marshal's occupancy limit.

Mariel lugged a wooden high chair though the crowd, and plopped it beside Ned's seat at the end of a long chain of four-tops. "You can feed him," Mariel told Ned as she maneuvered their tot's wiggling legs through the holes in the chair.

Because there was nothing on the Jorby's menu that suited Ned's father's new diet, Ned had the kitchen bake some salmon and steam some broccoli with chopped garlic just for his dad, and Gus ate mashed-up portions in solidarity. Ned couldn't help but notice that, aside from Mariel's salad, these meals were the only vibrant color on the table; every other guest, himself included, was eating shades of white and brown, but for the tiny sprigs of parsley.

Ned cut into his "Jorby's Special Cut" steak—actually just a chuck steak that, once upon a time, they used to marinate—and took a bite. It was like chewing a belt. He took in his father's plate and sighed with undisguised envy.

"You know, we're talking about serving stuff like this," Edward said. "Next January, we're launching a 'heart healthy' section."

"Dad, how come I didn't hear about that?"

"You weren't around for those meetings, I guess."

It was true. Since his dad's health scare, he'd taken half days off here and there to be with his baby son, to witness first steps and first words, to help this new soul discover the world. "Dad, I promise I'll be there more."

"You do your thing. They're not babies for very long. I always regretted not spending more time with you when you were that age."

This was true as well. There were only three pictures ever taken of his father holding him as an infant, and that probably represented the grand total of the times his father had actually held him. It was nice to hear that his father felt bad about this, but as a father himself now, Ned had no clue how any parent could live a life without regret. Like most parents, he just had to choose which regrets he could live with. His father had evidently chosen his.

THE FOLLOWING SPRING, Betty Miller passed away, suddenly, in her sleep.

She was only eighty, still sharp as a cocktail spear, and as recently as Christmas, seemed in good health. They said it was lung cancer, which was a shocker, because Betty was never sick in her whole life. Mariel and Floyd didn't even know if Betty had ever seen a doctor. Even if she had, it wouldn't have been like her to make her health issues someone else's problem; she would've been embarrassed if they were. This was a woman who would've wanted to die with her boots on.

Ned was ashamed by his first thought when he heard the news. He now felt that his victory was inevitable, like he was playing chess against someone who lost their queen early, quite literally. Floyd may have been the owner, but Betty was the soul and foundation of that supper club. To hear Florence tell it, Betty was the one who'd brainwashed Mariel into loving the place, and she'd certainly intended to do the same with Gus.

It seemed like the entire town of Bear Jaw was at her funeral. Because Betty was so beloved, the wake afterward was like a celebration. People gave toasts and speeches for hours. Floyd was tearful, but doing his best. When he gave his address to the mourners, he pointed at Gus and called him "the future of the supper club," but to Ned, the vigor seemed gone from that claim. It felt like a hope, not a promise.

"This is almost as much a funeral for the Lakeside, isn't it," Ned quipped to one of Florence's friends, a woman named Mildred.

"Floyd and Big Al will keep it going," Mildred said. "And Howie Gibson will run the bar. Don't you suppose, Florence?"

Florence didn't reply.

In fact, she hardly spoke the entire day and evening. She mostly stuck by her friends, and neither wept openly at the burial nor laughed at the stories told at the wake. The only person Ned ever saw Florence talking to was Big Al, out back by where the employees took smoke breaks. But Ned was too far away, and he couldn't hear what they were saying.

NED SPOKE WITH FLOYD only once, at the end of the night, and the exchange unnerved him.

"So, Ned?" Floyd asked him. "Are you going to come up and visit Mariel this summer every weekend like you used to?"

Ned laughed. "What do you mean?"

"Mariel's offered to come up and work the bar to help out. And don't worry about Gus. Lois is retiring. She and Mildred and Hazel are going to take turns looking after Gus when his mama's at work. But you should come up when you can."

This was all news to Ned. "I think Mariel and I still have to discuss it," he told Floyd.

AS A RESULT OF that discussion, Gus spent his second birthday at Jorby's.

His tastes in pretty much everything had evolved by his birthday that October. Now, Gus liked the garbage truck, his Fisher-Price Corn Popper, Richard Scarry's book *Cars and Trucks and Things That Go*, and getting the mail. If Ned and Mariel were understanding their son correctly, the main thing he wanted for his birthday was his own mailbox.

Florence insisted on giving Gus the mailbox before lunch, and when Gus's blueberry pancakes arrived, Ned had to tear the dang thing out of Gus's arms so he would eat, and much wailing ensued. Mariel also wanted to remove all of the ashtrays from their table, and by the time she'd dealt with that, Gus was playing with his mailbox again, thanks to Florence.

"Let him have it," Florence said. "You don't have to be so jealous just because Grandma makes him happy."

"What'd you order?" Ned asked his wife as the plates for the adults arrived.

"Crap. I think the waitress totally missed me."

"Here. I'll split mine with you." He'd ordered the grilled lake trout with a side of green beans from the new "Hearty and Healthy" section, and saw at a glance that a few others at the table had done the same.

He'd been able to attend more company meetings again. That was the only good thing about his wife and son being up north all summer.

He watched her take a bite. "This trout is actually pretty decent, isn't it?"

Mariel shrugged as she cut their son's blueberry pancakes into small, manageable rectangles. "You know, if we do the next birthday at home, we won't have to settle for *pretty decent*."

"You had him all summer up in Bear Jaw," he reminded her. "We'll discuss it."

"What's there to discuss? They really needed me up there. And in a few years they'll need Gus too. There's lots of little jobs he can do. Just like I used to do."

"We'll see," he replied.

In regard to his own job, Ned was finally taking a step forward. He'd spent three weeks working on a proposal for a location that'd be perfect for a new Jorby's. "You told me that I need to blaze a new trail," Ned told his father. "It's in a place you know."

For the record, the final decision wasn't Ned's. Yes, he'd specifically proposed Bear Jaw as a location for expansion, but he was honestly surprised that his father went for it, considering that its community area was well below their minimum population threshold.

"Now, the population on a weekend in the summer is mid–five figures," Ned's dad said to the board. Ned hadn't told him that; it was neat to see that his father had done some research of his own. "And the Majestic Lodge is a shithole. It'll be closed in a year or two. And there's nothing else up there."

"Besides the Lakeside," Ned reminded his dad. He started to feel kind of bad, even if the place was doomed. If it wasn't them, it'd be Perkins or Country Kitchen or maybe even Embers marching into Bear Jaw with a GRAND OPENING sign, hastening the Lakeside's demise. Mariel and Floyd would certainly understand that. He just didn't know when he'd tell them.

"As we've been saying," Ned's dad said, tapping his slimmer waist. "There'll finally be somewhere healthy to eat up there."

FLOYD CALLED MARIEL ABOUT a month later and told her the rumor he'd heard about Jorby's buying a corner lot in downtown Bear Jaw. She hung up the phone, called her husband at work, and asked him if it was true.

"Let me check on that," he said. "I'm not sure."

She hung up on him right then. She knew. She didn't speak to him for two days afterward.

When they broke ground on the new Jorby's in Bear Jaw the following May, Mariel didn't speak to Ned for a couple of days then, either. It felt like something her mother would do, and it got the point across.

When Mariel began to respond to him again, he'd tried his best. "They're so different," he told her. "There's enough room for both." He didn't actually believe this, but he supposed it was possible.

"And if there isn't room for both, the cheaper restaurant wins," Mariel replied.

"Other than stop the construction, what can I do? What would make you happy?"

And that was how, at last, Gus was finally able to spend a birthday at home.

ON THE EVENING OF Gus's third birthday, the temperature was in the high forties, winds were mild, and the skies were partly cloudy. The trees in the backyard had been dropping little bursts of red, yellow, and orange onto the grass; Ned had spent a few minutes after lunch raking leaves from the heated pool, and already at least a dozen more had found their way onto the water. Mariel had baked a cake in the shape of a *Tyrannosaurus rex*, Gus's favorite thing in the world, and had coated it in green frosting, his favorite color. Carla was there already, and the other guests would arrive any minute.

Mariel was excited to not be at Jorby's that day for countless reasons, one of which was because she'd invited some neighbors, including Julius Blackwell, an outfielder on the Minnesota Twins. He'd told Mariel that because the season was over, he might be able to make a quick appearance, especially because their son was a fan. Gus wasn't actually into baseball yet, but Mariel made him wear a Twins cap that day anyway in case Julius really did come by.

"Julius Blackwell would never come to a birthday party at a Jorby's," she told Ned. "This way Gus actually gets to meet him."

"If he comes," Ned replied, stepping out onto the back patio, grabbing the rake.

Ned had last seen Julius just a few weeks ago. When Julius waved from his black Porsche, Ned froze in shock and hadn't responded at all. He'd convinced himself that this awkward moment had offended Julius and there was no way in hell he'd now come to his kid's birthday party.

Gus came from nowhere, waddling behind him.

"Daddy, I help."

"Thank you, Gus," Ned told him. He'd taught his son to not wait to be asked to help, but to volunteer his aid, like Ned's mother always had. "Kneel here at the edge of the pool, and when Daddy rakes the leaves over to you, you pull them out."

"Okay, sure," Gus said, and his tone—like someone who'd just been invited to test-drive a Corvette—made Ned laugh.

"Daddy, what's funny?" Gus asked, confused.

"Nothing," Ned said, still smiling as he raked a cluster of bright leaves to the side of the pool. "There. Lean down and get them."

Ned heard what sounded like a semitruck honk twice, close to their house.

Ned shouted to his sister, who was in the living room, scrutinizing their record collection. "Carla, what was that?"

"I don't know." She held up the sleeve for *Murmur*. "How'd you hear about R.E.M.?"

"From you," Ned shouted, and the truck honked again. "Can you go check the door?"

"Just let me put this record on first." He saw her put *Murmur* on the turntable and walk away.

About a minute later, over the cheery wail of an R.E.M. song, Ned heard her voice again. "Hey, we need some help out here!"

"With what?"

"I can't tell you, it's a surprise for Gus! You can't let him come down!"

"Well, ask Mariel."

"She's out here already!"

"All right, hold on." Ned flailed his rake toward the last leaf in the pool one more time, and set the rake aside with a groan before turning to Gus. "Don't move. Just stay right there."

Gus nodded.

Ned ran to the front door, where he saw a large white box truck, and then Florence, conducting Mariel and Carla as they helped a gaunt young man, who Ned assumed to be the truck driver, preparing to move a fossilized *Tyrannosaurus rex* skull out of the truck.

"Where's Gus?" Mariel asked.

"Out on the back patio, I told him to stay put."

"Mom, go out there and keep an eye on him."

Florence didn't move. "But it's my surprise for him."

"Mom!"

"All right," Florence said, shuffling up to the front door. "Don't bite my head off."

Ned stood next to the driver, and with Carla and Mariel's help, hoisted the giant skull out of the back of the truck. A chorus of unathletic bodies grunted as the weight fell onto their arms.

"Be careful," the driver said. "It's about two hundred pounds."

Florence was now standing in the front doorway, watching them. "I just saw him, he's fine."

Ned could have been annoyed by her inability to follow such an easy request, but in the years he'd known her, he'd learned that being frustrated was a waste of time. She'd only ever do anything, even a favor for someone else, on her own terms. Like earlier that same day, when he'd sent her out to buy Pepsi and 7UP for the party, and she came back with Diet Rite, because that's what she liked. He knew who she was, so it was his fault for believing she'd act otherwise.

"Florence, where the hell did you get this thing?" he asked.

"I rented it," she said. "We don't have to bring it back until tomorrow. In case he wants it in his bedroom overnight. Now, be careful with it, it's millions of years old. It'd be embarrassing if you were the one to break it."

Ned strained beneath its weight as he backed toward the doorway. "Well, you really outdid yourself. It's not an actual fossil, is it?"

The truck driver shook his head. "Nope, it's a replica."

"Yes, it's an actual replica," Florence said.

"Mom," Mariel said. "Go back in and keep an eye on Gus."

"I want to see his face when he first sees it."

"You will, we'll call for you first. Now please go check on him."

"All right," she said, still not moving. "Just put it somewhere nice like the dining room table."

"Florence," Ned said. "That thing is going to damage any piece of furniture we put it on."

"Yeah, it will." The truck driver nodded.

Florence finally went back into the house, and about thirty seconds later, they had the giant skull through the front door. As they set it down, Ned was surprised to see Florence standing there in the foyer.

She looked at the skull. "Well, at least put a blanket over it."

Ned sighed. "Carla, go upstairs and get a blanket out of the linen closet."

"Gus!" Mariel shouted.

"Don't call him yet!" Florence scowled. "It's not even covered up."

Mariel shook her head. "I'm going to go get him."

Florence watched her daughter walk away. "She just hates that Gus likes my presents better than hers."

"I'm sure that's it," Ned replied as he heard Carla's footsteps coming back downstairs with a blanket. He was looking in his sister's direction when a sound came from outside, a scream so loud he felt it in every drop of his blood.

THE FIRST FEW SECONDS after that scream, the world spun on its axis, but then Ned touched the wall of the foyer and he felt his legs under him again. He heard the R.E.M. album playing in the living room, and for just a moment everything seemed normal. He almost believed it was. Then he heard the devastating sharpness of his wife's wailing, and his body willed him into motion. He had been disoriented for only a moment, but somehow he was the last person to reach the patio.

He saw his son, soaking wet, Carla kneeling over him, rigorously giving him CPR, his wife bent sobbing over her. Florence had stopped on the transom between the living room and the patio, and had fallen to her knees, her hands over her mouth.

And there was Gus. Gus's little chubby arm flopped beneath the fallen strap of his OshKosh B'Gosh overalls. His fingers were motionless. Ned caught a glimpse of his son's blue face, and knew right then.

"Keep going!" he yelled at Carla.

"I called the ambulance! They're on their way!" the truck driver shouted. Who told him to do that? Thank God for people.

"Let me know when they're here!" Ned shouted back.

The truck driver stood there, still holding the phone, tears in his eyes. Ned's sister was still giving CPR. Mariel was clutching their son's hand and howling. Florence was standing now and moving toward them. And Ned. Ned was paralyzed.

Then the doorbell rang. The paramedics.

Thank God they got here so fast. Maybe everything would be okay.

Ned ran to the doorway, and the person at the door, a handsome man in a dark coat, jeans, and a Twins cap, stood smiling on the stoop, holding a baseball bat with a bow on it.

"Is everything all right?" the man asked, seeing the panic in Ned's eyes. It wasn't a paramedic. It was Julius Blackwell. Oh, Jesus.

"Our son," Ned managed to say. He couldn't yet say what happened.

Their neighbor stepped inside the house just far enough to get a glimpse of Ned's sister doing CPR.

"Grab him and meet me at the end of your driveway," he told Ned, and then took off running as fast as Ned had ever seen a man run.

. . .

NED SPRINTED BACK TO the pool. "I think our neighbor's going to take him to the hospital."

Carla looked up at him. "But the paramedics are coming!"

"But they're not here yet!"

He tried to lift his son. Oh, God. He felt him. A flutter. He carried his son out the front of the house, pressed against his chest, to
where a black Porsche idled at the end of the driveway. "Hang on,
my little boy," Ned whispered.

"Keep giving him CPR!" Julius yelled from behind the wheel.

"I don't know it!" Ned screamed.

"I'll go with him, I'll go," Carla said, taking Gus in her arms,
and running to the passenger seat of the car.

Ned could not leave his son. "Let me drive, please," he told
Julius, who quickly stepped out.

Just then, a brown Plymouth Reliant approached the house. Party
guests were arriving. It was the security guard Edgar and his family.

At last, Ned heard the sirens faintly in the air.

YOU NEVER KNOW HOW you're going to learn the most important piece of news you've ever heard. For Ned, it was in the ER,
holding his son's cold hand, when the doctor paused in his work,
and asked for the time.

Mariel had already been sobbing. She'd known for a while. Ned
did too. He just didn't believe it. There's no way to understand
something that wasn't supposed to happen.

Without a word, the medical staff left husband and wife alone. It was just them and their son, just the family. Ned held his son's hand so tight. Ned could hear him say, "Daddy. Daddy, I help." But Daddy wasn't there. Daddy was too late. And now their little boy, that sweet, innocent soul, was gone.

SOMEONE ELSE FISHED GUS's Twins cap from the pool. Someone else returned the *T. rex* skull, someone else threw out the green cake, someone else took that R.E.M. album off the turntable and hid it, and someone else covered the pool and turned off its lights and heat. Ned later found out that Carla did all of these things, but at the time, he was merely grateful it wasn't him or Mariel, each of whom had been ground into dust that simply blew from one day into the next.

IT WAS MONTHS BEFORE Ned returned to work. Sometimes he'd get dressed and make it to the garage before he turned back. Sometimes he'd start his car. Sometimes he'd make it to the end of the driveway. Many times he wouldn't get out of bed.

MARIEL HAD BLAMED FLORENCE for everything. The *T. rex* skull, the surprise, the stalling, and most important, not going out and staying with Gus on the patio like she was told—all of it made Florence solely responsible, his wife believed.

"You don't blame me?" Ned asked her.

"We all were where we were that day because of her."

Ned didn't feel that anyone was to blame besides himself, because he was the one who failed, the one who left Gus alone by the pool in the first place. But he didn't have the strength to disagree with his wife, and she found solace in her focused anger. Ned knew Gus's death was his fault, but some small part of him felt relief that his wife blamed someone else. He was so poisoned against himself, he couldn't bear it if she was too.

AFTER A WRETCHED CHRISTMAS and quiet New Year's, Ned finally made it to work on January 8. He wondered if it was the solution. It wasn't. He'd never noticed before how every cubicle he passed on the way to his corner office seemed to have pictures of children on display. He couldn't see them without sadness and anger, but he couldn't very well tell these nice people to take them down, either. He just would learn to look the other way.

In meetings, everything sounded inconsequential. He took to quoting Ecclesiastes when people asked for his opinion. "It is all meaningless, like chasing the wind," he announced during a brainstorming session that spring. "What are we even doing here?"

"Reworking the kids' menu," his father replied.

"No, what are we doing as a company? Don't we have enough? We're a family business and we don't even know what's going on in our own families."

"Let's take fifteen," his father told the room.

"I'm sorry, son," his father told him after everyone left. "Should've excused you from this one. I wasn't thinking. Kids' menu."

"I need more time," he said then. It was April. It had been six months already. Only six months. One sixth of his son's life.

"Come over for dinner on Saturday," his father said. "We miss you."

NED COULD SMELL THE steaks grilling as he approached his father's door.

"Rare treat?" he asked Peg.

Peg shrugged. She looked hollowed out and fragile. He wanted to hug her, but he was afraid to; he was afraid of what it would do to both of them. This was a woman who'd spent almost every day she could with her only grandchild. Now, her grief seemed to him like a frozen lake in springtime. It was best to not take a step.

She must've felt the same way about them. Some people made Ned feel like his son's death was a virus. Get too close to Ned and Mariel, and maybe your child is next. The people who'd once been close with them had been completely rearranged, based on who was there for them now and who kept their distance. Although they'd shared so much when Gus was alive, Peg had kept her distance.

"Come on in," Peg said to them now. "Help yourself to some wine."

Carla was there, and both Ned and Mariel hugged her, but they'd seen a lot of her. She'd been their lifeline, buying groceries, ordering takeout, planning the funeral.

"What's the deal?" Ned asked her as he winced at the spread on the table. "How often do you let him eat like this?"

"It's not my call. He's been eating like this again for a while."

"How long?"

"You know," Carla sighed. "Since then."

THAT MONTH, a week into the season, the Twins traded Julius Blackwell to the California Angels, and Julius promptly moved. Ned never saw him again, except when the Twins played the Angels on TV, and he noticed, every time Julius stepped into the batter's box, he touched the gold cross around his neck.

Certainly, that cross was touched to honor a memory that had nothing to do with them. Still, when Ned watched Julius's eyes, which had the same compassion and strength that Ned had seen last October, he felt something else.

In the seconds before a pitcher's windup, in the sacred space in the sport of baseball where one player reigns over a realm of silence for nine other men, Julius paused just that one extra beat. In reading this peaceful gesture, Ned found a connection with their son. In a swing of the exact same make of bat that sat wrapped in a bow, undisturbed in their closet, he watched the memory of Gus, his sweet little boy, breathe in and out.

AFTER THE KIDS' menu meeting, it was another week before Ned went into work again. He had just made it to his office when his secretary rose from her desk.

"Mr. Prager," she said, and just looking at her, Ned knew something was wrong.

"What is it, Amanda?"

"Your dad's in the hospital."

. . .

NED ARRIVED TO FIND his father asleep, and Peg sleeping in a chair beside him. She seemed like she'd aged ten years since he'd last seen her.

The stolid, weary physician said that Ned's father was doing well, all things considered. He'd had a successful heart valve replacement and was expected to make a full recovery.

"How long is the recovery time?" he asked her.

She seemed to be carefully considering her words. "Maybe two months. Depends how he responds to treatment. And see that he follows my orders this time."

NED DIDN'T FEEL COMFORTABLE sitting in his father's room, next to his sleeping stepmother. Since the steak dinner at his dad's place, she'd gone silent, as she had before. No calls, no visits, no acknowledgment that she was suffering too.

Leaving her to sleep, he went to the waiting room, and thought over what he'd tell his father. He could not be the interim boss for two whole months. Maybe he could fake it for a week or two again, but two months, right now, and he might lose the confidence of everyone in the building. He'd give his father a list of names, people who'd do better at the job until Ned was ready. That list was everyone in the C-suite except Fritz Lauder.

AFTER SEVERAL HOURS, Peg appeared in the waiting room, just when *Wheel of Fortune* was getting interesting.

"Here you are," she said. "He's up, and he wants to talk with you alone before your sister gets here."

Ned had tried to call Carla a few times at her apartment, but it just rang and rang. It wasn't like her to not be here with him, but she'd always resented that Ned was the chosen heir, and probably didn't want to witness the passing of the torch, even a provisional one, if that's indeed what was about to happen.

"I'm ready," Ned said, and hoped he at least convinced Peg of that.

WHEN HIS DAD saw Ned, he smiled.

"Oh good, it's you," Edward said. "They told me this wasn't a severe one. Not severe, my ass. I don't know how many more of these I have in me."

"You can handle a lot, I bet."

"I gotta tell you something." His father sighed. "I'm gonna re-tire, effective immediately."

"Oh," Ned said. He was sure he couldn't hide his shock. This isn't what he wanted to hear at all. "Like, permanently?"

"Yep. I'm done."

He remembered when he felt a flood of overwhelming fear and duty after his dad's first heart attack. He at least had the energy then. "Really? Today? Why don't you come back once you're re-covered, and work for another year or two? Go out on top?"

His father laughed. "This is as close to the top as I'll ever get again. And I can retire whenever I want, and I choose today. Being that I'm still alive."

"Well, honestly, Dad, I don't think it's a good time for me to take over right now." Even if his dad held on for another six months, it might be enough.

"I don't think it's a good time, either," his father said, looking his son in the eyes. "I'm leaving the company to Carla. She's going to take over."

"What?" He was sure he'd misheard his father.

"At least for a while. She's been in the office all day, starting the transition."

"But you can't do that. The father–firstborn son thing is tradition."

"This company needs the best person for the job, that's the tradition. The heir has always been chosen. Nathan is older than me, and he got passed over too."

Nathan had hated restaurant work. He'd wanted to be a judge since he was a teenager, all because some random customer had said he'd be a good one. Ned, on the other hand, had always wanted this life, but somehow, he couldn't express all this right now. He couldn't even look at his dad. All he could muster in his own defense was, "Why?"

"You need some time off. And you should move out of that house, too, it's not helping."

"I know. We're working on it."

"And your heart hasn't been in your work for a while. You always prioritized other things. Even before what happened."

"Well, what about Bear Jaw? That was my idea, and it's happening."

"You know, Carla pitched it to me a week before you did. She's the one who gave me all the hard data. But she told me you were thinking about it, so we decided to give you the credit, to give you a little bit of confidence."

Carla. He'd told her, because he told her everything. And she undercut him.

"So, Carla's got the job, just for a while? Just until I'm feeling back to normal?"

His father shrugged, and that's when Ned felt it in his stomach. It was over.

"Let me know how I can help," Ned said, trying his best to seem dignified.

"You're a sweet, kind man," his father said, and sighed. "And that's not what we need."

Standing in the hospital elevator, completely alone for the first time in hours, Ned wept, and not because his father was right. Ned could agree that he wasn't cut out to be the boss, but it was still the only future he'd ever known. Any other job at the company would now feel like a demotion. Hanging around and being known as the one who couldn't hack it would be worse than not being in the family business at all.

TWO DAYS LATER, Carla came over to the house with a briefcase full of papers. Ned offered her a beer, and she turned it down.

"What's got into you?" Ned asked her. "Are you okay?"

"I don't want control of the company for a little while, Ned. I want control of it, period. I had my lawyer draft this contract. The only variable is the number. How much do you want to permanently relinquish any claim of ownership rights?"

"What?" Ned sat at a barstool in his kitchen, rubbing his temples with his thumbs. Not this, not now. It was too much to take. "Why?"

"Because I'll be good at it. I never thought I'd get this chance, no matter how hard I worked. But Dad is actually leaving it to me, now. And I just don't want any confusion about who's in charge."

"Just give me a minute," Ned said. The last two mornings, he'd felt like he'd woken up in a bitterly unfamiliar world. It was clear now that he'd be trapped here, in this disordered version of his life, and because of his own family.

His sister sat on the stool next to him. "Ned, I'm so sorry about what happened to you. You know this. I'm not taking advantage of your vulnerability. You know that this job wasn't a fit for you. Just tell me how much you want."

"I don't know." Even if he could sell his future, how could he put a price on it? "A million dollars?" He blurted out.

"That's a deal," Carla said. "I'll write that number here, you just initial next to it."

Oh no. He knew what a fast acceptance meant. "Wait a second. I don't even know if I can do this." If they were going to permanently take his destiny away, they could at least set him up for a good chance at another one. "I need more."

Carla sighed. "I can't go over one million. And only if you decide now."

"I'm your brother, Carla. Why are you being so cutthroat with me?"

"Because it's my money, not the company's." She smiled. "Jorby's isn't buying you out, I am. And you know how I am about money. I can't help it."

"How do you have a million dollars?" He barely had a fifth of that, at least liquid.

"I've saved the money Dad's given us since we were kids, and I had him invest it for me."

"Oh." Ned had no idea that his sister and his dad had become so close, and that she was privy to their father's financial acumen, and he somehow wasn't. Then again, he'd never asked. Initiative was a critical, even sacred, quality to their father. Everything made a lot more sense now.

"This isn't personal, Ned. I love you. But I actually have a vision for this company."

"What is it?" He was genuinely curious.

She laughed. "I can't tell you most of it. But I shitcanned half the C-suite this morning. I got security to escort that old pervert Fritzie out of the building. God, that felt good. New blood's coming in."

Ned almost smiled himself, thinking of it. "I would've loved to do that."

"You wouldn't have, though. And that's okay. We all know you're too nice for this. Dad agrees with me. It's the easiest decision of your life." Carla handed him a pen. "You can sell this house, get an extra mil on top of that, and maybe never have to work again."

Put that way, it almost sounded all right. "Carla, I can't make this decision right now."

"Yes, you can. You know it's right."

Ned shook his head. "There's one problem with you playing hardball. You want my signature more than I want to give it to you. Come back with a better offer."

When he closed the door after she left, it was the first time he'd smiled in a while.

·   ·   ·

NED DIDN'T TALK TO Mariel about it until dinner. She'd been having a good day, which was rare. A good day for her meant no crying, no anger, and no new exposure to any reminders of what they'd lost, either overt or subtle. Sadly, those reminders were everywhere, for both of them. Mariel did errands like grocery shopping as late in the evening as possible, when there would be a lower risk of small children in the stores. Every day she left the house, she'd said, felt like choosing to be punched in the heart by a voice, a fleeting image, or a word. It was getting a little better every day, she claimed, but he couldn't tell.

He had noticed her new compulsive habits, like how she took a certain indirect path to the mailbox and fanned their magazines on the coffee table in a particular order. He figured there were at least a dozen more he didn't perceive. While Ned didn't entirely understand them, he still did his best not to violate them.

He'd thought about Mariel's delicate well-being when he assumed that having his future taken away would be as devastating for her as it was for him. Either way, he had to tell her, and he did so as matter-of-factly as possible.

While she listened, she prepped their dinner. She didn't seem upset at all. She'd been looking forward to trying a new recipe, she said, so perhaps she wasn't being fully attentive. She'd bought vegetables from the co-op, and planned to prepare them with some weird grain and an unusual spice, neither of which he could pronounce. She cooked like this all the time now, and it was great, although there were days he snuck out later and bought himself a cheeseburger.

"Huh," she replied, after he'd explained everything, and then she checked the readiness of the unpronounceable grain. "Would it mean we won't ever have to eat at Jorby's again?"

"I don't imagine I'd care to."

"How much was the offer?"

"One million." He grinned slightly. "I'm holding out for more, though."

"Wow," she said, and stared at the simmering pot. "One million is a lot."

This isn't the life I was promised, he said to himself, for the first time, but instead told Mariel, "This isn't the life I promised you," which felt more important.

"I didn't want the man's career, I wanted the man," she told him. "Will it complicate your relationship with your sister? I love her."

"I love her too," he replied. "And yes, it will."

CARLA CAME BACK two days later with a surprisingly better offer. Two million. Hearing that number blindsided him. It seemed like such a victory, he couldn't refuse it. But as he signed the document, he didn't feel like a winner.

"I'm going to miss you," Carla said. "A lot."

He remembered the last time they went to Disneyland, when their mother was still alive. Ned was twelve and Carla was ten, and their mom gave them each twenty dollars to spend in the store. He wanted something that cost twenty-four, and Carla wouldn't lend him the difference, even though he knew she wouldn't spend one penny of her money. He remembered how mad he was, the whole rest of the trip. He knew he could've just asked his mom for the extra four bucks, but he wanted his sister to help him, and she wouldn't. It just wasn't who she was. She had a plan for her money, all along, he supposed.

He hadn't thought of that memory in years, until now.

"You made your choice," he replied. "I wish you success."

THAT NIGHT, Ned had just turned off his bedside lamp when Mariel's voice startled him.

"Hey. Do you want to move up north? Floyd could use the help."

"We could." He was surprised at how quickly he liked the idea. He was surprised that he could like anything. "He's got to be annoyed with that damn Jorby's already."

It had just opened three months before. They'd heard that there were lines around the block. Front-page news in the local paper. To some, Bear Jaw was a real town now, just by being a place worthy of a chain restaurant.

"It's devastating him. He won't speak its name or allow it to be spoken at the Lakeside."

The thought of supporting the opposition to the new Jorby's made him incredibly pleased. "Where would we live, though?"

"You didn't get your family's cabin in the negotiations, did you?"

"No, I didn't think to ask for it."

"Then we'll live in the one I lived in."

"God. Really? It was barely big enough for your stuff."

"So? We don't need all of this bullshit."

"I guess we don't," Ned said, taking in the bedroom, the vanity, and dresser, all of it new, and tainted by association.

"You know, Florence doesn't ever go up there. My grandma's

funeral was the one time. She and Floyd have never gotten along for some reason."

Ned thought about how they hadn't seen her in the six months since Gus's funeral. He didn't know if Florence had tried to reach Mariel since, but they certainly hadn't tried to contact her. Mariel still blamed her mom for their son's death, and the distance from Florence had hardened that blame into a way of life.

"Let's do it."

"I'll call the Realtor tomorrow," Mariel said, and smiled at him. Ned smiled too. "Wow," he said. "I'm actually looking forward to something." And then she touched him, in a way she hadn't in a long time. "You want to—?" she asked.

"I need more time," he said.

"All right."

"And I think only with birth control."

"Oh, I don't want another kid right now, either," she said.

"I might need a lot more time," he said. He would figure out a different way to please her. It still meant the world to him to make her happy.

"All right," Mariel told him. "You just let me know."

He'd already thought of something. "I just have one question," Ned said as he held her. "Who owns that empty plot of land across the street from the supper club?"

"Floyd does," she said. "Why?"

Just over a month later, on a Saturday morning in May, Ned went into Floyd and Betty's Lakeside Supper Club to use the restroom. Mariel was in the dining room, talking to two young men. Floyd was at the bar, playing cribbage with a dapper, serious-looking old man, and was the happiest Ned had ever seen him.

"Hey, Ned," Floyd said, turning around, smiling. He'd been more welcoming to Ned than expected, but Floyd was indeed thrilled to have the former Jorby's heir join his side. "What brings you over?"

"Private business," he replied, and touched his wife gently on the shoulder as he passed her.

"Can't you just go in the woods?" Mariel laughed. "Hey, I want you to meet Felix and Raul, our new busboys."

The young men waved, and Ned waved back. He appreciated her use of the word "our," but he didn't intend to spend much time in the supper club, at least for a while. He had a big job to do, starting today.

FIVE MINUTES LATER, Ned stood on a scrubby patch of dirt, breathing in the cold northern air. He stared across the street at the restaurant and thought he saw Mariel in the window. It was clear she was in her element at the restaurant; she had finally found some measure of contentedness, and they were both busy. She had a full-time job running the bar at her grandfather's supper club, and he had this project, which would take as long as it needed to.

Ned stuck the shovel in the hard ground, and wondered again how many bedrooms he should build in this house. *Maybe just one*, he thought. The blueprint had two, and he wanted two. But he wasn't ready to fill a second one, and he wasn't sure when he ever would be. He touched his chest where he last felt his son's quiet heart against his, and felt that silence again.

This time he spoke to it, and told Gus, *You can go. You can go, little son. Go, little son,* he said again and again, with each motion of the shovel.

A STATION WAGON STOPPED on the road, and the woman behind the wheel rolled her window down. He and Mariel had met her on their first day here, but now he couldn't recall her name. She was wearing a clear plastic rain bonnet, although it had quit raining hours ago.

"What are you working on, Ned?" she asked him.

He thought of something his father used to tell him, long ago, when Edward left them for weeks, on his trips to expand his empire and make more money than they'd ever spend.

"I'm doing something for my family," he replied.

She smiled and nodded as if she understood, but then remained there, looking at him, as if waiting for an explanation.

He decided he didn't owe her one, and turned away from her and returned to digging. A few moments later, she left.

That day, he dug for hours, through cold and fatigue. The man in him was exhausted, but the father in him was tireless. So much work lay ahead of him, but progress was being made, as incremental as it was. Deep into the evening, he kept digging. He dug until darkness fell on him and all the other fathers across the north, and all their families, large or small, gone forever or yet to come.

Ten

E veryone knows that the worst invention in world history is
the surprise. There's a reason they don't exist in the animal
kingdom unless murder is involved. Florence believed that's
what surprises were—emotional assassination.

Florence could tolerate making her wedding anniversary a public occasion, with an obsequious waiter and a stupid little dessert
on the house, but when she figured out that a surprise was in the
works, she wanted to go hide in the woods until the stroke of midnight.

By then, sadly, it was too late. After they'd driven north through
the Cities, just as they passed the sign for Sherburne County, Gustav's smile gave it away. It was a sentimental destination for him.
It meant something far different to her.

"No," she told Gustav. "Take us back home."

"I can't," he said, still smiling. It had been his dream, not hers, to get married the weekend after Thanksgiving, because it was his favorite holiday. She'd only acquiesced because she hoped it would mean their anniversaries would be small and private, safely overshadowed by a momentous family gathering. This unraveling scenario felt like an incredible betrayal.

"It's still quicker to go back. You'll save money on gas."

"No, I'll lose money, because I already reserved a deluxe suite up there. I mailed a deposit a week ago."

"At the Majestic Lodge?" She shook her head. "That's idiotic. You don't have to do that in the off-season. Hardly anyone will be there."

"Hard to say, it being Thanksgiving weekend."

"My mother and Floyd are coming down for Christmas anyway. I'd prefer to get all that awkwardness crammed into one trip instead of spread out over two. Because if we go up there, we have to see them."

"If we ever visited them, it wouldn't be awkward." Gustav winced. She'd never told him the reasons why, only that Floyd had always disliked her.

"Why did you think this was a good idea?"

"The Majestic Lodge is where we met," he said, looking pleased. "It'll be the perfect place for romance."

Gustav had put on a few pounds, but he was still handsome and confident enough to say things like "the perfect place for romance" with a straight face. Even so, the phrase was unnerving, because she knew what he meant.

"You want to do it there, without the thing." She still couldn't bring herself to say the word "prophylactic." It sounded like an instrument of Communist propaganda. Besides that, they'd talked about it. They'd keep using the thing until they *both* agreed to stop.

"You said you were open to it."

"Oh. Yeah." She did, perhaps, have one too many cocktails before the topic came up. Even if she was the one who agreed that their anniversary sex should be more memorable this year, procreation was not what she had in mind.

Still, most of her friends had started having kids more than ten years ago. It didn't appear to have killed them, at least completely. And now, she was closer to forty than twenty. Much closer.

Even so, for such a long time, she'd never wanted a child. She lost the love of her life over it. And there was nothing wrong with her life that a child would fix.

For fifteen years, Gustav had agreed with her. They traveled, ate in fancy restaurants, bought nice furniture, and enjoyed every minute of it. But about six months ago, he changed. He claimed it wasn't because he had a mild heart attack, but a week later he woke her up in the middle of the night and told her that he needed to be a father. He wanted a family.

"But we are a family," she told him. "You don't need kids to be a family."

He asked if she'd do it, for him, just one child, and because she said she'd think about it, he'd been wearing her down ever since.

Now they were going to attempt it, in her hometown, of all places. At least she'd get to spend time with her mother; it had been a while. She hoped she'd also get to see Lois, Hazel, and Mildred. Maybe she'd get to see Al Norgaard.

. . .

GUSTAV LED HER, arm in arm, up to the front doors of what was now called Floyd and Betty's Lakeside Supper Club, and opened them to reveal the same dim orange warmth, the same acrid cloud of cigarette smoke, and the same people.

"Surprise!" everyone brayed.

There he was, in the back, against the wall. Al Norgaard, smiling in his soiled white clothes, his scarred chef's arms crossed above a larger belly.

The last time she'd seen him was ten years ago, at her friend Lois's wedding to Howie Gibson. He was married then, to a woman named Cloris, who was as well-intentioned and charmless as a store-bought pie. Florence barely talked to Al that day, and it wasn't until his divorce that they'd really spoken again.

As Betty took their coats, she asked them how the weather was down in Winona.

"It's cold and grim," Florence said. "Same as here, same as everywhere."

"Oh, cheer up. You two and your friends all eat free tonight." Betty pointed into a large room that didn't exist when Florence worked there. "You've got a table for four, right by the stage."

FLORENCE AND HER HUSBAND were seated across from each other, with Mildred and her husband, Don Kochendorfer, on their right. Gustav had rarely eaten here, or at any of the other old rural restaurants that were now called supper clubs, and he was delighted when Lois came by with the relish tray. Florence wondered who was back there doing that job now. She would've gone back to the kitchen to see, but she didn't want to go barge in on Al, and make it seem like she was stalking him.

Gustav glanced up at the ten-point trophy rack above Florence's head, moved here from Archie's old house, which had been falling into disrepair. For years, Betty had been agitating to get that place torn down and have the space used for extra parking. Florence wondered if Floyd was keeping it around for Archie, in case he ever returned.

"Who's this handsome fellow?" Gustav asked the table.

"That one was about to wander into the road and get hit by a car," Florence replied. "His death saved lives. They're a menace up here."

"That's for damn sure," said Don Kochendorfer.

Lois Gibson, one of Florence's other best friends from school, appeared just in time to snuff out the awkward silence. It was hard to believe, but Lois had been a waitress at the Lakeside for more than fifteen years already, and while she was the same age as Florence, she already looked a decade older. Being on her feet all night in a fog of cigarette smoke had to do a number on a woman, Florence thought.

"All right," Lois said, surveying the table. "Four old-fashioneds, right?"

"With brandy?" Florence asked.

"What else?"

"What?" Gustav seemed surprised. He couldn't fix a radio, or change his own oil, but he knew a lot of things, like the ingredients in an old-fashioned. "They're supposed to have bourbon. Or rye."

"If you're German, or from Wisconsin, they have brandy," Lois told him. "Or if you're in a supper club. Which so far, you are."

Florence, eager to change the topic to help her husband save face, glanced at the bandstand, where an upright piano and a drum kit sat unattended. "Is there live music tonight?" she asked.

"Yep, most Saturdays," Lois replied. "Tonight it's a band called Safari Dan and the Super Dupers. You're lucky, they're not local. They must be decent, judging by the crowd."

Indeed, the joint was packed on a Saturday in November. Florence gazed around this new room, which was just a dream of Floyd and Betty's at the time Florence moved away. It featured not only the raised stage and PA system, but wood flooring laid down for dancing. The whole gambit had been a huge hit. Her mother mentioned that the Six Fat Dutchmen were the first band they'd booked, and that was a point of pride for Betty, to get a polka band that famous.

Once the drinks arrived, Gustav stood up, and raised his glass to the entire restaurant. "Everyone, let's have a toast to my wife of fifteen years, Florence Stenerud!"

"Please don't," she said, but everyone did it anyway.

Gustav was always doing normal, thoughtful things like planning surprise parties, booking suites at the hotel where they met, arranging dinners with her friends, and proudly making their anniversary into a public occasion.

She loved this man, she did. She loved his simple, steady ambitions, his confidence, and who was she kidding, his startling good looks. She loved his comfortable childhood and his adoring, financially stable parents. She also loved that he was the fun teacher that all the kids liked, even if she was the hard-ass they all feared and loathed. Not least of all, she loved the fact that they once wanted the same kind of future, even if it had been for different reasons.

Now she raised a drink to this man, thanked him, saw the wonderful father he would soon likely be, and never felt so scared.

It didn't matter if Gustav was the happiest, calmest, most easygoing man on the planet—and he was pretty close—the anxiety and sadness Florence brought to their genetic potluck was so powerful, even cut with Gustav's sweetness and light, it would doom some unlucky child to a life of profound unhappiness.

As Florence watched Gustav talk with Mildred, who'd had five children by age thirty, it occurred to her how overjoyed her husband would be with such an unruly brood. To her, the compromise was having a child, but to him, the compromise was having only one. Had Florence entered the Majestic Lodge through the employees' door that day long ago, and not the main lobby, maybe he'd have met someone who was an eager and wonderful mother. But often, that's not the way life works. People like Gustav end up with people like Florence, and children are born with their hearts already broken, for the mother they needed and will never have.

FLORENCE HAD FORGOTTEN SOMETHING important about the Saturday prime rib specials at Floyd and Betty's Lakeside Supper Club. They were ridiculously generous. They'd been that way since the Great Depression. Back then, Floyd saw the anxious faces on his customers, and saw people who'd saved up to have a special dinner for a birthday or anniversary. He felt that it'd be comforting for them to see so much food in one place, and wanted to let these folks know that everything was going to be okay. Now, it was impossible to scale them back, even if Floyd wanted to. In a time of plenty, the portion sizes here had a different meaning. They felt like an overt display of American success.

"I forgot how big these were," Mildred said when the prime rib platters arrived.

Mildred, of course, was already full from multiple trips to the salad bar. As someone who professionally made the twelve great salads of Western civilization for five years, Florence was no big fan of that newfangled invention. Florence figured she went to a restaurant to have people bring her drinks, cook her food, and serve it to her, without her having to move an inch, and she'd be damned if she was going to pay to get off her butt and assemble her own dang salad. What a farce. In the kitchen there should be a salad person who made all of them to order, and fresh produce shouldn't be sitting out collecting germs, which is how people apparently liked it now.

"Who wants another drink with dinner?" Lois asked the table. "Wait, this is on the house. Everyone's getting another."

By the time the dimensions of tomorrow's leftovers began to take shape, Lois came around to check if everyone was ready for their grasshoppers, and alarmingly, everyone ordered yet another round of what they were drinking instead.

Gustav was sitting sideways in his chair, staring at the empty stage, well on his way to being blasted out of his mind. "I thought that the band was supposed to be playing by now," he said.

"They're not here yet," Lois said. "Probably got lost."

Gustav looked around the room at the other tables of diners, most long since finished with their meals, languishing restlessly over their drinks. "There needs to be dancing!" he exclaimed.

"Can't argue with you," Lois said. "But no music, no dancing."

"May I, then?" Gustav asked Lois, indicating the stage.

"I'm not stopping you," Lois said. "Unless you're terrible, then I'll stop you."

"You know anyone here who plays drums?"

"Yeah," Lois said, scanning the room. "See that teenager over there? That's Paul Buckman, he plays in the high school band."

"Well, get him up there," Gustav said, and got to his feet.

Florence leaned back in her chair and crossed her arms as she watched Gustav play a few chords on the piano. "A little flat," he said, and glanced behind himself at the pimply Paul Buckman kid, who seemed thrilled to be up there. "Are those drums tuned the way you like?"

"Uh, sure," Paul said.

Gustav played an A-flat key. "Glenn Miller?" he asked Paul, and then played the opening riff of "In the Mood" with his right hand.

Everyone in the room reacted as if they'd been sitting in the dark during a power outage and the lights had just come back on.

In under a minute, Paul Buckman had an entire room stomping and clapping to his serviceable beat. Gustav, meanwhile, was a bit showy; watching him was like observing a talented child repeating what had earned him approval. In twenty seconds, there were a dozen couples on the dance floor, and then, quickly, a dozen more.

After the Glenn Miller song, some of Paul Buckman's friends from band were onstage with brass instruments fetched from their fathers' cars, and were rubbing the chill from the mouthpieces.

The kids were okay. Good enough, anyway. A few songs later, half the crowd was singing along with the music. People went home for instruments and joined the patchwork group onstage. The crowd and makeshift band moved in a tectonic shift of rhythm, and everything in the room that wasn't nailed to the wall moved along with them.

Florence hadn't been dancing in years, and dancing alone on the floor, she grabbed in the direction of a helpless delirium she didn't know she'd needed. For a few moments, control—control of her body, control of her desires, control of her fate—wasn't the first thing on her mind. She had, perhaps, never been safer in her life, and given that this must've been what she required for pure enjoyment, her body moved so fearlessly it surprised her.

AFTER AN HOUR, she needed a break, so she grabbed her coat and snuck out the back door, the one that only the employees used. She leaned against the outside wall and could hear and feel the music. Facing the cabins in the dim light, Florence tried not to look at the one she used to live in with her mother.

"You used to live right there," Al Norgaard's voice said, and Al pointed as he emerged from the shadows.

Florence nodded, crossing her arms, the sweat on her body freezing her beneath her coat.

"Now, I live in one," he said, slapping his cigarette pack against his open palm. "The one with the birdhouse. That's pretty neat, isn't it?"

"Did you make that birdhouse?"

"Yeah. I like birds. They're calming."

"I agree," she said, even though she didn't. She thought birds were obnoxious and meddlesome. He offered her a cigarette before he lit his own, and she waved it off.

"No, thanks. I still don't."

"Well, that's good, I guess. Does Gustav smoke?"

"He used to." He'd been forced to quit by his doctor after experiencing his heart attack, but she didn't want to talk about her husband's health issues. "How are you doing?"

"I envy him. Easier to quit when you're with a nonsmoker," Al replied.

"You going with a smoker?" She tried to make that question sound as casual as possible.

He took a long drag. "I'm thinking about it."

"Who is she?"

"You wouldn't know her. Her name's Kathleen. She just started working here."

"Kathleen Krammen? Has a little girl named Sarah?"

Al seemed amused, but not surprised. "How do you know?"

"I may not come up often, but I stay in touch with everybody. Lois and Howie helped her get this job here. Her husband died in Korea, I heard."

"Yeah, well, she asked me what my plans were next Monday.

And I said, 'Nothin', it's one of my days off,' and she said I should come over, because her brother gave her some venison, and it's too much for just her."

"You should go, Al. You should absolutely go."

"What if I don't like her cooking?"

"Whether you like it or not, you may never have to eat it again."

"That's true. But."

"But what?"

He looked her in the face, and there he was again, that boy who she'd watched for so long, while they worked together, during the greatest summers of her life. She had no business remembering that, not now. It did no one any good.

Al's eyes glistened. "She's not you."

He may as well have stabbed her in the heart with an icicle. "Why did you say that?"

"Because it's true."

"What am I supposed to do, just leave my husband and run away with you?"

"No, I'm not asking you to do that."

"What are you asking, then?"

"I know better than to ask. It's up to you." Al mashed his cigarette against the side of a trash can and threw the butt inside. "Well, I guess we should go back in. People may be wondering about us."

"I guess they might," Florence said, and led the way.

FLORENCE WAS BARELY BACK in the dining room before Gustav wrapped her in his arms and pulled her onto the dance floor. A motley group of locals onstage were butchering "It Had to Be

You." She was still flustered, and overwhelmed, but it felt incredible to be held, even by her husband, even to the worst cover of a song she'd ever heard.

"Let's just dance," she told him.

WHEN BETTY CAME OUT and finally turned the lights up, Gustav was back onstage, playing the Hank Williams tune "Move It on Over," with Don singing, and pretty well, for being completely drunk at two fifty in the morning.

"Hey, it's about time to vamoose," Lois said as she cleared their table for the last time, and looked up at Mildred. "I'll give you and Don a ride home whenever you're all ready."

"I'm ready," Mildred said. "But Don's still singing. He never gets to sing."

Just then, Betty walked back into the room, wiping her hands on a towel.

"I hope none of you are driving," Betty announced. "If any of you even took a bicycle here, I'm locking it up."

"Me and Gustav walked," Florence said. "We're staying at the Majestic Lodge." She realized now that her mother may have been a bit hurt that they weren't staying with her, but there was no way in hell she'd be having possibly procreative sex in her teenage bedroom. "It was an anniversary gift."

"Romance," Gustav whispered in her ear, and she laughed.

THAT NIGHT, he did his best, with whiskey breath and stumbling, tender hands in the strange, ridiculous confines of a luxurious hotel bed. He fell asleep immediately afterward, like he always did, and she was wide awake, like she always was.

She got dressed again in the dark and went outside. She found herself taking a walk up the road, in the direction of the Lakeside, and when she breathed, she felt the cold lake wind on her lips.

Eleven

Mariel, 1996

Nearly an hour after smacking her car into a deer, five minutes before the end of the church pancake breakfast where her mother still waited, Mariel found herself in a giant, freestanding garage, surrounded by machines. She saw a riding mower, two snowblowers, four air compressors, a couple of gas-powered generators, some outboard motors, a Weedwacker, and three motorcycles. Everything was used and dusty, but in decent shape. Faded toolboxes, dirty coolers, trash cans, worn dressers, and plastic bins lined the perimeter, and most of the floor was hidden beneath bags and boxes. Mariel had witnessed versions of such accumulations in garages and homes many times. Half the old men she knew had even more stuff, and much less space. She didn't judge, but it always felt like being on another planet, being on the property of someone who evidently didn't throw much away. Mariel forgot to look where she was walking, and stumbled over a Payless ShoeSource bag bulging with cassette tapes.

"I said, watch out for that bag," Brenda said, not unkindly. "You okay?"

It was clear what Brenda meant, but it was the first time in a while that someone had asked that question, and her desire to be honest almost overtook her.

"I'm fine," Mariel replied instead.

A border collie named Bronzie, who'd run out to greet them when they arrived, got in everyone's way as Mariel followed Brenda's request to help her flatten some cardboard boxes and lay them on the one open section of garage floor. While Mariel watched Brenda's son, Kyle, hang the deer on some kind of pulley system, she noticed he wasn't wearing a wedding ring, which seemed unusual for a good-looking young man in these parts with a reliable job.

He hadn't spoken to her much besides complimenting her shirt. He loved the Boss, he'd said, especially "The River."

"Thank you for doing this," Mariel told him. "My chefs are going to love it."

Kyle, focused on the deer, just nodded in response.

"Do you know them? Al Norgaard and Felix Peralta?"

"Yeah, just saw them at your grandfather's visitation," Kyle said, and stopped to look at her. "Again, my condolences." He must know almost everyone in Bear Jaw, she figured. The funeral home where he worked was the only one in town.

"Come on," Brenda said, already at the garage fridge, where she removed two cans of Blotz Light. "A morning like this deserves a beer."

Mariel followed Brenda out of the garage and across the freshly mown grass. Mariel hadn't drunk any alcohol since January, and would've flatly refused this beer twenty-four hours ago. The cold can felt like an occult object in her hand.

"Hey, I'm not proposing we get plastered," Brenda said. She seemed to be leading them toward a garden. "But if you want to, I got some stuff that's even stronger."

"Oh no, this is fine," Mariel said, cracking open the can, because it seemed like the agreeable thing to do. She thought about asking to use Brenda's phone to call the church, but she found that she was actually enjoying herself. While Florence had clearly decided that it was time to reconnect, she sure as hell didn't set the terms, and the direction Mariel's morning had taken was starting to feel like a welcome adventure.

Brenda set her beer on the ground as she stopped in her tracks to yank some crabgrass out of her lawn. Her house wasn't large, but the property was vast and private, enclosed on two sides by wind-break pine trees. Mariel suspected that Brenda might've had a husband, but she seemed far too relaxed to be married. "You take care of all of this yourself?"

"Yep, with my son's help," Brenda said.

"It's so organized," Mariel said, out of politeness, she supposed.

Brenda laughed. "Would hate to see your house, then. You should've seen the garage when Fred was alive. There was nowhere to even walk in there."

"Fred was your husband? I'm so sorry."

"Don't be, it happens."

Mariel was surprised to sense that Brenda meant this. She couldn't imagine ever reaching such a place after that kind of loss.

"Well, it's gotta be nice to have a grown son around."

"It was, when he lived here. He just bought his own place in town last year." Brenda grinned. "You know the purple house across the street from Our Savior's?"

Everyone knew the purple house. A nice old guy, Augie Stolze, had lived there forever. He gave out full-size candy bars on Halloween. "Your son bought it? Is he going to keep it purple?"

Brenda laughed. "I hope so. I'm not helping him paint that crap."

Now Mariel laughed too. It felt good. She'd already laughed more today than she had in weeks. "Wow, good for him, a young man with a good job and a house. You must be proud."

"Oh, it's all him. We just tried not to screw him up too much," Brenda sighed. "What about you? Any kids?"

Mariel just shook her head. That simple motion took all of her strength.

Brenda held Mariel's gaze, and nodded her head. "You wanna see the house? Come on."

On the way, they passed Brenda's unusual garden. Besides potatoes, there wasn't much in the way of vegetables, but she was growing cilantro, Florentine irises, and juniper shrubs. "Impressive herb garden," Mariel said, and pointed to a plant with bunches of flowers that looked a little like green dandelion heads. "What's that one?"

"Herb garden?" Brenda seemed surprised. "Oh yeah. My botanicals. That's angelica, right there."

"Botanicals." Mariel repeated the word as if she'd never spoken it before.

"You want some gin?" Brenda asked.

Mariel looked away at the clean, orderly looking little house, and back at this fascinating woman, who'd been living here, less than four miles away, for many years. Mariel didn't believe in fate, but she was tempted to think that Brenda had been hidden from her until she was ready to meet her.

"Okay," Mariel said. "What the hell."

TWO HOURS AFTER smacking her car into a deer, well past the time she was supposed to pick up her mother, Mariel was lying on the beige-carpeted floor of Brenda's living room, finishing her second gin martini, the best one she'd ever had.

Mariel didn't know if it was the gin that made her finally start talking. Or if it was the lack of judgment from the woman who distilled it. But Mariel finally spoke for the first time, to anyone, about yesterday's miscarriage. It was liberating.

As they moved from the kitchen to the living room to the living room carpet, Brenda split her attention only to mix more drinks. To her credit, Brenda didn't dispense any advice or pat words of comfort. The only time she addressed the topic, she said, "It's sad. I think we should take some time and be sad about it."

And so they were, drunk on gin and sadness into the afternoon, and it was perfect.

A little later, when Mariel asked, Brenda opened up herself, about her son.

"You know, I was fine, I didn't even want kids," Brenda said.

"Fred wanted to be a dad. He wanted a buddy to go hunting and fishing with."

"Yep," Mariel replied. "That's what men say."

"So we tried. For like, five years. And here the poor guy was shooting blanks the whole time. But Fred had a buddy down in Waseca who was adopting a girl from Korea, and we said, let's do that. And we lucked out. Kyle's the best person I've ever met in my life. I just feel bad we didn't think about what it might be like for a Korean kid to grow up in a place like Bear Jaw."

Mariel and Ned had also talked about adopting, enough to have had this conversation. Ned thought if they loved that child to pieces, which they would, everything would be fine, regardless of the child's race. He was probably right. But Mariel was the one worried about raising any child in a place where hardly anyone looked like them.

"Other kids can be awful," Mariel said.

"For sure. Other parents too. I know Kyle didn't tell me most of the bullshit he heard. I think he downplayed it just to get along. But I can tell ya, anyone who even quoted *Sixteen Candles* got thrown out of my house. As a mom, you know, you just see red sometimes."

Was Brenda presuming that Mariel knew the fury of a protective mother? What more did this woman know, or perceive? Mariel wondered if she'd said too much.

Brenda rose and walked to her kitchen. "Hey, how about another martini?" she asked, already pouring gin from an ornate crystal bottle into a stainless steel shaker.

"I shouldn't," Mariel had to say. "I have to be at work by two thirty."

"What?" Brenda seemed angry. "I can't believe they're making you go into work the day after a miscarriage. That should be illegal."

"Well, I'm the boss now," Mariel said, and it still felt weird. "It's my call."

"Then give yourself the weekend off, at least."

Mariel appreciated the argument but honestly couldn't wrap her mind around it. The Lakeside needed her, especially now, with Floyd gone. Maybe it would even be good for her.

"You should come by tonight. You know, I don't think I've ever seen you there before."

Brenda stared out her window as if watching a stranger come up the driveway, but the world outside was motionless. "Me and Fred used to go there a lot. In the sixties and seventies. I guess that was kind of the golden era."

"It still is," Mariel replied. People had said things like this to her before, but she didn't take it personally; they were usually talking about *their* golden era, not the Lakeside's. "Last summer was our best in a while."

"Back when we went, there were live bands, and the whole place would be hopping until three in the morning, and then Floyd would go back in the kitchen and make pancakes for whoever was still around."

"I remember." As a teenager, Mariel made those pancakes, more than once.

"There was a girl back there helping out sometimes, was that you?"

"Yeah. Only thing I ever made back there that people liked."

Mariel smiled thinking about it. "Whenever you come by, it's on me."

"I don't eat out or drink at bars around here. Nothing personal about the Lakeside."

"I get it. But I hope you change your mind." As she passed back through the dining room, Mariel studied the small array of cookbooks on a dusty shelf, a little curious about what Brenda cooked. She pulled at a familiar spine and smiled, impressed.

"You have the *Chez Panisse Menu Cookbook* too," Mariel called out.

"I have the what?" Brenda shouted back from the living room, where she was riffling through a shoebox of CDs.

The cookbook looked untouched. Mariel opened it and saw an inscription inside that read *From Paul, with Love.* Who was Paul? She closed it quickly and pretended she hadn't seen it. "This cookbook from Chez Panisse. I have this one. It's great."

"Yeah, I'm not going to make any of that whacked-out California bullshit. Way too difficult."

"You distill your own gin, and that's harder to do than anything in this book."

"Yeah, but I like making gin."

Bronzie began to bark outside. Mariel followed her host back into the living room, where they watched through the big window as Bronzie chased a passing car.

"She was hit by a car once," Brenda said. "Now, she hates them all."

"That's a tough way to live."

"Don't knock it." Brenda shrugged. "It gives her purpose."

. . .

By two o'clock, after two more glasses of water and a mug of instant coffee, Mariel felt sober enough to drive. She left with two coolers chock-full of venison. Brenda tapped the driver's side door and told Mariel to watch the road this time.

As she drove away, Mariel heard Bronzie chase her toward the county road, and stared ahead as a sheriff's patrol car crossed her path, sirens blaring.

Twelve

~~

When Gustav asked Florence, in August 1957, when she figured they conceived Mariel, she told him it must've been the weekend of the anniversary surprise party.

"Heck of a surprise," he told her, holding their newborn daughter in his arms.

"Not to me," she told her husband. "She was fifteen days overdue."

"You didn't even want to go up there," Gustav reminded her.

"That's right." She watched her baby girl's chin quiver in her sleep and felt an unmistakable envy. To start over, with no knowledge, no memory—what she wouldn't do to trade places with this infant.

Gustav handed Mariel to Florence with tears in his eyes. "She loves her mommy."

"We'll see," Florence said.

Florence felt she had good reason to be an anxious person, but she didn't know anxiety's true borders until she became a mother. For months, Florence couldn't sleep more than a few hours without waking up to make sure her daughter was still breathing.

"Mariel's fine," her husband always insisted. "Get some rest."

"It's an injustice that she won't remember any of this," Florence said, meaning the vigilant love and duty that infant care demanded. "Then she'd already know how much we love her."

"Yeah, but this is what's expected of us," he replied. "We earn it through what's not expected."

WHAT FLORENCE EXPECTED was one heedless, near-fatal disaster after another. Of course, she'd heard that she should let her daughter fall once in a while so she could learn how to pick herself back up on her own. Florence couldn't do that. Little Mariel was the most fiercely guarded middle-class toddler anyone knew whose childhood wasn't restrained by a strict religion or a medical condition. Even the childless couples in Florence's life were alarmed into offering parenting advice.

Her mother, who'd raised only one child, long ago, under vastly different circumstances, and Floyd, who'd rarely been around children, were so easygoing with Mariel, Florence knew they would've gotten that little girl killed or maimed several times.

Florence had just come back from the store with ingredients for potato salad when she saw her three-year-old daughter playing in the grass of Betty and Floyd's front yard.

She moved the groceries to one arm, scooped up her daughter in the other, and barked at her mom, Floyd, and Gustav, who were all sitting on folding chairs in the open garage, listening to the radio, drinking iced tea.

"What are you doing? She can't play in the yard—there's a road right there! And not even a curb! A car could just come and plow right into her."

They'd all experienced Florence's piqued alarmism enough that none of them even reacted anymore. Finally, her husband shrugged. "How about the backyard? It's fenced in."

Florence sighed. "Yes, but there are bees in the garden. We don't know yet if she's allergic."

"You survived way worse," Betty said. "We're darn lucky you didn't get polio."

"Honey," Gustav said. "She's going to be fine."

"I know she is," Betty interjected. "Because she's not like her mother."

That stung a bit, considering the source, but it was true. Mariel was brave. She was funny. She was affectionate. And she loved everything about Floyd and Betty's Lakeside Supper Club.

By the time Mariel was six, Betty often joked about abducting little Mariel, keeping her in Bear Jaw, and putting her to work in the kitchen.

"That's not remotely humorous," Florence finally said. "You say that one more time, and I'm calling the police."

Betty laughed. "You're just scared that she's going to want to."

Gustav was delighted by the idea of his daughter working for a family business. "She might learn how to cook prime rib," he said. "We'd save a lot by eating it at home."

Betty smiled at him. "We'll teach her anything she wants to learn."

In June 1964, Betty took Mariel on her first behind-the-scenes tour of the supper club, and her granddaughter came back enthralled.

"Too bad," Florence said, already in the car. "You're coming back home tonight."

"But, Mom!" Mariel yelled from the front steps of the supper club. "Grandma said I could stay the whole week. Or even more!"

"It's no trouble." Betty smiled. "We love having her around."

"Mom, quit undermining me. I don't think she actually wants to stay here for a week, I think you want her to."

Mariel wailed, "But I do, Mom!"

"She's only six," Florence reminded her mother.

"She's almost seven," Betty replied.

"She's never spent a night away from me." Just the thought made Florence's heart split apart.

"Then you could use a break. Normal people do this with grandparents all the time. Remember how happy you were with Gustav before you were a parent? You can have that again for a week or two."

"I wasn't happier," Florence told her mother. "There was just less to worry about."

"Go home. Take it easy. She's safe here."

Florence still couldn't leave.

"Mariel!" she called out, after she turned off the engine. "I'll stay right here for a while in case you change your mind!"

After waiting an hour in the recently paved parking lot of Floyd and Betty's Lakeside Supper Club, she heard her daughter's laughter come from the restaurant again. That girl truly loved it, and wouldn't want to leave anytime soon. It didn't matter. Florence would be there for her when she did.

Thirteen

~

Mariel, 1996

Mariel was at the intersection, watching a police car disappear, thinking about whether to make a right turn and follow its racket into town. Her mom had certainly been picked up from church by now, and was probably at Lois's or Mildred's. Mariel was already late for work and didn't need the wild-goose chase. If her mother's gesture today to reach out was genuine, Mariel predicted she would try again soon, and maybe things would go more smoothly next time.

Mariel had just flipped on her turn signal when she noticed Hazel's station wagon approaching her from the left, Hazel's arm waving from the open driver's side window. She'd barely rolled down her own window by the time Hazel's car swerved onto Custom Street and stopped, parallel to hers. Her neighbor's pink face was as bright as a birthday cake.

"You're alive!" Hazel shouted.

"So far," Mariel said. "What's going on?"

"Oh, jeez! We've been combing the whole area for you. Someone said they saw your car pulled over a few hours ago. I figured I could help, you know, because I remembered what you were wearing. Just in case you were murdered in the woods."

Mariel had to laugh.

"What happened to your car?"

"I hit a deer. Car still runs fine, though. Could be worse." The full story was none of Hazel's business. "By the way, who picked up my mom from church?" Hazel would know this, and Mariel figured she owed at least a free appetizer to whoever it was.

Hazel shook her head. "No one!"

"No one? What, did she walk home?"

"Nope. She's still there."

"Christ on a cracker," Mariel replied. "Why?"

"She said she's waiting for you to pick her up."

"Well, I'm going to be late to work now. Can you do it?"

"No, I can't."

"Okay, well, I'll try to find somebody, then."

"Well, I tried already, and I can't. Nobody can. People have been offering her rides all afternoon. Even Pastor Jeff offered to drive her. Your mom says she's going to wait there in the church until *you* come to get her."

This was the most Florence Jean Stenerud thing that Florence Jean Stenerud had ever done. If she was being this stubborn, it was probably because she was trying to make some kind of point. Mariel had no patience right then to guess what it could be.

Mariel shook her head and put her car into drive. "I gotta open the supper club, Hazel. Just tell her I can't do it today."

Hazel sighed. "Sounds good. See you at happy hour."

BY THE TIME MARIEL arrived at the Lakeside, Big Al had beaten her there and had let a few of the new hires in. It was a blessing to have inherited a place where people wanted to work. Her supper club was by far the best gig in the area for prospective waiters, and they rarely had to place an ad. Besides the local high school teachers, Mariel's best source for employee recommendations was her regulars, and two weeks ago, Hazel had referred a recent graduate named Cayla Graff.

In that brief span of time, Cayla had already become the best server in recent memory. Twenty years ago, someone like her might spend a few decades working here, fall in love with a co-worker, and build a life, like Florence's friend Lois had. Now, Mariel would be lucky if a kid as smart as Cayla lasted more than a summer.

Cayla watched as Mariel mixed drinks and set them down in front of certain barstools. "Hazel gets Betty's Lemonade," Mariel explained. "Edina Sue gets a Seven and Seven, and Paul Buckman gets a gin martini with three olives."

"Wow, awesome," Cayla said. She was taking it all in with more focus and enthusiasm than Mariel was used to from new hires. She reminded Mariel of herself at that age, right down to the frequent questions. "Is three olives a lot in a martini?"

Mariel nodded. "It's about three too many."

"Are martinis the main drink people order?"

"Distant third," Mariel said. "The brandy old-fashioned is number one. Just like at every other supper club. Betty's Lemonade is number two."

"And Seven and Seven is fourth?"

"No, but I do have to order extra Seagram's 7 just because of Edina Sue. In the old days, we would've kept a bottle just for her in a locker," she said, and pointed to the disused liquor lockers on the back wall.

"Why does everyone call Sue Shipps 'Edina Sue'?"

"Because she moved up here from Edina, sixteen years ago."

"That's what I thought," Cayla said, looking out the window at the first customers pulling into the lot. "It makes sense."

Cayla was a local, born of locals, so of course it did. Sixteen years was nothing up here. Sue Shipps would still be Edina Sue in thirty years.

Mariel recalled the day she got to know Edina Sue. It was Mother's Day, and she'd shown up at the bar alone, the first customer in the door. Any woman who goes out drinking alone on Mother's Day was probably Mariel's kind of person, and Edina Sue turned out to be a riot. About ten minutes later, a logging truck dropped its load on the one road heading in from town, so hardly any dinner reservations came for two hours, but once the road was cleared, more than a hundred carloads of aggravated, starving mothers and their families all came at once, like a herd of furious buffalo. Before and after the most brutal rush in supper club history descended on them, Edina Sue made Mariel and Betty laugh for hours. It was Edina Sue's idea to have them send every table free ice cream.

"Oh, one more thing," Mariel asked Cayla. "Are your tables ordering grasshoppers?"

Cayla nodded. "About a third of them."

"Here's the trick. Never ask a table *if* they want grasshoppers. You ask them *when* they want their grasshoppers. That's how my grandma bought me a car." Mariel glanced at the clock, and told the host to go ahead and unlock the doors. It was time for Saturday night to begin.

MARIEL GREETED THE REGULARS as they sat down in their usual spots. None of them had any idea what she'd been through since last night, which she supposed was comforting. What bothered her now was that she'd forgotten to fill the now-empty green cherry slot in the garnish rack with something else.

"Heard you were missing," Edina Sue said.

"Yep, just let me know if I turn up anywhere," Mariel replied.

With everyone at the bar content, Mariel stopped by the kitchen, where her two favorite employees, Big Al and Felix, were with their crew, awaiting the first ticket.

"Hey, boys," she said, pointing at the Koh-i-Noor walk-in freezer. "Don't know if you saw already, but I put some fresh venison in there for you."

"Venison?" Big Al smiled. "Wow. Where the heck did you get it this time of year?"

"Just got lucky," she told them. "Each of you, take as much as you want."

"Thanks," Big Al said. "I'll grill some up this weekend."

"I'll wait," said Felix. "You want to eat venison with fall produce."

"Good point, then I'll wait too," Big Al said.

Felix was less than half Al's age, half Al's size, and had been there one fifth as long, but Al knew Felix was the better chef, and treated him with respect. As Al mentored Felix in supper club cuisine over the years, and watched the younger man surpass him in skill, they'd also become year-round fishing buddies.

Mariel had first met Felix when he found his way up to Bear Jaw with his friend Raul in 1986, a couple of twenty-one-year-olds from a small town in Zacatecas. She couldn't imagine what that journey north must've been like, but she knew that things weren't always easy at the destination, either.

"I have one thing to say to those people," Felix said once about the locals who'd made him feel less than welcome. "'You think you can destroy me? You'd better think again.'"

"I like that quote." Mariel thought she'd heard it before. "Is that Pancho Villa?"

"No," Felix said, looking annoyed. "Slayer."

Like Al, Felix started as a busboy. Now, he and Al were the head chefs. Maybe it was an unlikely dream, assuming Felix wouldn't ever be tempted to take his talent elsewhere, but Mariel hoped he would carry the supper club's kitchen into the next generation, provided that the next generation still came to supper clubs.

"How'd you pick northern Minnesota?" she asked him one day

several years ago, after he'd been there a while. She'd tried to learn some Spanish—they had a private joke about a sign she'd written that read NO BASURA that he started taping to things like the time card tray and the door to her office—but it was clear that his English was improving faster than her Spanish ever would.

"That's easy. Lefse," he told her.

"No, Felix, I'm serious."

"I'm serious too. It's basically a potato tortilla, right? My kids love it." He glanced at Al. "Oh, and the fishing."

"Okay, but how'd you end up in Bear Jaw, of all places?"

He shrugged. "Raul's uncle, he worked at the Majestic Lodge. He said it was the best."

The Majestic Lodge, a beautiful, famous resort in its day, closed suddenly in 1986 after a series of ownership changes. The giant old building sat vacant for a long time, and rumors of more buyers came and went, until someone finally tore it down. In its place now was a strip mall with a dreary smattering of foolproof franchises: a tacky bar and grill called the Lodge House, a tanning salon, a video rental store, a no-frills barbershop, and of course, a Subway.

"You didn't know the Majestic Lodge was about to close."

Felix shook his head. "Two days after we arrived."

"It was a legendary place up here," Mariel replied. "My mom used to work there. That's where she met my dad." It wasn't the only important thing that happened there, according to family legend, not that she'd blithely roll that particular tape.

Raul soon moved to Duluth with his uncle to work at a hotel, but Felix had stayed in this small northern town, saved money for his mom and girlfriend to come up from Mexico, and raised a family. His biggest concern now was the cost of hockey equipment for his five-year-old son, Brandon. He'd become a hockey dad, and when he wasn't here, Felix was practicing with his son.

Mariel watched from Felix's station as Cayla delivered the first ticket of the evening. Prime rib platter, which they would serve more than a hundred times that night. She'd tried to take a more active role in the kitchen once, and actually missed the work, but there was no use repeating the same crushing blunders. Her seasonal vegetarian specials, featuring fresh Minnesota produce, were all abject failures. Some of it she was able to smuggle onto platters beneath a hunk of protein, but she ended up giving most of those gorgeous, delicious ingredients right back to a local farm, as pig feed.

It was only on Tuesdays, her day off, cooking at home alone, where she felt things like creativity and pleasure in a kitchen. She'd long accepted that the Lakeside's duty was not to introduce new food as much as it was to honor old food, to respect the customers' loyalty to the known and beloved, and create every night a simple sacrament out of ground chuck and pot roast and fried trout.

SEVERAL HOURS LATER, behind the bar, when things appeared calm for a moment, Mariel looked up Brenda Kowalsky's address and phone number in the local white pages and transcribed it into a red address book, with the annotation *gin*.

"When you're done writing poetry, I'll take another," Hazel said, pushing her empty glass forward. "So, what were you doing on Custom Street today?"

"Just driving around, trying to clear my head." Which wasn't a lie.

"Know who lives down there? Paul's old fling, Brenda Kowalsky."

Paul Buckman had already left and gone home to his wife, but Mariel glanced at his usual barstool just to make sure. "Who's she?"

"You don't know about her? She was a teacher at Bear Jaw Elementary until she slept with Principal Buckman here."

"Paul wasn't the only one," Edina Sue said. "She slept with a bunch of married guys."

"She slept with Paul?" Mariel asked. Brenda sleeping around back in the day, she could see that. But Paul Buckman? He looked like Mister Rogers, but less sexy.

"Yeah. The district shitcanned her for it. It was a huge deal."

The news was heartbreaking. But it explained some things. "When was that?"

Hazel spoke up again. "I think eighty-two, or so."

That was the summer that Mariel didn't come to Bear Jaw at all, and the name Brenda Kowalsky would've meant nothing to her back then in any case. Mariel had no kids in school, didn't go to church, and rarely went to town except for groceries.

"So, he's still the principal, all these years later, and she got fired?"

"Neither of them got divorced, so there's that. Which is amazing, considering what Brenda did."

"Come on!" The double standard made Mariel furious. "She slept with one married guy, once!"

"Uh, no," Edina Sue said. "She slept with other guys too. All dweeby Paul Buckman types. Smart, married men with good jobs. Mostly they were onetime things, I guess, but still, she got around."

"Yep," Hazel interjected. "And nobody knew until the thing with Paul Buckman blew up. Then all the dirty laundry came out. Mariel, I can't believe you never heard this."

"I wasn't here," Mariel replied. "So what happened, then?"

"The wives, they just shut her down," Edina Sue said.

"Yep. She could hardly go out in public anymore. She'd show up at a restaurant, and people would walk out," Hazel said.

"Whether or not Brenda had slept with their husband," Edina Sue said.

"That's awful." Mariel shook her head. "I don't see why people had to behave like that."

"Well, what if it was your husband?"

"I don't know. I'd get him screened for gonorrhea."

Hazel frowned. "Seriously."

"Okay, I'd be upset, sure. But if Brenda came in somewhere I was eating, I wouldn't walk out. Especially if she only slept with some other dude. That's ridiculous."

"Hey, I don't make the rules," Hazel said.

"You kind of do, Hazel. You have a choice to be a decent person or not. What are you trying to say, that your dirty laundry isn't as dirty? Or is it just that you're incapable of compassion and forgiveness?"

Edina Sue and Hazel froze and stared at her.

"I never left a place when I saw her," said Edina Sue, who then excused herself.

Hazel just sat there like a small child who'd been yelled at.

"Another drink, Hazel?"

"Oh, sure," Hazel said, and sighed. "By the way, I passed on your message to Florence."

"And how did she take it?"

"Fine. Our whole quilting club went to see her. We brought her a hot dish and some three-bean salad."

"Wait a second. At the church?"

"Yep."

"Tell you what, Hazel. I'm locking the doors here at one, and after cleanup, I'm going to bed. And so should she. She's not spending the night there."

"We'll see, won't we," Hazel said.

THE NEXT MORNING, Mariel heard that Florence had indeed spent the night at the church. Mariel's mother reportedly had the best sleep of her life on the couch in Pastor Jeff's office, and some idiot had donated more pillows and blankets to make it even more comfortable. At the crack of dawn, some fellow seniors, apparently with nothing better to do before morning services, brought Florence breakfast and coffee. They returned later, toting along a picnic lunch, along with the day's newspaper and a Scrabble board. That evening they returned yet again with supper and set up a little cribbage tournament.

Sooner or later her mother would have to shower, and that's when the white flag would go up, Mariel guessed. As often as Florence extolled the virtues of her childhood's many privations, there was no way she would go another day with only a women's bathroom sink for personal hygiene. Mariel knew her mom's pride was even greater than her stubbornness.

Her mother had also chosen the wrong weekend to test Mariel's mettle, not that Florence could've known that. It still hadn't occurred to Mariel what her mother's point might have been, but she was certain her mom must have one, besides making her daughter look selfish or indifferent.

On her walk to the supper club—*her* supper club—Sunday morning, it finally dawned on Mariel. This was Florence's protest over a decision made twenty years ago. If that were the case, the only thing that Mariel could do to make her mother happy would be something she'd never even consider.

Mariel heard the chatter of birds above as she unlocked the door to her restaurant, and looked forward to the pleasant day ahead.

Fourteen

Every summer, Florence drove her daughter up to Bear Jaw. It made Mariel so thrilled to be up north with her grandparents at that damn supper club that Florence gladly leveraged that desire against all of her daughter's other preferences. *I can buy you those cutoff jean shorts, or you can go to the Lakeside next summer. You can go tubing with your friends, or you can go to the Lakeside next summer.* Mariel thought this was punitive, but it was merely a dose of how the real world worked, that choices had consequences.

"Enjoy it while it lasts," Florence would tell her daughter every year.

"I think I finally know what you mean by that," Mariel said one summer, when she was seventeen. "I used to think you meant my time up here. Or the summer in general. But it was never about me. You mean the Lakeside itself."

Although everyone knew that Florence would sell it as soon as both Betty and Floyd were gone, Florence had tried not to be too public about that fact. Depending on how you looked at it, the writing was on the wall for places like the Lakeside anyway. On Florence's drives to and from Bear Jaw, it seemed like the Cities were getting a little closer every year. Florence had noticed how towns she thought were too small to have a Country Kitchen or a Jorby's or a Pizza Hut now had these places. There was no such kind of restaurant in Bear Jaw yet, but one day soon there would be.

"Don't get too attached, that's all I'm saying," Florence said. "Anyhow, instead of spending every summer working your butt off up there, you should have some other experiences."

Returning home through St. Paul, Florence drove into the city and onto Grand Avenue. She slowed the car as she approached a white house, a green house, and finally, the big yellow house. It needed a new coat of paint, and there was a new door, but otherwise it was almost exactly the same. She didn't know who owned it or even if they were open to selling, but soon—perhaps very soon—she'd have enough to make an offer no reasonable person could refuse.

BY MARIEL'S SENIOR YEAR of high school in 1975, she seemed to have taken her mother's recent advice to heart, and it created a whole new problem for Florence.

"I want to go to college out of state," Mariel informed her mother one September afternoon in the kitchen, while Gustav was in the garage watching a Vikings game.

"Oh, no you're not," Florence responded immediately.

"I just want to experience another place, like you said," Mariel replied.

"That's not what I meant. I was trying to say you should have some other work experiences. I know some of your friends detassel corn in the summer."

"Jeez, Mom, that was like five years ago," Mariel replied, with a disgusted look, as if such honest labor were beneath her. "I'm not even saying I'll move anywhere permanently. I just want to see what life is like somewhere else."

"Like where?" Florence had to remind herself to not automatically think of a doomsday scenario. There were some colleges in Iowa and Wisconsin that were closer to Winona than Minneapolis. "I hear Iowa has some very good schools. Were you thinking Iowa?"

"Nope. California and Ohio."

"No way."

"Dad thinks it's fine."

Florence laughed. "Your father thinks everything is fine. And I bet everything actually is fine to him. I might think so, too, if I'd been born with his advantages."

"Well, you can't stop me from applying."

Florence knew that her daughter was right. She couldn't stop her. She'd kept her girl safe for so long, and the reward was always going to be abandonment. She just didn't think the terms would be so extreme.

"Well, I imagine you can get in anywhere you apply." She'd been so proud of her daughter's test scores and perfect GPA, and now they'd be used as weapons of anarchic liberation. Those smarty-pants friends of hers, Cathy Cragg and Mary Blace, were certainly to blame for some of Mariel's big ideas. "Where are Cathy and Mary looking? Are they choosing to stay close to family?"

"Mary is hoping to get into Northwestern, and Cathy wants to go to Notre Dame."

"Oh," Florence replied. She knew neither college was in a state that bordered Minnesota. "Well, you should apply somewhere close as a safety school. Somewhere like Winona State."

"I'm not going to college a mile away. Duluth, maybe." Mariel walked to the fridge and removed a beer. "Look, Mom. I'm not doing this to leave you. I'm never going to not be your daughter. But this is for me."

Florence was so distracted by what her daughter was holding, she barely heard her thoughtful words. "You're not old enough for that."

Mariel frowned and walked away. "It's for Dad. And I've had beer before. It's gross."

"You're right, it is," Florence said after her. It felt good to agree with her daughter, even if they were both lying.

She thought about joining her daughter and husband out in the garage, and pretending to like football just to spend time with them. It sounded like fun, or something close enough to it. But she couldn't move. The thought struck Florence that a year from now, her daughter would be somewhere far away, and Gustav would come inside himself to get a beer, and they'd have a dull conversation about whether to buy a garage fridge, and it might be the only memorable exchange she'd have all day.

There had to be a way they could both be happy, mother and daughter. There had to be.

One day, later in the fall, Mariel left for school shortly before her parents left for work, as she always did, and Florence watched as she put her college applications in the mailbox. *There she goes*, she thought, *three different futures in three different envelopes*. As Gustav started their car, she walked out to the mailbox to look at them. Pomona College, California. Oberlin College, Ohio. University of Minnesota Duluth.

She slid each envelope in her bag and joined her husband in the car.

"What do you have there?" he asked.

"Mariel's college applications. I thought I'd bring them to the post office myself during my break. Just to make sure they get there."

"That's thoughtful of you." He smiled. "Isn't it exciting? I'm so proud of her."

Florence took a deep breath. "Yes. So proud."

"We might finally have an excuse to visit California." He turned up the radio before he put the car in drive. "Look, they're playing 'Surfin' Bird.' It's a sign."

"Yes," Florence said, although she didn't believe in signs. At least not this one.

THAT AFTERNOON, in the post office, she walked in without looking at anyone, pushed one envelope into the slot in the wall, and gently slid the other two into the trash, addresses facing down. Then she went to the window and bought some stamps.

During her short walk back to the elementary school, she almost went back to the post office twice. But then she reminded herself that what she did was for the good of the family—the entire family.

MARIEL WAS PLEASED TO receive an acceptance from Duluth, but as the weeks passed, she was confused about why she never heard from the other two. Someone suggested that she call the admissions offices, but Florence told her it would look desperate, and hurt her chances, if she still had any. Mariel, being her father's daughter, remained optimistic for a while, but soon came to regard their silence as her fault, that her application was unworthy of even a response. The change in outlook was sudden. It was the first time that Florence ever witnessed her daughter acting so anxious and defeatist. It reminded Florence of herself, and not in a way that felt like any kind of victory.

She knew what she did was terrible, and there was no way to ever make it up to her. "Maybe you should phone their admissions offices after all," Florence suggested at last.

By then, Mariel's hopes were already dashed. All of her college-bound friends had replied to their acceptance letters, and were showing up to high school wearing their college logos and colors. "I don't want to call them just to hear them tell me no," Mariel finally decided, and that was that.

GUSTAV AND FLORENCE DROVE Mariel to the University of Minnesota Duluth the following August, and by then, everyone seemed satisfied about the destination. Once Mariel was situated in her dorm room, had met her roommate, Amy, and had exchanged the final, weeping embraces with her parents, it was only then that Florence couldn't bring herself to move.

Gustav finally walked her to the car, where she froze up again. "She knows where we parked. Let's stay here for a while in case she changes her mind."

"She won't change her mind," Gustav said, starting the car. "I'm starving. There's a Jorby's right here. That okay with you?"

"I'm not hungry," Florence said, even though she was.

"She seems happy," Gustav said, staring at the college buildings. "That's what counts. You should be too. She went to college in state, like you wanted."

PERHAPS NO ONE in the family was happier than Betty Miller, who bought Mariel a car as a belated graduation present, and drove it over the next day. "It's selfish of me," Betty said. "Now you can hop on over from Duluth and work with me anytime."

From then on, summers, breaks, and even some weekends found Mariel working at the Lakeside. She learned jobs she'd never tried before, and proved herself able and enthusiastic at all of them. She especially loved working with Betty and Howie Gibson behind the bar as their barback, and they loved working with her too.

On Mariel's nineteenth birthday, Betty and Floyd gave her a hell of a surprise.

"MOM," MARIEL SAID, her voice trembling over the phone. "Betty and Floyd changed their will. They're leaving it to me. I'm going to be the sole owner of the Lakeside. I thought you should hear it from me."

Florence sat down in her kitchen, and rested the receiver on the table in front of her. She stared out the kitchen window, at her neighbor's rosebushes, as she heard her daughter's voice repeating, *Hello? Mom, are you there?*

Florence stared at those bushes as she heard those words again and again as they rose in pitch, and finally surrendered as the line went dead.

THE FOLLOWING SATURDAY while Gustav was in the garage watching the Twins, Florence drove to St. Paul, up to Grand Avenue. Hearing the honking behind her as she went slowly up the block, Florence saw the white house, then the green house, and then nothing. The big yellow house was gone. In its space was an empty lot of brown dirt surrounded by a chain-link fence.

She parked, and stumbled to the restaurant across the street from the space where her home had been.

"May I help you?" the host asked. His name tag read RICO.

"What happened to the house across the street?"

Rico glanced in that direction. "I don't know. They just finally finished tearing it down. I hope they make it a parking lot, honestly."

"When was it sold?"

He shrugged. "Before I started working here. Maybe a year ago. Would you like a table?"

"No, thank you," she said. She had to tell someone what that place had meant. "I used to live there."

"Hmm," he replied, gently nodding, with a polite smile. Florence heard the door open behind her, and she moved out of the way to let two women approach the host station. Once Rico had greeted them, she caught his eye again. "It was a Winthrop house," she said, her voice almost breaking.

He looked back at her without enthusiasm. "Okay. Have a good day, now," he said, and guided his customers to their table.

NOBODY REMEMBERED anything anymore. But Florence remembered. She remembered the smell of lilacs, the dust motes in the sunbeams, the laughter on the staircase, and she remembered running, many times, up the porch steps, and once, in the dark of night, running away. She remembered looking out the screen door, at family coming up the staircase, long-gone aunts and uncles and baby cousins from her father's side. Lately, she envisioned that one day she'd be standing there again, watching her own daughter and grandchild coming up those steps, smiling, overjoyed to be home.

As she left the restaurant, Florence stared through the fence at the dirt, looking for answers, but dirt gave the same reply it always did. *See you soon enough*, it said.

A short, worried-looking woman with a little girl, each carrying grocery bags, approached from down the sidewalk. A local. Perhaps she would know why the house had been torn down.

But as the woman and her daughter got closer, Florence couldn't speak. She tried, but everything she thought to ask suddenly seemed pointless.

The woman glanced once in Florence's direction as they passed. Florence watched as they reached the far end of the block and turned out of sight.

Just then, it came to her. *Make her happy*, she wanted to tell the woman. *Make her happy, while you can.*

Fifteen

Mariel, 1996

That Monday afternoon, Mariel's new waitress, Cayla, showed up for work with a string of red, white, and blue Christmas lights around her neck, and wore an American flag apron she'd brought from home.

"What's with the getup?" Mariel asked. She'd never told any of her employees to do anything more than their jobs.

"I hope it's okay," Cayla said. "I thought I'd wear this on the Fourth, but figured I could try it out first, on a slower night?"

She watched Cayla work a booth where two longtime customers, John and Mary Sands, were ordering dinner. They were big-city lawyers who'd retired a while back and moved to Bear Jaw. Mary was Ojibwe and had grown up in the area, was tirelessly active in the community, and had many friends. Cayla was talking to Mary and John like she'd known them for years, and maybe she had. Watching Cayla laughing with them, Mariel became startled by a fleeting thought. She caught herself wanting a daughter, and imagined she had one, someone very much like Cayla.

On her way back to the bar, Mariel made a sudden detour to her office, and closed the door, keeping the lights off. She took a few deep breaths, and let the desire pass through her, until her heart was hers again.

BACK AT THE BAR, she learned a disturbing piece of news from her mom's friend Hazel. The pastor's office at Our Savior's had a private bathroom with a shower stall, and Florence was allowed full use of it whenever she pleased. Refreshed, Florence took her place in the lobby, reminding people, "My daughter knows where I am," whenever anyone asked.

AROUND SIX THIRTY, Brenda's son, Kyle, showed up, still in his suit from the funeral home. He ordered a Jameson neat.

"Here for your mom's coolers?" she asked him. He looked as objectively handsome in that suit as he did gutting a deer in a bloody apron.

"What? No," he replied. "But my mom does want to know how late you're here after you close."

"Usually about an hour. Why's that?"

"She doesn't like crowds so much."

"Well, then she'd love it here right now."

Kyle grinned politely. "It looks like you're doing okay to me," he said, glancing back at the half-full dining room behind him.

A woman with a fresh perm and acid-washed jeans, who'd been sitting alone in a booth, smoking and staring out the window, returned his glance with the piqued expression of a meaningful but misremembered acquaintance.

Kyle turned back to face Mariel, his eyes and posture betraying no memory of this person. *It must happen to him all the time*, Mariel figured. Of course people have some recollection of *him*, given his unusual, crucial role in their fresh grief. But how could he remember them all? He must see hundreds of the bereaved every year, their losses each as fleeting for him as falling leaves.

"Got big plans for the rest of the weekend?" she asked him, just to make conversation, although she was curious what a young guy like him did for fun around Bear Jaw.

"On my way to Minneapolis," he said.

She laughed. "You leave now, you won't get there until after ten."

"That's true."

"What's there to do in Minneapolis after ten?"

Now he laughed. "Oh, lots of things."

She didn't know whether this was an invitation to ask. It sounded illicit. The thought occurred to her that he might have been some kind of playboy, or gay, or just in need of something else Bear Jaw didn't provide, which was a lot. For year-round residents, Bear Jaw's singles market was brutally limited—it often seemed that locals didn't sleep around until after they were married—and the town would have an active volcano before it had an active gay scene. For all its natural beauty, Bear Jaw still had a lot of ugliness. People here liked to say they rooted for the underdog, but some of them got real quiet when the underdog was different from them. A few days after Floyd passed away, Mariel had finally put a rainbow flag sticker on the door, far less afraid of losing business than she was of losing her heart.

But no one had yet said anything negative about it to her face, and whatever bullshit they said behind her back she could live with. One thing was certain. As kind a soul as Floyd was, she didn't want to know what he would have said, being a man of such a different generation.

"By the way, I gotta ask," Kyle said, and for some reason she thought he was going to ask her about the flag sticker. "What's the deal with your mom?"

Mariel was so surprised to hear the question from him that it made her take a step backward. "How do you know about that?"

"I live right across the street from the church. She's sitting in the lobby like a statue. I hear that she's waiting for you. I'm just curious, are you gonna get her, or what?"

"No," she said, without thinking.

"Awesome," he said, and smiled.

"Thanks." She noticed he'd raised his right hand to give her a high five, which, after a confused moment, she returned.

"Stand your ground," he said. "I don't know your mom, but I've met her friends. I know how these people think."

"Yeah, they're a little stubborn."

"You have no idea. I can keep an eye on things for you and give you routine reports." Kyle stood up, finished his shot, and left a ten-dollar bill on the bar as he turned toward the door. "Stay strong," was the last thing he said before he left.

Mariel heard Kyle tell somebody, "Pardon me," as he opened the door, and she turned to see a tired young family hovering by the unattended host station. They evidently didn't see the sign that, around eight fifteen, had been turned to read PLEASE SEAT YOURSELF.

"Would you like to be seated by a window?" she asked the parents.

The father didn't seem to care either way. "That's fine. Do you have high chairs?"

"Yes, we do," Mariel said, though it had been a long time since she had needed to locate one. She glanced around the room; the servers were all slammed. She'd be seating this family herself.

Mariel looked down at the little boy. He was wearing a green T-shirt emblazoned with a roaring cartoon *T. rex*, and his attention was fixed on the northern pike mounted on the wall behind the host station. It was about three feet long, and its predator teeth and lifeless obsidian eyes had captivated countless children since Mariel was a child herself. This little boy suddenly dashed over to it, a single hand outstretched toward the fish's mouth. Mariel instinctively grabbed him, pulling him backward, a stranger's child, now openly whining in her grasp.

"I'm sorry, I don't want him hurting his finger on those teeth," Mariel replied, handing the boy off to his mother.

"I can see that," the mother said, taking in the large sign just above the fish that read DO NOT TOUCH. "Thank you."

She seated the family and was proud of herself that they didn't seem to sense anything off about her. She was pleased that they could look right into her eyes and not see her heart falling into her stomach. She took their drink orders of two ice waters and a cup of milk like a perfectly normal person, and even smiled.

"Oh, and that high chair," the father reminded her.

THERE WERE TWO high chairs already on the floor, and the only other one she could find was dirty, its cushions gunked up with post-toddler crust, so she lugged it into the women's bathroom to clean it off. Feeling its familiar weight under her hands made her arms shake, and she was relieved to set it down in a quiet, unoccupied room. She took a moment, a deep breath, and then got to work. She dabbed some pink soap on a paper towel, wet it under the spigot, and scrubbed against the high chair's seat cushion, as she'd mindlessly done many times long ago, when it was a simple activity lost in a frenzy of exhausted hours.

This time, she was careful, even loving. It would look as a good as new, she'd decided. But she couldn't even get halfway done before she'd started sobbing.

As she wiped her eyes, Mariel heard the door squeal, and saw the woman with the perm and acid-washed jeans take a few steps in and pause by a pink stall door. Who knows what this woman thought, but she barely hesitated. She walked right over to Mariel and hugged her.

Mariel's body collapsed into the stranger's embrace. Did this woman understand? It didn't matter. There was no end to the journey Mariel was on. Any moment of grace was a refuge.

She could be so grateful for the three years she knew her son, and so furious those three years were all she'd been given. That meant there were moments like this when it seemed like she had barely moved forward, and that was okay. Keeping it together is overrated, she believed. There are no prizes for false composure.

Long ago, she had to give herself permission to break again and again, as often as she damn well pleased, and she knew she'd keep breaking forever. Perhaps it wasn't the only way through grief, but it was hers, and she welcomed it. She would break until there was nothing left, until she was nothing or something else entirely, another woman perhaps, one who could feel something like forgiveness.

Sixteen

≈

Mariel, 1996

ater that night, about thirty minutes after close, when Mariel
and her teenage janitor, Mo Akbar, were cleaning up, she saw
a familiar silver-haired woman standing outside the entrance,
peering through the glass. Mariel ran to open the door.

"Hey," Brenda said, looking around as if the restaurant were
completely unfamiliar.

It was hard for Mariel to disguise her joy. She couldn't stop
thinking about how last Saturday she'd spent hours simply *talking*,
and to someone who wasn't an employee or a customer, but a friend.
She'd slowly lost touch with Cathy Cragg, Mary Blace, Amy Thyren,
and all of her other old childhood and college friends over the years,
and these relationships were something she realized now that she'd
dearly missed.

"Let me go grab the coolers," Mariel said. "They're here in the office."

"What? Oh, who cares. I know where you are if I need 'em," Brenda said. She led Mariel to the bar, where she removed a familiar ornate crystal bottle from a Red Owl grocery bag. "I got a proposal for you."

"Oh," Mariel said, eyebrows raised. "Are we gonna have some gin now?"

"Sure. But here's my offer. I sell you one of these bottles for twenty bucks. You sell it for four bucks a shot. Everyone wins."

Mo wandered over to the bar, still holding his mop. "What's that?"

Brenda pulled off the cap. "It's homemade gin, want to try it?"

"Hell yeah," Mo said.

Everything was happening too fast, or at least too fast for Mariel.

"He's eighteen," Mariel stammered.

"So what?" Brenda replied. "I had my first shot of gin when I was nine. Kid, you've had gin before, right?"

"Nope," he said, and watched Brenda pour the shot.

"Vaya con Dios," Brenda said as she handed it to him.

Mo raised the shot glass to his lips, and sipped it like a bird. Mariel waited for him to wince. Instead, his eyes widened. She saw curiosity and wonder shift the ridges and valleys of his face. He sipped it again, and gasped this time, evidently feeling the alcohol's radiant burn, but all the while he was smiling. "You made this?" was the first thing he said. "How?"

"You want to come by sometime, I'll show ya," Brenda said. "Been doing it for thirty years. We used to make our own beer too."

Now Mo seemed really impressed. "You made your own beer?"

"Both of you, just hold on a minute," Mariel said at last. "Brenda, I don't even know if we can have that behind the bar."

"Sure you can, just set it there." Brenda walked around to where Mariel was standing, and wedged her bottle among the gins and vodkas. "See, like that."

"Why not, Mrs. Prager?" Mo asked. "You run this place, don't you?"

Mariel couldn't argue. "Okay, fine."

Brenda grabbed a brandy snifter and filled it a third of the way with gin. "You want ice?"

"Sure," Mariel said, and watched Brenda drop in a trio of cubes. Mariel then took the glass and held it to her mouth, tilted it up, and felt for herself, once again, what just blew Mo's mind. "Thank you," she said at last.

"You're welcome!" a man's voice shouted playfully. Under the bar lamps, Ned Prager appeared, in his plaid shirt and jeans, still as attractive to her as he'd ever been.

MARIEL NEVER ADMITTED TO Ned that this was the room where she had first noticed him. Like most kids without siblings in an adult world, she was wildly attentive to others her age, and by the time she was eleven, the cute, cheerful boy who'd come up every year with his family had suddenly seemed intriguing in a more intense way. A couple of years later, the boy's father was with a younger wife, and the boy seemed somber and moody, which, at the time, only increased his appeal. Even so, by the time he was in his late teens, he'd dropped the sad-sack look and came to exude a calm kind of confidence.

She'd never once spoken to him. Even during the two years she'd worked as a waitress, Mariel had never been given his table, not that she would've wanted it. She was content watching him from a distance, and knew, like many other cute older guys she'd seen in the supper club, that he'd soon be showing up with girlfriends and eventually a wife.

What made him special was that he was the rich tourist boy most of the other girls went nuts over. The other waitresses knew all about him. The Pragers were *multi*millionaires, they said. It was stupid the way some of her co-workers threw themselves at him, perhaps because of that very reason. Some of them even slipped Ned their phone numbers. He never called them, which only made them even crazier about him.

Then, one summer, when Mariel was taking a break from the kitchen to learn bartending, there he was. Crossing a room toward her. He extended his hand and smiled, and she was a goner. She surprised herself when she invited him out that night, and even more when she kissed him.

She had to deal with shit from the jealous waitresses for a while. She didn't care. Mariel, the gawky, overweight bar trainee, had bagged the catch of Bear Jaw Lake. She'd won, and done it without trying. And she and Ned had been together ever since.

"Hey, come here," he said, bolting behind the bar to kiss her.

He was energetic in the way he often was whenever he returned after a weekend of baseball games with old friends. She might have found this nice, if she could forget how her presence would soon dim his wild joy, reminding him of the sadness that had become their marriage's strongest ligament. For a while now, they'd been like bricks with no mortar, all of the heaviness with none of the stability.

He still kissed wonderfully. She released his lips, and told him, "It's so good to see you."

For some reason, he was wincing now, his expression troubled.

"What are you drinking?" he asked.

That was how he found out.

ONE OF THE MOST difficult tasks for a polite Minnesotan is the job of quickly clearing a room so two people can have a private conversation. Ned was the nicer one, by far, and Mariel closed a bar six nights a week, so in situations like these, she took charge.

"Mo, see you tomorrow," she told him, and then nodded at her new friend. "Brenda, I'll come by in the morning."

"Anytime." Brenda nodded back. She got it. And she left the gin.

By the time the front doors closed, Ned was already crying. She sat next to him and cried along, in silence.

"When?" he eventually managed to ask.

"Last Friday night," she said. "I didn't want to ruin your trip. I'm sorry."

"Why are you sorry? I get it." Ned took a deep breath. "I know they said it might not work the first time, but I had hoped it would."

She noticed that Ned didn't even utter the abbreviation "IVF" when they were in private. Maybe because it had been hard for him to accept that he had fertility problems too. Mariel expected it for herself, being thirty-six when they actively began trying to conceive, but he hadn't. He'd put on a happy face about it, and cheerfully went under the knife and got a TESE procedure to extract his unmotivated sperm, but only after eighteen months of denial. It had been such an arduous and painful journey for them both, and after all of it, here they were, once again, a childless couple.

Mariel remembered the miscarriage she'd had long ago, before giving birth to Gus, and didn't say what was on her mind. "Me too," she said instead.

Ned put his hand on her shoulder. "If you want to take some time before we try again, that's okay."

"I want to do it again as soon as possible."

"Yeah," he said, and wiped his eyes. "Let's do that. But tell nobody this time."

Mariel thought about how so much of her own mental peace, right now, relied on the maintenance of certain secrets and withholding information. She supposed everyone's life was like that. How exhausting it all was. Her heart ached when she reflected on how her mother had never trusted her with so much of herself. She wondered if things would've been different if she had.

Mariel and Ned sat in silence for a while, at the bar, until finally, she dropped a few cubes in a rocks glass and poured her husband some gin.

"Try this, it's excellent."

He sipped it, and then instantly poured more in his glass. He lifted the bottle again to top Mariel off, but hesitated, glancing up to check her reaction.

"Please," she said, and watched him fill her glass.

"Tell me some good news," he said.

"I got in a car accident," she replied.

. . .

WHEN MARIEL FINISHED telling him the entire story, Ned seemed confused.

"Wait a second. She's still there? At the church?"

"Yep."

"Wow." Now he seemed impressed. "How long are you going to make her wait?"

"Until I'm ready to get her," Mariel replied, and damn, it felt good to say.

"A few days? A week?"

Mariel had no idea.

Seventeen

~~~~~

Mariel, 1996

TWIN CITY TALKER, THURSDAY, AUGUST I, 1996

ELDERLY MINNESOTA WOMAN WAITS FOR RIDE FROM DAUGHTER

By Cinthia Specht

On a Saturday in late June, Florence Jean Stenerud's daughter Mariel Prager promised to pick her up at the Our Savior's Lutheran Church pancake breakfast up in Bear Jaw. Now, over a month later, Mrs. Stenerud is still in the church lobby, and she's still waiting. Refusing all other offers of transportation on principle, Florence is seen by many in the area as a hero.

"So many parents have experienced this kind of

careless neglect from their adult children," friend and local resident Mildred Kochendorfer said. "Florence knows how they feel, and they know how she feels."

The five weeks spent waiting at the church for a ride home is believed to have shattered the unofficial, unverified record for public passive-aggressive waiting more than thirty years ago. In September 1965, Verna Swenson waited twenty-four hours at Mickey's Diner in St. Paul for her son Mitch, when Mitch got the date wrong by a day.

When informed of setting a possible record, however, Mrs. Stenerud seemed unimpressed. Although she wouldn't go on record, the pastor at the church, Jeff Staley, attempted to speak for her. "I don't know about that term, passive-aggressive," he said. "Maybe it's the other person who's being passive-aggressive. You know, it takes two to tango."

Meanwhile, Staley, Kochendorfer and other Bear Jaw residents have rallied behind their stubborn friend, bringing Mrs. Stenerud food, changes of clothes and entertainment. Several Scrabble, Yahtzee and cribbage tournaments have been held, and a meat raffle featuring a visit from former Minnesota Vikings head coach Jerry Burns attracted a standing-room-only crowd last Thursday. Mrs. Stenerud has also received hundreds of letters from other seniors offering support, prayers and shared grievances. She seems nonchalant about the attention.

"I told her to take it one day at a time," Burns said after meeting her. "Just sit down there in the lobby and give it 110 percent every day."

Both Mrs. Stenerud and Mrs. Prager declined several requests for comment.

Mariel had to admit that the senior community at Our Savior's had indeed done a truly impressive job reinforcing what was becoming known around town as Fort Florence.

According to Kyle Kowalsky's routine reports, the church had cleaned out an office for Florence's use as a bedroom. During daylight and evening hours, there were also church services, Bible study groups, post-funeral luncheons, quilting clubs, and the occasional wedding that apparently welcomed Florence's participation. She was suddenly the most helpful person in town. It was maddening.

"What are these people thinking?" Mariel asked. "Do I even want to know?"

"No one is against you personally, Mariel," Kyle said. "It's just that everyone loves Fort Florence. Except you and me."

"What's it like living across the street these days?" Mariel asked him.

"It's like being in the middle of the state fair, all day, every day, if you hate the state fair," he said, and sipped his third Jameson, not smiling. "It must end."

THE NEXT MORNING, in an attempt to get her mind off everything, Mariel decided to help Big Al and Felix in the kitchen. She could lose herself in the work in a way she couldn't at the bar, at least until Big Al started talking to her. As they worked on a batch of Jutta's Kartoffelsalat, he told her that he had to apologize.

"I brought food to your mom yesterday," he said, setting down his potato peeler. "I'm sorry."

This was a surprise. She thought he was on her side. And besides, Florence didn't need Big Al's help, not at all. "It's fine," she said. "She's your friend."

"I'm glad you see it that way," Al said, getting back to work. "Because I've been helping her out in other ways too."

"You have?"

"Oh yeah, a lot," Al said. He seemed relieved to be admitting it. "You know, she didn't expect to inherit Floyd's house. She's got to clean all his furniture and stuff out before she can even move her things up from Winona."

Bear Jaw had long been the one place in North America safe from her mother, but now with Floyd gone, Florence was apparently coming home. It was too much to comprehend. "Sounds good," was all she could say to Al.

"I told her I'd take care of it," Al said. "And you know, I also called her friends down there, to bring in her mail and water her garden and everything."

"I figured someone has to do all that," Mariel said, even more annoyed. "It's been over a month."

"Wow," Felix said, looking over at her from where he was dicing peeled potatoes. "Your mom's a real stick-in-the-mud, huh?"

"Yep," Al interjected. "That's for sure." Al's voice had a tone of mild, amused admiration, common among older Minnesotans when speaking of another older person's illogical stubbornness. "But underneath all of that, she's a good person."

Mariel looked over at Felix, hoping for any gesture of support.

"I only met her one time, at Floyd's funeral," Felix said. "She helped me remove a wine stain from my tie."

"I guess I'm glad everyone else gets to know the generous side of her," Mariel replied. "Growing up, I was only ever told what I couldn't do, never what I could do. And anything new or different or far away was always dangerous or bad."

"Come on, you were her only child," Big Al said. "She was just being a worried mother. I bet when you were a parent, some of what she did made perfect sense."

"It did not. And how's this for perfect sense? When Ned and I lived together before we got married, my mom refused to even set foot in the place. She said we were living in sin."

"Yeah, I can understand that," Big Al replied.

"Because you were," Felix said. "At least to her."

Mariel set her knife down. "What's the matter with you two? You're supposed to be my best friends. I need a little validation here."

"Hey, I don't actually believe it's living in sin," Felix said. "And Al doesn't, either. He visits his granddaughter's house all the time."

Big Al shrugged. "Well, they *are* getting married."

"Oh, damn," Felix replied. "McBroom finally asked her? When did he do that?"

"Last weekend."

Big Al nodded with pride. His granddaughter Alexandra's long-time boyfriend, Jeremy McBroom, had been the first local hockey player in thirty years who made it to the NHL. To become the only person in Bear Jaw more universally beloved than Florence, you apparently had to play for the Hartford Whalers.

"Well, good for you and your family, Al," Mariel said, still a little frustrated, but relieved at the sudden change of topic. She was murderously weary of the amount of space her mother had claimed in her life without even being present.

"You know, Mariel, two of their guests just canceled. Would you and Ned like to come to the wedding?"

"Is it after Labor Day?"

"Yeah," Big Al said. "Saturday the seventh. Will Ned be in town?"

It was a fair question. Since finishing the house a number of years back, Ned had spent a lot of time traveling around the state, buying and trading baseball collectibles. What was supposed to be their guest bedroom had mutated into Ned's "baseball room." There were worse hobbies that could consume a husband, for sure, but besides the occasional gig helping other people build their own homes or cabins, he was seemingly gone chasing after baseball paraphernalia too often to hold down a regular job. Of course, they each needed a distraction from their grief, and she supposed this was his. She just wished it were something that didn't require travel.

"I'll make sure he is."

"Why are they getting married so suddenly?" Felix asked. "Al, is your granddaughter pregnant or something?"

Al glanced at Mariel, then at Felix. "We should change the topic."

"Oh, right," Felix said, looking abashed. "I'm sorry."

It was sweet of them to care. "It's okay," she told them, but they looked back at her as if they didn't believe her. "You can talk about Al's pregnant granddaughter."

Just speaking those words made her feel more thick-skinned than she was. Since she and Ned decided to try again, loose talk about other people's easy or unintentional pregnancies didn't upset her quite as much. Maybe it depended on the circumstances. She wished she could tell both of these guys right now how excited she was for her and Ned's next embryo transfer, which was right around the corner. But she didn't need everyone knowing all that.

DRIVING SOUTH TO THE Cities with Ned happened rarely enough that it still made her think of riding in his inherited black Mercedes, with all of her possessions, so fiercely in love, all those years ago. Now, they each packed enough for just one night, and she was drinking from a gallon jug of water, feeling indescribably anxious.

When they arrived at the clinic, some awful woman was in the lobby with her three-year-old. *They shouldn't allow that*, she thought, and almost said something to the receptionist. Thankfully, the woman was summoned by her OB after just a few minutes, and Mariel could fill her bladder in peace next to Ned.

The new OB, Dr. Ellen Bucher, was kind and serious, with nothing sentimental, New Agey, or overly personal in her style, and Mariel supposed that was fine. Either this would work or it wouldn't.

In no time at all, Mariel was lying back at a slight angle, holding Ned's hand, awaiting the second embryo transfer of her life. When talking about what would happen in the days to come, Dr. Bucher used the word "blastocyst." Nobody here said the word "baby," of course, and a blastocyst was pretty damn far from being a baby. But it was what all this hoopla meant.

Last time, Mariel had eight fresh embryos implanted. One stuck, until it didn't. Now she was getting just one. Dr. Bucher was all about trying new things, and she was confident. "You still have three more embryos on ice we can try if this doesn't work. Or we can go through the process of making fresh ones again."

Three more.

She didn't know if they had the money to start over again. She was grateful they still had the resources to do this at all.

Building a new house from scratch hadn't been cheap, and the supper club took as much extra cash as they could give it. Even still, they had a little money left from selling the Sunfish Lake house, and some from Ned's payout, after setting half of that aside for retirement. With the rest of the money, they'd planned to travel, and maybe even buy a cabin or condo somewhere. Then they needed help getting pregnant.

Now, all of it was nearly gone. Of course, they had one great asset that could help them keep trying, but Mariel didn't want to have to choose between her supper club and a baby. She wanted both. The future of one would depend on the other.

A NURSE BROUGHT IN a long syringe, confirmed the contents were theirs, and in a moment, it was done. Mariel had to remain recumbent for a while. She'd never held Ned's hand so tightly, but asked him to keep quiet. She didn't want him to say anything that might jinx it. She stared at a painting on the wall of red birds on a wire, and tried to think positive thoughts.

THEY DROVE INTO MINNEAPOLIS to have dinner at Lucia's, her favorite restaurant, and Ned asked what she wanted to do on her birthday, which was coming up.

"Can I decide that day?" Why did she pose it as a question? She certainly wasn't requesting permission from him.

"I don't see why not," Ned replied.

"It may not involve you," she told him. "I need to not think about things."

IT WAS THE LAST birthday of her thirties, and she knew the one person she wanted to spend it with, the only person with whom she could truly forget the previous thirty-nine years, and still know her just well enough to have a good time.

When Mariel approached Brenda's little house, and saw Bronzie and Brenda running toward her car, she knew she'd made the right choice.

"Happy birthday!" Brenda screamed. "You're almost forty! Let's get shit-faced!"

"I'm taking a break from alcohol." As she stepped onto the driveway dirt, she saw Brenda wobble in the grass. Good Lord, she seemed shit-faced already.

"You have to get drunk on your birthday. Those are the rules!"

She wondered how she would phrase it to Brenda. "I'm pregnant," she said finally.

Brenda seemed confused. "Since when?"

"Since last week."

"Damn," Brenda said. "Well, that's a dumbass thing to do before your birthday. You couldn't have waited until after?"

"It's not how my cycle worked out." Mariel nodded. "But otherwise, you have a point."

"Well, good luck with it. Kids are great. My only advice is don't take any advice. Now let's try to somehow enjoy ourselves anyway."

. . .

BRENDA LED MARIEL INTO her kitchen. A perfectly simple brown cake awaited them, covered with thirty-nine blazing candles, framed by two glasses of viscous golden wine.

"Ta-da," Brenda said. "It was the only cake recipe in that book you keep blabbing about." Brenda opened a kitchen drawer and revealed a copy of the *Chez Panisse Menu Cookbook*, and opened it to a bookmarked page. "Yeah, the Olive Oil and Sauternes Cake. Jesus, it was a bitch to make. But I think I did it."

Mariel had tears in her eyes. "You made me a cake from a Chez Panisse recipe?"

"Yeah. I tried, anyway," Brenda said. "I had to schlep to the Cities to find this Sauternes stuff. That shit ain't cheap. But it's not a problem, it's your birthday."

No one had ever made Mariel a Chez Panisse recipe before, let alone something like Olive Oil and Sauternes Cake. It was beyond anything she'd even dream of asking for. And yet, there it was, shimmering beneath the flickering candles counting the last year of her thirties, made by a woman who probably hadn't used a whisk before, let alone an eight-inch springform pan. It didn't even matter if the cake was any good. It was the most beautiful thing anyone had done for Mariel in a long, long time.

"Just give me a minute," she said, dabbing her eyes.

"Here," Brenda said, grabbing a glass. "Have a sip of this schmancy wine. It'll be fine."

Mariel couldn't take it, because her hands were covering her face, because she was crying.

Brenda hugged her, and after a few moments, asked, "You wanna try the damn thing?"

Mariel got some tears on the cake when she blew out the candles, but even with the tears and candle wax, it was the best cake she'd ever eaten.

Afterward, Brenda announced she was going to grab a beer from the garage fridge, and when Mariel followed her, she noticed that the space was a little emptier; two of the air compressors, a motorcycle, and a few other things were gone.

"Thinning out your air compressor collection?" Mariel asked, and laughed.

Brenda didn't laugh back. "I got bills to pay. Life is expensive."

"Oh," Mariel said. "I'm sorry."

"Don't be," Brenda said. "My husband was a mechanic. He didn't leave me much money, but he did leave a whole garage full of shit. It's done me all right."

Mariel stared into the vast garage, and sniffed the oily air, and bet it still smelled the same way it must've smelled ten years ago, when Brenda's husband was still alive.

"Well, pretty soon you're going to run out of machinery to sell."

"Sure." Brenda gave her a look. "By then, I'll be getting social security."

"I have an idea," Mariel said. "Let's go out. My treat."

"Ha," Brenda said. "Go out where?"

"Come on," Mariel said, already walking to her car. "I'll drive."

"I told you, I don't go out around here. I don't know what you've heard, but I don't have the most stellar reputation."

"You think I give a damn?" Mariel replied. "If anything, I'm impressed. Sounds like you had a good time."

"It was all right."

"Were you trying to get pregnant?"

"I got the exact son I always wanted." Brenda smiled.

"I didn't mean to get too personal."

"You know, I just like sex. And married guys are great. You know where you stand. You don't have to make them dinner, or deal with their shit. I shoulda just kept it out of the workplace."

"That's what blew everything up."

"Yep. I wasn't a home-wrecker until it all went public. And I'll tell you, I didn't wreck any homes that weren't halfway wrecked already. But that was it for me. People didn't want to be seen as having my back, you know." Brenda laughed. "So I'd only eat at a restaurant if I hated it and wanted to ruin their day."

Mariel smiled. "Then I know exactly where we can go."

Eighteen

≈

Mariel, 1996

W elcome to Jorby's," claimed an unenthusiastic young woman in a crisp, calico-patterned top. "Is your whole party present?"

"I hope so," Brenda replied.

The young woman grabbed a couple of laminated menus from a shelf behind her podium and led Mariel and Brenda into the dining room. When people started to notice Brenda, the ambient chatter in the restaurant suddenly lowered enough that Mariel could hear the country music station playing softly in the kitchen.

The delicate social beehive of Bear Jaw had been smacked with a baseball bat, and Mariel felt the stings of a hundred whispers. These people really didn't let things go. She wondered what it must be like to live like that, and then caught herself.

Brenda, for her part, seemed to be enjoying it. "Yep," she said as they passed within punching distance of a few judgmental stares. "There's a guy I slept with. There's a wife of a guy I slept with."

Word would no doubt get back to Fort Florence about this, with a velocity that would impress Chuck Yeager. Mariel Prager, eating lunch with the sexually liberated local pariah. They were led toward the two-top booths that lined each side of a long stunted wall in the middle of the restaurant, and were shown to one right in the center of the seating area.

"The waitress will be right with you," the hostess muttered, and vanished.

"Fuckin' A," Brenda groaned as she plopped into her seat and picked up a menu.

"I've been wondering, why didn't you ever move?" Mariel asked her friend.

"I can't afford it, and anyway, where would I go?" Brenda laughed, and glanced around. "Hey, there's Frank Morrow. I bet his wife won't let him wave back to me."

As Brenda waved to people who didn't acknowledge her, it occurred to Mariel that she was a lot more unsettled being in this restaurant than her outcast friend seemed to be. This Jorby's had been the one dark feature of her former life that was difficult to forget.

After Ned's father passed away in 1987, Carla inherited and sold their Bear Jaw lake house. In the years since, they rarely saw her, and when they did, it was strange. They spent one Christmas with her at her new place in Marine on St. Croix, and she gave them such lavish gifts it was uncomfortable. She'd bought a Tiffany tennis bracelet for Mariel and a Commodore Amiga for Ned, and got them both an all-expenses-paid trip to Australia for New Year's. The following Christmases, Carla was in Vienna and then Tokyo, and although she invited them and offered to cover their travel, they declined. It all felt equally generous and impersonal. Ned said at the time that the woman who Carla had become didn't seem like his sister anymore.

Maybe he just couldn't handle what Carla reminded him of. She was the person from Gus's party whom they'd seen most recently, and by now it had been several years. A year after Ned's dad died, his stepmom, Peg, married an old high school sweetheart, a widower with a huge family, and now lived somewhere in Michigan. It seemed like everyone had moved on but them.

AT LEAST NEITHER SHE nor Ned felt a lost opportunity whenever they saw a Jorby's. Mariel certainly never did, and Ned had come around. Ned claimed he didn't even envy Carla anymore. The security and future of the family business had been in far better hands with his sister; even he'd admit that. It had been impressive to see Jorby's expand into a restaurant group with chains like Yucatan Lou's and Il Vecchio Mulino that were even more popular than Jorby's itself. What broke his heart was how they'd all left him behind, and done better than ever before.

What broke Mariel's heart was that the Jorby's franchise here in Bear Jaw was still apparently doing fine, or at least well enough to hurt the Lakeside. She remembered when they first moved up here, Jorby's had lines out the door on Saturday nights, and a ninety-minute wait for Sunday brunch. A ninety-minute wait, at a place with no lake view and the color scheme of a dentist's office, where almost all the food arrived frozen, even the bread. But it was cheaper. Goddamn it, a burger here was half the price, and a steak, two thirds the price. Mariel could run circles around their food, but they still had her by the numbers.

Mariel sighed. "Words can't describe how much I hate this place."

"Lighten up," Brenda said. "I was thinking about the steak. It's pretty cheap here."

"You get what you pay for."

"Then you should get the Sensational Sampler. Look, it's got mozzarella sticks, onion rings, skin-on fries, chicken niblets, and deep-fried cheese curds."

"Wow, that sounds fatal." Mariel saw that the "Hearty and Healthy" section was now a full page. It still looked as bad as everything else. "But I guess if I'm gonna eat frozen food from a plastic bag, I may as well go all in."

Brenda glanced around the restaurant. For the first time all day, she looked worried. "Does this joint have a bar?"

"No. And if they did, it would be light beer and boxed rosé."

"Sounds perfect. I'd kill for either of those things."

Mariel looked around. "Wonder when our waitress feels like coming over."

ANOTHER TEN MINUTES PASSED of laughing and insulting menu items before the thought occurred to them: they were being actively ignored.

"What do we do? Do we call them on it?" Mariel asked. Like

most people she knew, Mariel feared almost all varieties of public confrontation, but she had a hunch that Brenda didn't.

"Too easy," Brenda said. "So, we're invisible. Let's find out how invisible we are."

Mariel glanced at a recently vacated four-top that hadn't been cleared yet. "Those people at that table hardly touched their side of fries." She was thinking about getting up to grab a single fry, when Brenda reached over, grabbed the whole basket, and plopped it down between them.

"Bingo," Brenda said, starting to shake the ketchup bottle. "Still warm, even."

Mariel, starving, went to town on them, without a word.

"Hey, don't forget to breathe," Brenda laughed. "Don't you want ketchup?"

"No. It's all sugar. If I'm going to eat sugar, it's going to be worth it."

Brenda stood up. "Roger that."

Mariel watched as Brenda walked purposefully toward Jorby's famous rotating pie tower. She returned, just as confidently, with a blackberry pie. "What did you do?"

"Only one person who works here noticed me," Brenda said.

Mariel looked around and saw that every visible employee was now watching them. "They're all noticing you now."

"Wow," Brenda said, cutting herself a slice of pie with a butter knife. "The manager must've literally told everybody, '*Ignore them, and they'll go away.*' Want a piece?"

Mariel shook her head. She'd grown up in Florence's house, where stealing was a mortal sin.

"I'm just not in the mood for pie," Mariel said. "After that wonderful cake you made."

"Try just one bite."

Mariel was nervous. She didn't do things like this. By now, every employee and many customers were watching them. Still, no one was doing anything about it.

"Come on." Brenda held out a fork. "It'll go to waste otherwise."

The pie had no soul, but it wasn't terrible. Mariel tried another bite, and another.

She hadn't even sliced off a piece; she was just scooping chunks out of it, chowing down.

"More!" Brenda commanded. "Faster!"

She felt young and ridiculous, but Mariel obeyed, churning the pie to her face like a speed-eating piglet. Maybe she was even snorting a little. Brenda was laughing so hard, Mariel started laughing too. Finally, she lifted a fat, gooey piece that looked way too big for one bite, and opened her mouth to meet it anyway.

"Get it in there!" Brenda yelled.

Mariel laughed so hard, it fell out of her mouth. She wiped tears from her eyes and splotches of thick blackberry filling from her lips and cheeks. She took a deep breath, and made the mistake of glancing around the restaurant. To say that no one else shared in their joy was an understatement. She'd lost herself. She was a local business owner and this was wildly irresponsible. She pushed the pie away, wiped her face, and took a few deep breaths to calm down.

Brenda frowned. "Well, I'm full," she announced. "No use hanging around this flea-hole."

Mariel watched her friend rise, and when Brenda's back was turned, left a ten-dollar bill on the table, which would've easily covered the pie. No one said a word to them as they walked out to the parking lot.

. . .

OUTSIDE, IN THE WINDLESS, greasy air burned by deep fryers and car exhaust, the restaurant's American flag hung on a twenty-foot pole like a shop rag. A teenager drove by, blasting rap music from his parents' minivan, probably imagining he was somewhere cooler, somewhere much less safe. A pack of long-haired college-age kids were leaning against the shaded wall of a bait shop, and a young tattooed dude in a sleeveless shirt smashed out his cigarette butt with the toe of a black boot.

There were still a few young people who stuck around this town, which cheered Mariel. Maybe there was a good cook or server among that crowd over there. Maybe even a bartender who could hold down the fort in about nine months.

Brenda looked at Mariel. "You paid for that pie, didn't you?'

"Yeah," Mariel admitted as she opened her unlocked driver's side door.

"You're a good person. And I love that about you. But those people in there disrespected us, so screw 'em. Someone had to do something devious."

Mariel looked again at the careless long-haired youths. They probably did something devious every day. "I can be devious," she said, and turned the ignition.

THAT AFTERNOON, before the supper club opened, she decided to take up Brenda's subtle challenge. Florence was being childish, so why not Mariel? Maybe if Mariel sank to her mom's level, her mom would get the message.

She called up one of her vendors and arranged to have five cases of canned mandarin oranges, her mother's least favorite food, delivered to the church in two days. Florence would look like a jerk for turning down such a donation, but she sure as hell wouldn't eat them, so she'd just be forced to sit there in the lobby, surrounded by stacks of something she despised. The thought made Mariel cackle, and feel slightly guilty, and then cackle some more. Brenda might be proud.

THAT NIGHT, AS THE supper club filled with people, Mariel watched from the bar as Cayla moved gracefully among her tables. Mariel thought if she didn't have a child, if she miscarried again and again, she'd leave the Lakeside to someone like Cayla or Felix. She thought then about how the word "miscarriage" is horrible, *miscarry*, how it blames the woman, as if she failed or made a mistake, when it's the embryo that's unviable. When she wanted nothing more in the world than to carry. When she wanted nothing more.

RIGHT AFTER HAPPY HOUR ended that night, Felix surprised her at the bar, holding what looked like a freshly baked lattice-top blackberry pie with one candle in it. As Felix handed her the pie, he called his daughter over.

"This is Sonia's first pie," Felix said, putting his arm around his bespectacled little girl, who grinned up at Mariel. "She practically made it herself."

Good Lord, she couldn't touch one more bite of a blackberry pie. But after all the regulars sang her "Happy Birthday," Mariel pinched out the flame, and she waited for Felix to cut her a slice as Sonia's beaming eyes sought Mariel's reaction.

A COUPLE OF DAYS HAD passed by the time Kyle Kowalsky came by the bar again. Before he even asked, she was pouring him a whiskey, neat, how he liked it. He looked like he needed it.

"I just can't take it anymore," he said. "The constant noise and activity over there. It's getting worse every day. That generation, man. They're unrelenting. This morning was the last straw. We have to admit it, your mom is winning."

It was disappointing to hear this. Kyle was still her only public supporter in her standoff with her mother, and she appreciated his enthusiasm.

"What happened?" Mariel didn't really want to know.

"She's ordering food in bulk! There are trucks dropping off pallets of canned fruit at eight in the morning! She's stocking up provisions like it's a bomb shelter."

Mariel couldn't help but laugh. "It must've been the mandarin oranges," she told him. "I sent those over."

Kyle downed his shot, and frowned. "But why? This is out of hand. Why don't you just talk to her? That's a thing people do, you know."

He left a ten-dollar bill on the bar, and wished her good luck.

THE NEXT MORNING, while Mariel was crossing the road to open the Lakeside, Hazel's white station wagon suddenly rolled up and stopped in the road.

"Hey!" Hazel shouted, a bit too cheerfully.

Mariel braced herself for the bad news. She soon noticed Hazel had on makeup. It was unsettling.

"Hazel, you sure look gussied up." Up close, Mariel could also see that the flower-print dress Hazel was wearing looked brand-new and expensive. It made Mariel think about how infrequently she had cause to wear nice clothes herself these days. Her sentimental favorite was a sleeveless silk Pierre Cardin dress that hadn't left her closet since 1982, except to move closets. It was a garment for another person of another time, but she couldn't part with it. "And that's something I've never seen you in before."

"Got it at Dayton's a long time ago, off the clearance rack," Hazel said, and gave Mariel a weird smile. "By the way, I hear you've been blacklisted from Jorby's."

Mariel couldn't decide if she was offended or not. She'd never been blacklisted from anything in her life. She thought about it for a couple of seconds, and then looked at Hazel and said, "Awesome."

This didn't seem to be the reaction that Hazel was expecting. "Yeah. *Black*listed. They said that you and your companion stole a pie."

"Well, Hazel, I beg to differ. I paid for the pie."

"Well, all I heard was that you took it without asking."

"Yeah, that's true," Mariel said, and smiled at Hazel. "It was a blast."

Hazel smiled and nodded, which from her meant she either didn't agree or didn't understand. Then, she glanced at the dashboard clock. "Well, I better skedaddle. Want me to pass any messages on to your mom? I'm on my way to the church."

"Nope," Mariel said, and looked over Hazel's makeup and clothes again. "So what's happening there? Is my mom hosting high tea service?"

"No, she's serving the world's largest ambrosia salad. Some nit-wit accidentally sent her a ton of mandarin oranges, so she got her friends together to put them to use. Florence isn't even having any. She's giving it all away. That's how generous she is."

Mariel opened her mouth, but she was out of words.

"But that's not why I'm dressed up. Jason Davis from KSTP-TV is there reporting on it."

Florence was going to be on television. *No*, she thought. *No way*. She didn't want to know more. But of course, Hazel just had to tell her.

"Yep. He's doing a feature on your mom for 'On the Road.' One of those human interest stories, I guess. I always wanted to meet Jason Davis. Ever since he went to the North Pole. He won an Emmy for that, you know." Hazel had a habit of speaking proudly of the accomplishments of Minnesota celebrities, as if they were relatives.

"No, I was not aware."

Hazel tilted her head toward a square dish in her passenger seat covered in pink plastic wrap. "I went ahead and made him some lemon bars."

Mariel envisioned Jason Davis and his whole TV news team setting up in Kyle Kowalsky's front yard, getting establishing shots of the church. Kyle was going to be livid with her now.

"Well," Hazel said, beaming. "I don't wanna keep you. See you at happy hour."

. . .

MARIEL DIDN'T WANT TO think about happy hour, because her two part-time seasonal bartenders, Brian and Ruth, were both leaving at the end of the month, the barback wasn't ready, and looking further ahead, she had no idea who could cover the bar if she was going to be lucky enough to have a baby.

"Hey," Ned said, walking through the front door. When he popped by like this, it was usually because someone had called for her at the house. He always walked the messages over because it was exercise. "Edina Sue just called. Something about your mom being on TV."

"Yep. Just heard." A thought occurred to her that, at the time, felt like a Hail Mary pass. "Hey, do you want to work the bar for a while? Like, if we do have a baby and I can't be here?"

"I've never bartended before," Ned replied. "Do you think I can do it?"

"Absolutely," she told him.

THAT EVENING, SHE GOT to watch Ned up close as he filled water glasses, replaced empty bottles of brandy and schnapps, and yakked with the regulars. They were joking, talking about the Twins, making weather predictions, the usual bullshit. It was wonderful.

It reminded her of when she fell in love with him. Undeniably there'd been a part of her that was attracted to Ned because he seemed to understand and enjoy the supper club. That's why the

Jorby's up here felt like such a betrayal. Although Ned had made up for it, it wasn't until now, watching him working for free behind the bar, that she truly forgave him.

HE DID HAVE ONE habit that was unproductive for a bartender. When he spotted an older or disabled person entering the supper club, he ran over to open the doors for them, even when the host was on duty.

"I've never left the bar once to open the door for anyone, I promise you," Mariel told Ned after he escorted a couple to the exit.

He looked surprised. "I just assumed it was in your nature."

"Nope," Mariel told him. "Why the hell would you think that?"

Ned laughed. "Remember the summer we started going out? I'd been obsessing about you since the previous Christmas, because of something you did."

"What did I do on Christmas?" She honestly had no clue.

"You were at the Jorby's in Central Minneapolis, and I saw you hold the door for an old woman in a wheelchair. It's what made me fall in love with you."

"I've never once been to the Jorby's in Central Minneapolis," Mariel said.

"Really? I know it was you."

"I hated Jorby's. You knew that."

"Huh. Didn't I tell you this?"

"Probably. But I was falling in love with you so hard, I'd have agreed with anything you said."

"Well, it's my story and I'm sticking to it." Ned turned to Hazel,

Paul Buckman, and Edina Sue, sitting at the bar. "Did you all hear this? What do you think?"

"It sounds to me like everything turned out fine," Paul said, in his school-principal voice.

"I'm not getting involved," said Edina Sue.

"Florence is going to love this," said Hazel.

THE REGULARS, WHO KNEW Ned already, had warmed up to him quickly. Even John and Mary Sands, who normally sat in a booth, tonight sat at the bar to talk with him when they came in an hour later.

"Did you hear what happened at the Lodge House?" Mary asked Ned and Mariel.

The Lodge House was the bar and grill in the strip mall down the road. It was popular with tourists because of its two-for-one margarita pitchers, and unpopular with many locals because of what results from two-for-one margarita pitchers.

"What happened, another satisfied customer wind up in a ditch?"

"Remember that huge new deck they built in back, that went over the lake? Well, part of it fell into the lake."

"Oh, jeez. Was anyone hurt?"

"There's three people in the hospital, but nobody died, thank God. It was early and not that crowded yet. But yeah, they're shut down for now, indefinitely."

"Such a tragedy, and right before Labor Day." She felt a little guilty thinking that she'd likely get their customers, especially at the bar. The only other places with a liquor license within fifteen miles were Crappie's, which was a dive for young townies, and the VFW, which catered to old townies.

"Ned's going to have to learn to mix faster," Mary said, and pointed at him. "Two more old-fashioneds."

Ned laughed, and Mariel watched him grab the glasses from above without looking, while never breaking his smile at Mary. There, in that moment, was a glimpse of the confident, happy young man she'd met so long ago. She didn't know until then how much she'd missed him.

ABOUT AN HOUR LATER, Big Al came out of the kitchen and asked Mariel if they could talk privately in the office.

"I have a favor to ask," he said, standing in the open doorway anyway. "It's a big one, so you can say no."

"Does it involve my mother?"

"Nope," he said.

"Then I'll probably say yes, but ask me anyway."

"Well, Alexandra and Jeremy are looking for somewhere to have their wedding reception. They were going to do it at the Lodge House, out on their new patio, but you know what happened there. Can you help them out? They can pay you three grand."

She conjured the memory of her Lotus 1-2-3 spreadsheet in her mind; they probably didn't top three grand on the first Saturday after Labor Day any year, anyway. As loyal as Al and his family were to the Lakeside, and as important as Jeremy McBroom was in this community, they should probably do it for free.

"Just one problem, Al," Mariel replied. "The cost you quoted. It's not how we do things around here."

. . .

SHE WENT BACK TO the bar to tell Ned, who was shocked at first. His scorched-earth capitalist upbringing still clung to him sometimes, but he was coming around.

"I guess this is one edge we have on Jorby's," he told her. "This is something they can't ever do."

"You mean, give away free food and drinks for five hours? I don't suppose."

"Yeah," he laughed. "But more than that. I mean, they wouldn't give back like this to any community. Maybe sixty years ago, they would. But I'll tell you this, from the meetings I went to, if Jorby's comes to a town and can't figure out how to take far more than they give, they wouldn't bother existing in that town. It's what they're designed to do."

"What about Central Minneapolis? Didn't that franchise lose money?"

"Part of a long game to make inroads with a particular demo. Also, cheaper labor costs." Ned looked like he was remembering a bad dream.

"So you're in?" Mariel asked.

"Why not. I'll break out my old tuxedo. What are you wearing?"

"I have something in mind," she said.

"Where's the ceremony, Our Savior's?"

"Yep." Mariel sighed. "Fort Florence."

"There's going to be a lot of people at this wedding," her husband quickly reminded her. "There's no rule that says you have to interact with your mother at all."

It was a liberating idea, but Mariel knew that it was as impossible as eating a single mini-donut. Her mother was more wary of making a big scene in public than just about anyone Mariel had ever met, but that didn't mean there wouldn't be interaction. Far from it. It would be the emotional equivalent of a chess match that lasted for two hours without a single piece being eliminated.

"Oh, we might not speak, but we will definitely communicate."

"So, to be clear, you're going?"

"I wouldn't miss it," Mariel said. "No matter what happens."

Nineteen

≈

Mariel, 1996

The following Sunday, "On the Road" featured the segment starring Florence Jean Stenerud. Mariel didn't allow it to be aired in the bar, but Ned taped it, and watched it alone on the TV in his baseball room after he and Mariel got home from work.

"So. My mother's fifteen minutes. Do I want to know?"

"Nope," said Ned.

"How'd she come across, in one word?"

"Heroic," Ned said. "Maybe that's too mild. I rewound it, if you're curious."

Against her better judgment, Mariel told him to put it on.

Her mother looked older than she did at Floyd's funeral. And the TV crew lighting didn't do her any favors. But none of that mattered. It may have even helped Florence's cause to look frail, ghostly, and overwhelmed.

"Oh, I'm just fine," was the first thing she heard Florence say. It's what she said when she wasn't just fine. Then she said, "I've spent the night in worse places." That, to Mariel, was her mother's *get-me-out-of-here* cry for help.

Sure, with the editing and the softball questions, Florence's so-called plight was framed favorably, and footage from the ambrosia salad giveaway made the whole shebang seem like a party. There was a generous crowd at the potluck dinner the news team had filmed later that day, but apart from the desserts, the food didn't look that appealing. Mariel noticed too many pans of scalloped potatoes, bowls of creamed peas, and pots of cheap boiled franks. And amid it all, Florence didn't seem as proud or defiant as Mariel had assumed she would be. If anything, she seemed worried. Mariel watched it again, never taking her eyes off her mother's face. For the first time, Mariel looked at her warhorse of a mother and saw somebody vulnerable.

So why was Florence still there?

"What did you think?" her husband asked her.

"I think I'm going out for a walk," she said, and went down to the lake, to listen to the water, and think.

THE FOLLOWING MORNING, Mariel woke up with three mosquito bites, one mild headache, and two consequential decisions in the front of her mind. The first was to make an appointment with her regular local doctor.

"I'm going to see Theresa next week," she told her husband. "And I think I want to go alone."

"We're supposed to go see Dr. Bucher, you know. Why do you want to see Theresa first?"

"I want to hear it from a friend," she told him.

As she walked to work that afternoon, Mariel stared up at the beautiful, rusty sign bearing her grandparents' names. If she were lucky enough to have a child, Betty and Floyd would be little more than an abstraction. If the Lakeside were going to be meaningful to them, this child would have to make it their own somehow, whatever that looked like. And it occurred to Mariel that morning that she wanted a chance to make it her own first.

Nothing interrupted her commute, besides a pudgy squirrel she named Vamoose. Fifty-four seconds, door to door. She went straight into the kitchen, where Al and Felix were already prepping.

"Al, I need you to bring food to my mother," she told him.

He seemed pleasantly surprised. "What? Really?"

"Yeah," she told him. "And I want to make her something a little different. With Ned working the bar tonight, I can help you."

That afternoon, Mariel cooked in the Lakeside kitchen in a way she hadn't for ten years. She made some of her favorite dishes, which she'd never scaled up before. Wild rice cranberry pilaf. Iron Range–style porketta sandwiches. An heirloom tomato salad with basil and balsamic. As they cleaned up, one realization struck her. Mariel hadn't eaten at her own restaurant in many years—she went home for a quick dinner every day after happy hour—but she would eat all of this.

"One more thing, Al," she told him when he left to deliver the food. "Tell my mom and her friends that you're coming back tomorrow. Just don't say it's from me."

She kept this up for the next three days, making new dishes every time, and by the third day, it seemed like half the town was in line at Fort Florence to eat delicious food that they thought was from Florence's old friend Big Al.

ON THE AFTERNOON OF the fourth day, after lunch, Mariel got in her car and drove in the direction of town, and on the way, stopped by Brenda's. Bronzie came out to meet the car, but otherwise, everything was calm. It was the first time in a while she'd seen Brenda sober, and it pleased her.

Kyle was there, too, cleaning a motorcycle. He gave Mariel a friendly nod, which was a relief, considering the mood he'd been in the last time she saw him.

"Hey," Mariel said. "I'm going to go get my mom. I just had to tell someone."

"Thank God," Kyle said.

Brenda laughed. "Why? In case you hit a deer again, and get killed this time?"

"You know what I mean. I just need to talk it over a little." Mariel had never had a big sister, and realized, right now, that's whom she'd be speaking to, if she did. "Do you have any advice, or words of wisdom?"

"Nope. What, you want a Hallmark card? Just go do it already."

Kyle said, "Right now's a good time. It's usually pretty quiet there around now."

"Thanks," Mariel said. "It's just hard."

"Sure it is. It's a good story you've been telling yourself all these years about the terrible thing your mom did. But think of what you can have if you let that go."

"What?"

"Jeez, I don't know. That's up to you, isn't it? Now get."

UNTIL TODAY, MARIEL HAD never thought much about how sneaky churches were in America. Three years ago, right after they'd decided it was time to try for a baby, she and Ned went to Europe, for what they thought would be their last vacation as a couple. There, the churches were imposing monuments in the town centers, visible for blocks, even in small villages. Here, in small-town America, most were nestled in the quiet residential areas. They crept up on you like salesmen, and were in your face before you were ready.

Mariel sure wasn't ready. On her right, here was the church, a one-story white building with a modest steeple, and as Kyle predicted, it was quiet. She gave it a long look, and decided to drive around the block one more time.

She thought of her dad, and how much she missed him. If he hadn't passed away while she was in college, so many things may have ended differently. He'd have loved Gus so much, and Mariel wouldn't have hesitated to trust any child with him. If they were fortunate enough to have another baby, the logical part of her mind concluded that she would never again trust her mother. With her mother living far away, and no direct line of communication between them, Mariel wouldn't have had to think any more about it.

Now, for whatever reason, her mother was moving back here, where her daughter lived and worked. She wanted to reconnect with Mariel, that was obvious, and her way of going about it, while self-serving and childish, might have ultimately been considerate. However ridiculous her mom's church stunt was, it was far better than Florence strolling into the supper club unannounced and sitting down at the bar. It was a meeting that gave Mariel all the time she needed to prepare for, knowing that she wouldn't accidentally run into her mother anywhere else.

Even as Mariel stepped out of her car, there was still a part of her that wanted to get back in and drive home. Since the first day she'd decided to get pregnant again, Mariel had thought about raising a child who would never know a single grandparent, even though one was still alive. Most of the time, with the years of silence, and her mother so far away, it was easy to accept. Often it felt rational. But it never felt good.

If she were lucky enough to have a second chance at being a parent, she wondered if she, too, had the strength to give someone a second chance.

FLORENCE DIDN'T GLANCE UP as Mariel opened the door. Her mother was sitting in a gray plush recliner, a pillow behind her head and another at the small of her back, staring into a book of crossword puzzles. She seemed healthier and more like herself than she had on TV, less pale and sweet. Up close, it hit Mariel again that this was only the third time she'd seen her mother in about ten years. Florence was an old woman now, no doubt the same warrior, just in more sophisticated and deceptive armor.

"Mom," Mariel said. "I'm here to pick you up."

"Well, in a minute," Florence replied, not looking up.

"Mom," Mariel repeated. Outside, a lawn mower engine roared to life, and the noise finally jarred her mother out of the pretense of deep focus. At last, Florence set down her pen and book of crosswords and looked up at her daughter. Mariel's mother's expression was, surprisingly, kind.

"Let me go get my stuff," Florence said.

Mariel watched her mom rise and walk into the nave. "I'll be out front in the car," she said, grateful that no one seemed to be around.

Mariel stepped outside, and took a deep breath. A few tears escaped her eyes. She wiped her cheeks, and looked around to see if anyone was watching her. Kyle's purple house across the street and all the other homes nearby were still. The only person she saw was a teenage boy on a John Deere riding mower, who didn't seem to care about the woman having a major life event fifty feet away. Which was just as well. While she waited for her mom, she watched him continue a dispassionate course through the vast church lawn, and smelled the prudent, tangy odor of fresh-cut grass.

ABOUT TEN MINUTES LATER, Florence came out, loaded down with bags and gifts.

"Let me help you," Mariel said, stepping forward.

"It's my crap," her mother replied. "I can carry it. Pop the trunk."

Mariel did as she was told, and saw the jerry can and the jumper cables, remembering the last time she opened this trunk.

Florence shook her head at the front of the car as she approached. "Well, my suspicion was correct. You did get in an accident. It's what happens when people drive with their head in the clouds like you do."

FLORENCE TURNED OFF Mariel's car radio immediately after the engine started. Mariel decided to leave it be, but it further alerted Mariel that the intervening years had made her mom no less frustrating, whatever else they may have done.

"Well, Mom," she said as they drove out of the parking lot. "I guess you won."

Florence seemed genuinely confused. "Win what? I didn't win anything. Every day there was a loss."

Mariel drove in the direction of Floyd's house. It was just under a mile, and wouldn't take long. "I'd say becoming more popular and famous, and getting what you wanted all counts as a win."

"I didn't get what I wanted."

"That's right, you wanted me to pick you up two months ago," Mariel replied, and recalled her theory about why her mom pulled this stunt in the first place. "Right after I officially became the full owner of the supper club. Which you wanted to sell, and probably still do. You wanted to talk me into selling."

"No, it wasn't that at all." Florence's voice sounded peaceful and sad. "I got over that a long time ago. I'm grateful the Lakeside is yours."

It didn't seem like her mother was lying. "What, then?"

"I wanted to hear it from you," Florence said, staring straight ahead.

"Hear what? An apology?"

"No," her mother replied softly. "Al told me you might have had a miscarriage. If that was the case, I wanted to hear about it from you, not from somebody else."

"I knew it," Mariel said, and stepped on the brakes. "Damn it. I can't get anything past him."

Florence gazed out her passenger window. "He's known you your whole life. He knows you like a father would, believe me."

It's true, he did. And Al told Florence everything. Always had.

Florence looked over at her daughter. "Are you okay to drive?"

"Yeah," Mariel said, gently stepping on the gas. "But I still don't completely understand why you had to sit in that church for so long."

"I just wanted . . ." Florence began, and paused. "I just wanted to be someplace you could find me for sure, whenever you were ready."

"You could've gone to Floyd's, I'd have found you there."

"Until last week, I didn't even have any furniture there," Florence replied, and sighed. "I thought the church was a good place. But when it was clear you weren't coming anytime soon, everybody had to go and make a bunch of hoopla about me waiting for you. All the publicity was their idea, not mine. I didn't want to talk to that paper or be on TV. I just wanted to see you, whenever you were ready."

Mariel wasn't sure what to make of all this. She lingered at a stop sign for a few seconds just to process it all for a moment. She hadn't considered for a second how Gus's death and the ten years since might've affected her mother. She'd thought about how a loss like that can change everyone it touches, but simply hadn't believed that her mother was capable of change, ever.

"Thank you, Mom," Mariel managed to say.

"I understand why you didn't want to see me all these years," Florence replied.

Mariel stared ahead at the next stop sign. She couldn't yet say it wasn't her mother's fault. "It was an accident," she said, which was the best she could do.

"No, no, long before that, you had plenty of reasons." Florence shook her head. "I know I wasn't a good mother. But I'm here now if you still want one."

Mariel nodded. "Yeah," she said. "That'd be fine."

It was one of those brilliant last days before the school year began, and everywhere, kids were running around outside, squeezing the last drops out of summer. Up ahead on the right, two little girls in tank tops, probably sisters, sat at a folding table by the end of their driveway with a cooler, a pitcher of red liquid, and a sign that read COOL-AID.

"Look," her mother said. "Look at those little girls."

"Want a refreshing beverage?" the older child asked as Mariel's car pulled up even with their table. Behind the kids was a stunted white house with an empty kiddie pool and a decorative, uncomfortable-looking wrought iron bench in the yard.

"No, thank you," Mariel called back to them. "I have to take my mom home," she added, as if these kids needed an excuse.

"Yes, we'd love some," Florence told them. "We'll pull over and be right there."

Mariel groaned. "You don't like Kool-Aid. And neither do I."

"That doesn't matter. Come on."

Mariel pulled the car over to the side, and Florence had her door open before the engine was off. She addressed the two girls, asking their names and their ages. They were Lainey and Kerensa, and they were seven and five.

"You look pretty," the older one said to Mariel.

"And how do I look?" Florence asked them.

"Like a grandma," the younger one said.

"You used to sell lemonade, with your friend Mary," Florence said.

Her mom had the friend wrong. It was with Cathy. "You're right, Mom," Mariel replied, and then turned to the girls. "How much are your drinks?"

"Seventy-five cents apiece or a dollar for two," the older one said.

"Can't pass up a volume discount." Mariel gave the younger one a dollar as the older one filled two cups. "What's the flavor?"

"Red," the younger girl said, handing over a cupful of sticky colored liquid.

"I believe you," Mariel said, and glanced at the wrought iron bench. "May we sit?"

"You're paying customers, so that's fine," the older girl said.

Mariel took a sip of her Kool-Aid. The kids had evidently made it without adult supervision. It was disgustingly sweet.

Florence grimaced at the taste, and set her cup on the grass as she sat. "I should thank you for the dinners the last couple days," she said. "You're still one of those organic health nut people, evidently."

"Dang. I wanted people to think it was Big Al."

"Oh, no one believed that for a second. Why didn't you just say it was from you? That would've been nice."

"The last time I tried to serve healthy or local food to this town, it was a failure. And Big Al's reputation as a chef is way better than mine. Anyway, it's all part of some larger plan. I'm glad you liked it, though."

"And thanks for the mandarin oranges. That was you, too, wasn't it?"

"Yes. Regretfully."

"You know, *The Guinness Book* is certifying that ambrosia salad as an official world record. I told them that you were a contributor and your name should be on it too."

"I'd hate to be left out of such a distinction," Mariel replied. She wouldn't say it, but she was also somehow comforted to hear that her mother hadn't changed completely. "Beautiful day out," she said, just to change the topic.

Florence frowned. "It's a bit breezy."

"It's nice. Probably good for me to get more fresh air, get out of all that smoke."

After a moment, Florence opened her mouth to speak, but paused.

"What were you about to say?" Mariel asked.

"I don't know if I should ask this."

"You may as well."

"You're pregnant again, aren't you?"

How did her mom know? From one comment about fresh air? Her mother had always been a fiercely selective listener, so it was jarring whenever she revealed the depth of her perceptive abilities. "I think so. I hope so," Mariel replied.

Her mother's voice was faint. "Can I hold your baby, even just once?"

"I'm not even sure if we'll have a baby."

"I know you will. I know it."

"Ned may take some convincing."

"Of course."

"If it works," Mariel began, and then said something that, twenty minutes ago, would've surprised her to even think. "We might need your help again."

"I can't help," Florence said firmly, like it was an assertion of a fact. "I can't be left alone with a baby. Not ever."

Mariel looked away from her mom to the Kool-Aid stand. The smaller girl had been left by herself while the older one had run inside. At first, the little one seemed pleased to be in sole command, but after about ten seconds, she looked worried.

The little girl started calling her sister's name, Lainey, again and again.

"That's up to you, Mom," Mariel said.

When Lainey still didn't appear, the girl screamed the name. What a wondrous pair of lungs this child had. She screamed, louder and louder, until it reduced her sister's name to raw syllables, and didn't sound like a word anymore, but a primal emotion, shredding through the breeze.

"Can you take me home now?" Florence asked.

As they rose from the bench, they watched the little girl wail, as her voice touched the trees, shook the red out of the paper cups, and sweetened the earth, searching everywhere for her sister.

"What?" Lainey replied as she bolted out of the house. "What, what, what?"

"Nothing," the little girl said, and went back to pouring Kool-Aid. "I'm okay now."

Twenty

Mariel, 1996

ariel's appointment with Dr. Eaton was the Tuesday after Labor Day. She stuck with her plan to go alone. Whether the news was good or bad, she wanted some time with it herself.

DR. THERESA EATON HAD once been a waitress at the Lakeside, twenty years ago. For those two years, she had worked harder and made more tips than anyone, but didn't ever seem to spend the money. She took a bicycle to work, and never went out for drinks at Crappie's afterward with the other servers and cooks. People laughed when she said she was saving for medical school, but here she was, the ob-gyn for almost every woman within a thirty-mile radius. And with Dr. Eaton around, many more little girls in Bear Jaw got the idea to be doctors someday. That's not why she came home to practice, Dr. Eaton told Mariel once, but it was a big reason she stayed.

WHEN DR. EATON TOLD Mariel the words "you're pregnant," she just nodded and then asked to hear it again so it could sink in.

"Can I give you a hug?" Dr. Eaton asked.

Dr. Eaton knew everything. Only two other people did. "Please," she said.

Of course, she'd hoped for it every waking minute since the embryo transfer, but she wasn't prepared for how it would feel to hear. The past couple of months collapsed into this moment instantaneously, like a hundred filthy pennies exchanged for a crisp dollar bill. She was pregnant again, and tried to keep the fear of losing it again from flooding her heart.

"Did you go see that specialist I told you about?" Dr. Eaton asked.

For just a couple of seconds, Mariel considered saying, *No, it turned out nothing was wrong with us, it just happened, it was a miracle*, and maybe Dr. Eaton could see all of this on Mariel's face, because she spoke again before Mariel could reply.

"Like I told you, you are the way you are," Dr. Eaton said. "There's nothing wrong with that. Everybody needs help sometimes. You just needed help with this."

She could never hear those sentences enough. It's lonely, to not feel like others, to not experience their apparent ease or success. For the first time, Mariel felt ashamed that she'd tried to hide what she viewed as a deficiency. It was the shame that was isolating, not the need for support. Even if she'd never had another child, she was less alone for admitting she needed help, and accepting it.

Even if she lost this one, too, she had a partner, a job, and a home she loved. She lived a life that must've seemed easy and successful to many, one that many could not earn without a lot of help. She reminded herself that if this didn't happen, to merely have this glorious life was no failure.

"I'm pregnant," Mariel said.

Dr. Eaton nodded, smiling back at her. "Say it louder, for those in the back."

"I'm pregnant!" Mariel shouted. Her voice seemed to shake the walls, rattling the magazine rack and the framed anatomy posters. It felt so incredible, she screamed it again.

"That was good," Dr. Eaton said. "I think they heard you in Bemidji."

THIS TIME, she felt different. If this particular embryo jumped ship, she'd made up her mind there would be no shame in it. The conversation she'd had with Ned about waiting three months seemed rooted in fear, and she didn't want to feel afraid. That weekend at Alexandra and Jeremy's wedding, Mariel told a few people whom she could rely on to spread the news, like Hazel, and told friends like Big Al in private. There was one important person left by that evening. When she arrived back at the Lakeside for the reception, she couldn't find Felix. He'd missed the ceremony to prepare the food.

Ned nodded toward the exit door the staff used. "He's out in the back parking lot."

"What's he doing out there?"

"Well, Jeremy McBroom wanted to say thank you to Felix for making all the wedding food, so he gave Felix's son Brandon a bunch of hockey equipment. Enough skates, sticks, pads, and helmets to take Brandon through high school."

Mariel knew the cost of this stuff. "Maybe he should sell it and buy a boat."

Ned laughed. "He should. The kid's only five. We don't know if he's any good yet."

"Well, now he can find out," Mariel replied. "So Felix is still out there?"

"Yeah, I think he's going to stay out there until he can look like he hasn't been crying."

"All right. What can I do to help?"

"Nothing," her husband said. "Felix and Cayla handled everything. Just relax and enjoy yourself."

"That's one of the top three things a husband can say."

"One question," Ned said, watching Cayla and the rest of the crew as they set wild rice pilaf and heirloom tomato salad in the two buffet lines. "This looks like what you make at home. The couple chose this?"

"Nope," Mariel replied. "You get a reception for free, you better believe it's owner's choice."

"I love you, but . . . heirloom tomato salad? I don't know."

"Half these people were just lining up at Fort Florence to eat it. I know they'd never order it before, but now that they've had it, they might."

"Order it? Like from the menu?"

"We'll see," she said. Many of the best supper clubs outside Minnesota, like the Dorf Haus and the Turk's Inn in Wisconsin, or Northwestern Steakhouse in Iowa, had something different that made them stand out. Maybe, as with these places, the distinction would be a draw.

"I'm usually an optimist," Ned said. "But I'm going to hold my tongue."

"Everything's ready," Cayla told them.

"Thanks, Cayla," Ned replied, then nudged Mariel and whispered, "By the way, she kicks ass. I know you're not charging the couple, but you're paying her, right?"

"Yep, everyone. Nobody works for free on my watch."

Ned surveyed the room and banged a fork against his champagne glass. "Everyone, take your seats," he said, although most of the guests had seen the food being laid out and were seated already.

Big Al raised his champagne flute. "Hey, to Mariel, for making all of this happen!"

In a moment, everyone was on their feet, all of her friends and neighbors, smiling, applauding, and shouting her name.

She wasn't sure why, but she was crying. It was mortifying to feel tears rolling down her cheeks in front of everyone she knew.

"Thanks," she said, wiping her eyes, taking a breath. "Congratulations to Alexandra and Jeremy. We're glad you could celebrate here at Floyd and Betty's Lakeside Supper Club."

Big Al raised his champagne flute again. "Mariel's Lakeside Supper Club!"

Hearing him, of all people, say that made her start weeping again.

"Quit staring at me!" she shouted, wiping her wet cheeks. "What the hell is everyone waiting for? Dinner's on."

Twenty-One

Mariel, 1996–2000

For the next few months, Ned tried to convince Mariel to change the restaurant's name to Mariel's Lakeside Supper Club, like Big Al said, but Mariel wouldn't do it. For starters, the supper club was no longer just hers.

Julia Ellen Prager had been born the following May, and from that day forward, every decision that Mariel made about the supper club was meant to make it last for her daughter. Sometimes that meant things she'd wanted to do, like enforcing a no-smoking section, but often it meant things she hated to do, like raising prices and running the place with fewer employees. It also meant trimming menu items, including the heirloom tomato salad. Ned had been right about that one. People hardly ordered it, even when the tomatoes were in season and incredible.

Three years ago, ditching menu items, cutting staff, and jacking prices would've made Mariel lose sleep. Now at least she was exhausted for better reasons.

Julia was on her feet by eleven months, brazenly exploring the world. She didn't speak more than a few words until she was two. She also slept like a rock, fourteen solid hours a night. It was a little scary. Mariel asked their pediatrician if a baby could have too much sleep. No, the doctor laughed. Let her be.

That was the hardest thing to do.

"I feel like I still have to keep an eye on her at all times," Mariel told Ned. "But I won't. I won't be like my mom was to me."

"You're not your mom," Ned replied, which was still comforting to hear, even if Florence had lately been helpful when needed, and kept her distance when not.

Julia had been home a week when she first met her grandma. It was on the curbless front yard of Floyd's old house—where Mariel had once played as a child—that Mariel first gave Julia to Florence to be held.

Mariel couldn't remember ever seeing her mother cry, but Florence began to sob as Mariel reached out with her newborn baby. It was at least fifteen minutes before Florence could compose herself enough to hold her new granddaughter. She said nothing the entire time, except to whisper in the infant's ear.

"What are you telling her?" Mariel asked.

"That's between us," Florence replied.

They'd even asked Florence to babysit the nights while Mariel and Ned were both at work, but Florence said she still wasn't ready to be left alone with a child. Mariel wondered how long it would take. In the meantime, Brenda filled in, eagerly. "Your little girl will learn a thing or two from me," Brenda promised.

. . .

Because Julia was born in May, Mariel had to be back at work within a few weeks for tourist season. It was all right; it was. She could run back home anytime she wanted to check in on her little girl, which she often did. Besides, Big Al and Felix really needed her in the kitchen on Friday and Saturday nights in the summer. Sometimes, Ned stayed with Julia while Mariel relieved him behind the bar, but often, during Julia's wonderful and enervating first years, she got to be the one at home.

"I'm only here at work half as much," she told Edina Sue, a few days before Julia's third birthday. "But I'm twice as exhausted."

"You have a toddler," Edina Sue said. "Or did you forget?"

"I wasn't nearly this tired last time," she said. She could talk about Gus now, although people rarely spoke of him unless she did first.

"You're older," Edina Sue said. "Or did you forget?"

An hour later, Mariel had to leave work early. Since around Christmas, she'd felt like she had a cold every day, and even with the weather getting warmer, she still had a cough. More than anything, she felt like she could've fallen asleep right there, standing up at the bar.

Ned was down in the Cities, at a Twins game with his friends, so Julia was with Brenda that night. Mariel called Brenda and asked how it was going.

"It's like babysitting an elderly forest ranger. She just wants to wander around outside and look at trees. If I don't know the name of a tree, she gets agitated."

"Sounds like my girl. I'll see you both in a few minutes," she said.

It used to be that Mariel's favorite thing in the world was her commute to work, but now it was her walk home.

Her little girl was on the other end. Imagine being able to say a thing like that! The walk back took fifty-one seconds, or the total time it took to gather and empty the ashtrays on the bar. Mariel felt her heart beating, and felt her muscles ache, and felt her lungs fill with cool spring air. She noticed a crow on the power line, and named her Rosetta. She smiled at the light on in the living room across the road. The drapes were pulled open and she could see her daughter's head in the window.

I'm almost home, honey, Mariel whispered.

She sat on the side of the road, just for a minute, to watch her daughter for a bit from a distance. Julia was inside, climbing on the furniture, which she wasn't supposed to do, and she was laughing. Mariel was so tired, and the ground felt surprisingly good. She lay down, just to see what it was like, and felt the cool gravel against her cheek.

A minute later, a Borglund Services truck drove by and stopped in front of her.

"You all right, there?" asked the driver.

"I've never been better," Mariel said.

"You don't look so good. I'm calling an ambulance."

Mariel couldn't see her daughter anymore, just the giant black wheel of a truck. But she knew she was there. She knew her daughter was home, and that she was happy.

Twenty-Two

Julia, 2000–2014

J ulia Prager's earliest memory was of the noise. She was three years old, standing on the low bookshelf beneath the bay window in her parents' living room, her little hands pressed against her ears. The grand finale of the Fourth of July fireworks show exploded over the lake, violently assaulting her senses, and for no good reason, as best she could tell. Her grandmother stood behind her, holding her, in case Julia stumbled backward, so Julia had no escape from this pointless, overwhelming aerial chaos.

"That's it," her grandma Florence said, when the last bangs echoed over the trees and the final bright cinders plummeted toward unsuspecting trout. "No more until next year."

"Good," Julia replied, according to family legend. She has no memory of saying it herself. All Julia remembered after the terrible cacophony in the sky concluded was the welcome peace and darkness that followed, which she realized she vastly preferred.

It was the first preference she made that felt engrossing. Just as some children love dinosaurs, princesses, or cars—eagerly permitting these things to colonize their clothing, dominate their activities, and preoccupy their thoughts—Julia loved quiet.

GROWING UP IN THE north woods of Minnesota, one would assume that quiet was everywhere, and it often was. Around age seven, if Julia was the first to awake on a winter morning, she'd go outside, where a pale, subtle world embraced her. She adored its pristine hush, but also when it whispered to her in the crack of ice beneath a boot or the conversation of birds. She especially loved the throaty, gurgling croak of ravens, and later in the season she'd hear cardinals, singing what sounded like *what-what-what-what-what-cheer-cheer-cheer-rrrr*. What cheer, she'd whisper back.

Winter was her cathedral, and the snow-decked trees its endless pillars, and although it was quiet, it wasn't empty. The silence coaxed voices into her imagination, voices of the past and future, voices of animals and people both common and divine.

At the end of her walk, she'd sit near the lake, until the racket of the first passing vehicles revealed the *real world*, with all of its dull burdens and insufficient promises.

Julia disliked summer, but truthfully, she'd never gotten to know it. The term "summer vacation," a tautology to many children, was to her an oxymoron. She and her father went on their vacations in March over her school's spring break, when they went at all. From Memorial Day weekend to Labor Day every year, Julia rarely went farther than ten miles from home. Most days, she simply crossed the street. Since she was a child, her summers were spent at Floyd and Betty's Lakeside Supper Club, where her father, the owner, ran the bar.

UNLESS SHE SHARED A staff meal with her dad in the office, Julia ate dinner with him only one night a week, and she'd rarely see him on evenings and weekends unless she was at the Lakeside too. That was the life of a kid whose parent ran a restaurant, and when she was little, she didn't mind. The people back then, especially Big Al, Felix, and Cayla, were not just nice, they made their jobs look like something you'd want to do.

Her father used to say that Julia wasn't raised by a village, she was raised by a supper club. As a small child, she sat at the bar, sneaking Maraschino cherries, colored and drew at the maître d' station, and looked for little things she could do to be useful. She was the one who'd first asked to help. By the time she was eight, she was sweeping the front steps, doing salad bar maintenance, and filling glasses of ice water. By age ten, she was pushing the big vacuum through the dining rooms, and helping clean the kitchen, taking the rubber mats off the floor and hosing them off out back where the cooks smoked. Her father gave her half of her take-home pay, squirreling the other half away in a savings account, in case, he emphasized, she *chose* to go to college.

It didn't take long for these tasks to lose the sheen of novelty and become work, but her dad loved having her there, and it was an easy kindness to please him. She could be patient. Each day was either winter or one day closer, when she'd have her quiet.

SHE WAS TEN WHEN her father first told her about her future. On a muggy July afternoon, Julia was folding napkins with him, enjoying the meditative qualities of repetitive labor, when he said, "I'm glad you like it. You're going to inherit this place."

Julia's first reaction was to be scared. "When?" she asked.

"When you're twenty-one. It was your mom's decision, because she was the owner at the time."

"Whew," Julia said. That seemed like an eternity away. "But I thought you were the owner now? Could you change that?"

"No, it's in a trust," he said, and smiled as he thought of a way to explain it. "Remember *Return of the King*?"

They'd just rewatched the whole *Lord of the Rings* trilogy again a month ago, so of course she did. "Why? Am I Frodo?" She'd much prefer to be Sam.

"No, thank God. Remember how Gondor had a steward, while it awaited a real king, from the royal bloodline? I'm the steward, and you're Aragorn."

"Oh." Now it seemed like a lot of pressure again. "I'm glad it's a long ways off."

"Your mom originally wanted you to have it when you turned eighteen. But I thought you needed a few more years to learn a thing or two."

Julia nodded. Her whole life she'd heard stories about what her mother had wanted, but never directly, at least that she could remember. Her sole memory of her mother was of her pale and bed-ridden, sick with the lung cancer that wasn't caught in time.

"Just stay here with your mom," her father had said, and she did. She was only four and a half years old, so there was no school or work like there was for everyone else. Someone had to be there in case something happened. That made Julia think that nothing would, as long as she was present. She spent as much time as she could in that bedroom, watching movies with her mom, and sat reading by her bedside, just letting her mother stare silently at her every day for hours.

Ned, Florence, and Al relieved her when they could, and sometimes Brenda and Felix, but after a while, Julia decided she couldn't leave the room. In darkness and sunlight, she listened to her mother breathe, convinced that her presence was essential.

And then, early one morning, Julia dozed off in her chair. She awoke to hear no breathing. Just the birds outside.

"No, Dad," Julia cried, after her dad came in, already sobbing, and told her that her mother was gone. "I was here. She can't go while I was here."

But one glance, and Julia knew. The woman she knew as Mom was no longer in the body she saw. Mariel Prager, her mother, was elsewhere.

JULIA HAD NO MEMORY of her mother's voice, but she knew that there was no place on earth her mother loved more than the supper club, and her mother would speak to her there, someday, somehow.

"I'll learn whatever you want me to," she told her father.

"I'll still be around to help," Ned said. "Unless you fire me."

Julia couldn't imagine her father ever doing anything else besides running the supper club. Now, he'd said many times he was much happier just being a bartender, and didn't enjoy any of the work that came with being a boss, but he was good at it. She was vaguely aware that lately he was worried about the economy, and while it was true that there had been fewer customers for a while, Julia hadn't noticed any other ill effects from this intangible phenomenon. The phrase "the economy" meant about as much to Julia as the words "menopause" or "al-Qaeda," subjects of concern for adults that held no shape in her head.

"I always thought you'd run this place forever," Julia replied.

"Your mother, she would've," Ned said. "What makes you say that about me?"

She knew he was genuinely curious, which is why she felt ashamed that she couldn't articulate it. It was simply evident. Most adults that Julia had observed seemed happy only when they were either unproductive or productive on their own terms. Her father's happiness was fundamental, and infectious to almost everyone. Apparently, he was once a solitary, handy guy—he'd helped build the house they lived in—but only when called upon to make repairs around the place did he hint at this ability. Now, the talents he demonstrated were social. Her father was one of the three best listeners she'd ever met, and the other two were dogs.

"It seems like you're doing what you were born to do," she told him.

He'd told her once that he didn't know how much he'd flourish and be appreciated behind a bar, or how much he needed to flourish and be appreciated. It also felt good to be in a social environ-

ment after the years he'd spent distracting himself, he'd said. Julia
had seen pictures of how her bedroom once looked—so full of
baseball crap that she could hardly see the floor or the walls. Her
father had traded it all for one item, a 1952 Topps Mickey Mantle
rookie card in "very good" condition. He was pleased to make it his
final transaction.

Now, running the Lakeside bar every night, he said, the sadness
he'd felt long ago seemed like another lifetime to him. Ned otherwise scarcely spoke of the time before Julia was born. It was weird
to think of a completely different country inside her father, whose
borders didn't seem contiguous with what Julia could observe. And
one day, he'd be giving her something from beyond his own past to
inherit, a legacy that went back generations.

"I didn't always love it here," he said. "But I do now."

Julia knew she should love this place like her parents and great-
grandparents did, or at least hope that she would. She was sure she'd
wake up one day and look forward to coming here as much as she
looked forward to walking through a winter forest at the eggshell
break of sunrise.

She was still just ten years old, and there was something entic-
ing about having her future decided for her. She let this idea move
her thoughts around until there was enough room for such a future. "Well, I love it too," her ten-year-old self told her father.

FIVE YEARS LATER, she did not.

By then, the only things she liked about working at the Lakeside day to day were the money and the convenience. She'd been
working here in some capacity for half of her life, she realized, and

not only had she yet to sense her mother's presence, she started to wonder if she ever would. It occurred to her that this building had killed her mom. Although smoking hadn't been allowed indoors for many years, the scent still clung to the walls and carpeting enough that if she were her mother's ghost, she wouldn't come back here.

Either way, this place, which had been in her family for three generations, and been in business nearly a century, would be hers in six short years. As she continued to understand herself and what nourished her soul, she tried to find ways the Lakeside could make her happy.

One thing she enjoyed was listening to the vendors who came in on weekdays, especially Madeline Roy, the forager who brought in ramps and morel mushrooms every spring.

"Want to come out with me sometime?" Madeline asked.

Julia was thrilled to go. Madeline was Ojibwe, and although most people knew her as an accountant—she did Ned's and Felix's taxes—she'd been foraging since she was a kid, and had knowledge of the local forest that most people didn't. She was extremely smart; she knew multiple names and uses for just about everything in the woods. For all the time Julia had spent in nature herself, she'd never known how much of the forest was edible. Julia stared into an expanse of the north woods she'd never been to, and couldn't wait to explore in this new way.

"Once you learn how to see the edible world, it's everywhere," Madeline said, handing Julia a bright orange safety vest. "Right there, that maple tree. Take a few leaves home and fry them in a pan."

Julia walked to the grand old maple and carefully pulled at the nearest green leaf. "So, they're like ghosts, in plain sight."

"They're not ghosts. They're alive. Hold it in your hand before you take it."

It was marvelous to be out in the woods with Madeline, at least whenever Julia could forget why they were supposed to be there. The truth was, being on such a single-minded treasure hunt disturbed the sense of sanctity she got from the forest. She felt like a thief in her own temple.

The second time out, she decided not to take anything, just absorb knowledge.

"You don't seem happy," Madeline observed, just the two of them in a cluster of old trees, over three miles from the nearest road.

"I don't like my job," Julia admitted.

"I know," Madeline said. "But I notice you're unhappy now. Do you know why?"

Julia nodded. "To me, it's restaurant work being out here," she said. "And I don't want the forest to feel like restaurant work. I want the forest to feel like a forest."

"I get it," Madeline said.

LATER THAT SUMMER, Julia wondered if she'd enjoy distilling. She didn't enjoy gin, or any alcohol, but she knew her mother had, and distilling gin seemed like a calm, scientific discipline that rewarded knowledge of plants and nature. It had also been a few years since she'd been to the farm of her old babysitter, and she missed the place.

When she hopped off her bike by Brenda's garage, she could smell oil and metal, but the garage was empty. A strange car was in the driveway, and around back, she saw Brenda's son, Kyle, who now lived in the Cities, sweeping his mother's patio.

"Hey!" Kyle smiled. "Brenda's at her class. Want some sweet tea?"

"Sure," Julia said. She'd always heard how much her mother liked Kyle, and it was easy to see why. He was content in a way that put people at ease. She didn't even like sweet tea, but when he offered it, she didn't think twice, as if some of what made him happy and peaceful were somehow stirred into it. "What kind of class?"

"She's getting a CNA certification," he said, closing the sliding screen door behind him as he went into the kitchen. "I'm thrilled for her. She's bored and lonely and could use the money."

"How's the new place?" It felt like such an adult question to ask, and she was pleased with herself.

"Can't complain," he said.

"You miss it up here? Besides your mom?"

He looked around and shook his head. "I don't know. Honestly, I'm a lot happier being down where my people are."

She wondered what kind of people he meant, and also wondered if she'd find them, for herself, someday. All this seemed like too much to say. "That's awesome," she replied, opening the screen door for him as he came back out with the tea. "What else is new?"

He laughed. Was she asking too many questions? Or were these questions *too sincere* coming from her? Most of the time, especially at school, she didn't say anything, except to her friend Grubbs, who also never said anything. It was death to be sincere at school.

But this was a person who got the hell out of Bear Jaw, and he was cool for an adult, and she was genuinely curious.

"What else? I'm learning Korean. It's awesome."

"Do you have people you can speak it with?" She hoped she wasn't being nosy.

"Some other Korean Americans, and a few really patient Koreans, yeah. It's not just about the language, but the culture. I also met some other Korean adoptees that found out their history, their birth names. They have the most beautiful Korean names."

"Are you going to change your name?" Julia was intrigued; she'd never met anyone before who had done that.

"Maybe. I've never really felt like a Kyle Kowalsky. We'll see. How about yourself, how's school?"

"Good. Just looking for some extra work. I guess I was wondering if your mom needs help with her distillery."

"Oh." He seemed amused again. Maybe it was humorous, a girl her age asking to make gin. "She doesn't really need help with that. She only does it now like twice a year. I'm sure she'd teach you sometime, though, if you really want to learn."

"I don't know," she said. Already the idea seemed ridiculous.

"How's that crazy grandma of yours doing?"

Julia was surprised that he asked, because Kyle never seemed to like her grandma. Apparently it was because of something that happened before Julia was born. It was a story she'd heard only parts of, and it didn't make any sense. "She's great," Julia told him. "Never been better."

"I don't get it." Kyle shook his head. "People say that every time I ask about her."

. . .

IT MAY HAVE BEEN TRUE. Florence had been the one person in the family who'd managed to get out of spending her whole life at the supper club, and she was clearly better for it. In her grandma's house, Julia felt no limits or expectations; it was the one place besides the woods where she could forget about her future. For most of her childhood, Julia would go there straight after school, putter around in her grandma's garden with her, stay for dinner, play cribbage after, and sometimes spend the night. She was devastated when she had to start going to work instead.

She finally started looking forward to her shifts once she persuaded her dad to hire Grubbs. Mina Grubbs was her only friend at school—the one other girl who loved books, who liked birds and nature well enough, and who could respect quiet. They finished second and third in the class every year, always behind Kristen Spencer. Kristen wanted to go to a top university and become an obstetrician, which was annoyingly admirable, and far too much work. Still, they might have been friends with Kristen, if Kristen had been allowed to have a phone. Grubbs and Julia each got their first phones for Christmas because of each other; their parents coordinated it. Neither made a major decision without consulting the other. Most decisions were major.

UNLIKE JULIA, Grubbs made art, texted boys, and had older sisters, and listened to their music, women like Beyoncé and Dessa and Robyn. Julia loved all of this. Julia also loved that despite being an A student, Grubbs was not always an upstanding citizen or a good influence.

On Julia's fifteenth birthday, sadly, she was both.

"I told your dad I'd do the dinner shift," Grubbs said at school that morning. "I have an idea, though. How about you work with me?"

"Ugh," Julia replied. "I'm not spending my birthday at work."

"Come on. We both need the money. Besides, what else were you going to do tonight?"

Grubbs had a point. Julia's dad was working; he gave her a present that morning—a pair of hiking boots she'd wanted—but they were celebrating her birthday the following Tuesday, as usual. Her grandma went to bed at nine, so that wasn't exactly party central. And if Julia wanted to eat out somewhere, the only other real dinner place around Bear Jaw was Jorby's, which was dismal. It was run-down, the food was crappy, and only old people ate there anymore. You could tell the servers were pissed to be there too.

As it stood, the Lakeside had the only decent food within thirty miles. So for now, she supposed she could be in the mood for fried torsk and Kartoffelsalat.

"All right. But we're not working next year on my birthday. Promise me."

A YEAR LATER, it turned out that Julia spent her sixteenth birthday at the Lakeside, too, because Grubbs was also working there that night, which meant that there was no place Julia would rather be. By then, they were each servers, making bank, getting hit on by creepy randos, and reveling in a private language of inside jokes.

"Got any Darcys tonight?" Grubbs asked her that night at the service bar. Darcy was their code for a hot guy, and Smerdyakov was their code for a creepy perv. Cool or interesting women were Emmas, while girls they knew and hated or women who were demanding customers were all Verucas, regardless of age. None of the other waitstaff understood these literary references, except the last one, so Julia and Grubbs relished saying them.

"Nope," said Julia. "Just a whole friggin' table of Smerdyakovs."

"God," Grubbs said, already glaring at them. "They say something?"

Julia had become accustomed to this. Grubbs thought Julia was hot enough to be a model, which Julia thought was kind but wildly incorrect. If she were ever a model at all, it'd be for something dull, like safety goggles or raisins. She was "cute," and that was all, or at least cute enough to get hit on by gross or strange guys at school and in public.

"Yeah. They told me that stupid 'I'll have some fries to go with that shake' line."

"They're wasted, right?"

"Nope, I don't even think so."

Grubbs didn't enjoy dealing with creeps any more than Julia did, but she was awesome at it. Unlike Julia, Grubbs had actually become hot, but to her credit, Grubbs used her looks as cover to defend her friends and offend strangers.

"Let me take 'em," Grubbs said. "It's your birthday. I'll handle the Smerds."

"This is the best birthday present," Julia said.

"Just wait until after work," Grubbs said. "I have a surprise."

· · ·

AFTER WORK ON WEEKENDS, a lot of the Lakeside staff went to Crappie's for drinks, while the oldest and the youngest employees went home. Tonight, though, the hottest guy in school, Travis McBroom, had invited Grubbs to a bonfire, and Grubbs asked if Julia would like to come with and party with the popular kids. This, apparently, was the surprise.

"Sure," Julia said. She'd never been invited to hang with this crowd before, and supposed she was curious about what they were like outside of school.

It was exceedingly dull. All they really did was share inside jokes and drink, which Julia didn't do, and no one ever asked her any questions.

"Maybe I should take you home?" Grubbs asked her after an hour. It was the first time at the bonfire that someone had spoken to her.

Julia knew what it would look like to these people, and to her friend. "Please," she told Grubbs.

ON JULIA'S SEVENTEENTH BIRTHDAY, she awoke at dawn. She stepped down the hillside toward the water, treading carefully over clusters of old snow that looked like bleached, miniature ruins of once-great cities. She walked along the lake, and stopped between the janky strip mall and the shore. Behind her, part of the strip mall was being built out, and a dirty bald eagle sat on the edge of an open dumpster. It reminded her that she'd volunteered to work that night, even though her dad said she didn't have to.

She just wanted to make as much money as she could before she left.

A week ago, her father had driven her to Kenyon College to visit, and after she set foot on campus only once on a blustery spring day, there was no question in her mind that she'd be going there if she got in. Her father was quiet about it, which meant that he was against it, but he did admit that the place was beautiful. He told her that in life there's often more than one correct choice.

"On your next birthday, you get the money we saved for your college education. So if you want to buy something instead, you can. Like a car."

She didn't even have a license. "I don't want a car."

"You know, when your mom found out she was inheriting the Lakeside, she almost dropped out of college right then. You don't need a degree to run a supper club."

"Can we not talk about this now?"

"All right," he replied. "What's Grubbs up to tonight?"

It wasn't that she and Grubbs had had a huge argument—nothing that dramatic.

After Grubbs started seeing Travis McBroom, she and Julia had slowly drifted apart. Julia didn't even go to prom. Grubbs went with a group of five couples. Grubbs had sex. Grubbs said she was in love. Grubbs had a boring story about eating an entire edible, thinking it was a normal cookie. Grubbs had gross dick pics on her phone and not just from Travis. To Julia, talking with Grubbs now was like watching a sordid YouTube channel, the kind that parents would try to get banned. After a while, Julia grew tired of listening without having anything to say.

By now, working with Grubbs at the Lakeside was almost like

working with anyone else, and it almost didn't even hurt anymore. If she and Grubbs had to enter a ticket at the same time, she'd let Grubbs go first, and wait at a distance, instead of talking like they once did. She got used to it.

"HAPPY BIRTHDAY!" SHE HEARD her grandma say. The voice surprised her, because Florence didn't drive, and never came to the Lakeside. "I would've just popped this in the mail, but then Mildred offered to drive me. For you," her grandma said, holding out a lavender envelope, which Julia guessed contained a check for fifteen dollars, Florence's birthday gift to Julia every year of her life.

"Thank you, so much," Julia said, and hugged her, although her grandmother was most certainly not a hugger. It was like hugging an anxious postcard rack.

Florence followed her to the bar. "There's a little extra this year because you're going to be leaving us soon, aren't you? So, how was the visit?"

"It was awesome. If I don't get in, I don't know what I'm going to do."

Florence stared past her at something on the wall, behind Ned, and leaned forward. "I know that man. That's Archie Eastman."

No one seemed to know what she was talking about. It took a bit to even find the picture she was pointing at. "This one?" Ned asked, taking down the picture of Julia's great-grandpa and another old man on a canoe trip. "Mariel took this picture. She said it captured her grandpa's essence."

"Yes! Yes!" Florence yelled. Julia had never seen her grandmother so riled up. "That's him, I know it's him. That's Archie Eastman."

"Yeah, I think that was his name. He'd come up and visit Floyd sometimes. I suppose you never would've met him."

She smiled at the picture, and tears were in her eyes. "They're together."

"Yeah. They almost look like a couple," Ned said, and laughed. "What do you think, Florence?"

Florence didn't say a thing.

Twenty-Three

Julia, 2015–Present

By the following June, Julia knew she was about to lose more than another teenage summer to the Lakeside. Whatever joy and serenity she was once able to set afloat in her mind every day was capsized, again and again, by the demands of tourists, the entitlement of locals, the sad presence of Grubbs, and the vigilant hope of her father, all amid the usual restless noise. Even when a brief spell of peace descended, the bitter clang of a dropped fork or the graceless blast of a soda gun tortured her concentration at viciously random intervals.

That summer, some competition to the Lakeside was moving in on two fronts. A couple named Brian and Susan, who'd grown up in Bear Jaw, gone to college, got married, and moved back, just finished building their new brewery down the road at the end of the strip mall. And since it opened, a chain called Yucatan Lou's, which Julia knew was owned by her mysterious aunt Carla, had been the new popular place in town. It hadn't hurt their bottom line a lot, her father said, but it did hurt them.

"Can't you call her and ask her to find a different location?" Julia asked her dad. After all, it was his sister. "Like Park Rapids, or Nisswa, or anywhere else?"

Her dad laughed. "I wouldn't know how to call her if I wanted to. I think I'd have to just drive to her house and yell at the gate. I haven't even met her children."

Julia just nodded. She'd only ever seen a picture of her cousins once on a Christmas card, and that was years ago, when they were babies.

"Anyway, I'm not too worried yet," Ned said. "I'd be more worried if I owned the Jorby's in town."

"I thought Carla did." They never talked about Carla, so Julia had no idea.

"No, she sold Jorby's off a while ago, to people who sold it to private equity. The company she runs now is called P2H. Stands for Prager Powell Hospitality. They're the industry leaders in innovative restaurant concepts."

"What does that even mean?"

"It means they're already onto the next thing. Like you."

She wasn't sure if her father meant that as a diss, but he wasn't wrong. It was all she could think about.

THE DECEMBER MORNING she found out she was accepted to Kenyon, Julia was at home with her dad. She knew he wouldn't be as excited as she wanted him to be, but she had to tell him.

"You know, you don't even have to go to college," was his reply.

He may as well have punched her in the heart.

"God," she said, wiping the tears from her cheeks. When she was a kid, he'd been such a great listener, and he still was, to the customers. But it had been so long since he'd truly listened to her. "Can't you please at least *say* you're proud of me?"

"I am," he said, sitting up on the sofa. "I'm just saying you don't have to leave, if you don't want to. You're going to be my boss in a few years."

"I'm aware," she said. "But when I'm twenty-one, it's still mine to do with as I please, right?"

He seemed to sense what she'd implied. "The supper club's been in your family almost a hundred years, you know. You don't know all the work your mom did to keep it going. All for you. I know you can be like her, and find a way to love it."

She had no idea how she could ever be like her legendary mother.

Her father didn't bring it up again, but he didn't have to. It hung in the corner of her brain and cast a little shadow onto every thought she had about her future.

JULIA GRADUATED FROM high school second in her class, behind Kristen Spencer, and even with the anticipation of leaving for college, she was able to forget the other part of her future that was considered certain. By the time tourist season began, Julia and her father were too busy at the supper club to talk about how she was another year closer to being the boss. According to her father, there was still so much she had left to learn.

In the meantime, she actually enjoyed the summer, as much as she ever had. She spent afternoons gardening with Florence, rented pontoon boats with her dad, and shot the shit with Brenda, at least whenever Brenda was not with one of her home health care patients. She even hung out with Kristen Spencer. They went on long walks in the woods, and freed from the social constraints and academic stresses of high school, actually got to know each other for the first time, a month after they'd both graduated.

"Come by the supper club and I'll hook you up," Julia told her new friend.

Of course, the next few weeks she was as slammed at work as she'd been in years, but Kristen came in on many Mondays and Thursdays. She took a seat by a window and read a book while she ate and talked with Julia during Julia's breaks.

It was lovely, until one Thursday evening in mid-August. "I'm leaving early for college," she told Julia. "But I want to thank you."

"For what? Excellent service?" Julia took after her father in that she often made light of situations when she was sad.

"No, the service was terrible. I want to complain to the owner," Kristen said, and smiled. "No, seriously. When I come home now, I have something besides my parents to look forward to."

It was a nice thing to hear, but also a bit chilling, if she understood Kristen correctly. Julia wondered what she was missing, that everyone seemed to see her future here but her. "I'm going to college too," Julia replied, in a way she hoped didn't sound defensive.

"I know, I mean on breaks and stuff."

"I don't know how long I'll be here," Julia said.

"Oh," said Kristen, and her smile fell. Now she looked like the withdrawn, quiet girl she'd been before Julia got to know her. "Please stay in touch, then," she said.

ON SATURDAY, AUGUST 15, the lake was roaring with boats and people, and traffic congested the ring road. It was hard to conceive that in a week, Julia would be on a beautiful college campus in rural Ohio to start a new life. Tonight would be her last Saturday night shift at the supper club for a long time.

She'd beaten her father to work, and watched him walk in and glance at her like she was just another unremarkable and expected part of the scene.

"Julia," her father asked as she tied her apron around her waist. "I just realized I left my phone back at the house. Can you go back and get it for me?"

Her father knew that Julia enjoyed any opportunity to leave the supper club for any length of time. But something felt off. Her dad seemed a little sad. "No problem. You all right?"

"Absolutely." Ned nodded. "It's going to be a busy night."

"More kids with birthdays?" They'd seen a lot of those lately.

"No, two wedding anniversaries."

Wedding anniversaries were highly preferable; there was much less cleanup and the tips were better for about the same rate of turnover. They also usually meant alcohol, and because her mom had improved the wine list long ago, there were actually some expensive options on the menu. Anniversaries were usually when people ordered them. "Sweet. Can at least one be in my section?"

"I think the plan is to give you both of them. And Brandon Peralta is celebrating his birthday here, and you get that too."

"Oh." The other servers would be pissed. Felix's son, Brandon, was the biggest deal to come out of this town since Jeremy Mc-Broom. Ned always comped his food, but Brandon always left a big tip. "You should give at least one of these tables to either Delaney, James, or Frances."

"They'll understand," her dad said. "You've earned it."

SHE HAD TO WAIT for a gap in the traffic before she could cross the road. She was in no hurry to get back to work, but she dashed up her driveway anyway, and took her shoes off just before she opened the door.

That's when she saw it on the dining room table. A large basket with a bow on it, with a huge sign that read I'LL MISS YOU, JULIA.

She walked over to it like it was a sleeping animal. Right away she saw the Kenyon College sweatshirt. Her father must've bought that in secret when she was exploring the campus solo. Next she saw the book titled *Birds of Ohio Field Guide*. There were two bottles of nice red wine with a note: *Share with your new friends*. Then there was a little card, with a cheesy image of a common yellow-throat leaving a nest. Inside was written *I am so proud of you, love, dad*. She started to cry.

In another time, she would've automatically taken a picture of everything and texted it to Grubbs, with a half dozen OMGs. She thought about texting Kristen, who had a phone now, but she didn't know her well enough yet. Instead, she sat on the floor, and cried alone.

. . .

JULIA WALKED INTO THE restaurant a couple of minutes before five and realized that she'd actually forgotten her father's phone. He was behind the bar, pre-pouring the drinks for the regulars.

"I'm sorry, I forgot it," she told him.

Ned smiled. "That's okay, I had it with me this whole time."

It felt a little awkward to hug him right there in front of everyone, but she just had to. She didn't say anything, because if she did, she was afraid she'd start crying again. Perhaps for the same reason, her father was quiet too.

THE FIRST ANNIVERSARY PARTY was an older couple who asked to be seated at the bar. She'd seen these two in here a million times. They were retired lawyers named John and Mary Sands. *Treat them special*, her father had told her. *Give them free stuff.* Julia went along with it, but it was never a practice that she completely understood. These people were probably the richest year-round residents of Bear Jaw, and no customer besides Brandon Peralta ever got more things for free. Her father was already making them a pair of gin martinis that Julia knew they wouldn't be charged for.

"Would you like a table tonight?" she asked them. They never did, because in Julia's lifetime, they never ordered food, just cocktails, but it was an anniversary reservation, so it seemed appropriate to ask.

"Just here to have a drink," Mary Sands replied.

"In case you get hungry, I should let you know that the prime rib platters are going fast."

"Those are memorable." Mary smiled. "But we don't eat like that anymore."

She wanted to ask why. It was probably health related, not that Julia had the time for such a conversation. "Please let me know when you need another round, then," Julia said.

EVERY TABLE IN THE original dining room was now taken, except for the reserved eight-top in the center of the floor, and for some reason Julia kept banging her hip into the chairs as she passed them. She'd always come home from this job with bruises and cuts. It was depressing compared with the calm ease that Felix and her father possessed, or folks like Big Al and Cayla back when she was a little kid. The way her father moved behind the bar was like watching the shadow of a cloud move across a meadow. Julia wondered what she'd have to do to inhabit such natural joy in this building.

Of course her parents wanted her to inherit this place; they'd molded this old restaurant into an expression of their own taste, and a place that accentuated their own interests and skills. It had seemed easy for them, which must've been why Ned assumed it would be easy for Julia. *Just make it your own*, her father always insisted.

"Make it my own?" she had replied a few years ago. "I'd tear the place down and plant a bunch of trees."

Ned laughed in response.

"You think I'm joking," she'd told him. "I'm not."

. . .

WHILE WAITING AT THE service side of the bar, Julia's left elbow knocked over a stack of promotional coasters for N. W. Gratz Artisanal Bitters. As she bent to clean them up, Grubbs appeared, to pick up drinks for a table in her section. Grubbs now worked only in the larger dining room—the windowless one they rented out for wedding receptions sometimes—while Julia worked only in the original room. There was still just one bar, though, and often enough they were here at the same time, forced into an awkward diplomacy.

"Hey," Grubbs said. She was still glowing with the immunity of the popular, even months after graduation. "When ya leaving?"

"Next Friday," Julia said.

"Wow," Grubbs said, taking her tray. "Well, good luck."

"Thanks," Julia mumbled, and tried to find the peaceful place in her mind, the snowfall, the hush, the birds.

BY SEVEN O'CLOCK, the supper club was in the hot, frantic throes of a summertime Saturday night. People were standing two deep at the bar, and not complaining about the wait, but talking to old friends and strangers. That eight-top in the center of the dining room was finally occupied, with Felix's famous hockey player son, Brandon, and his family and friends. Brandon had been playing for the Cleveland Monsters minor league team, and was about to report to preseason for the Columbus Blue Jackets of the NHL, hoping to make the roster. He was a famously nice and generous guy, the kind of person you wanted to see succeed.

Even so, Julia was far more impressed with Brandon's sister, Sonia, who'd earned a full ride from Illinois, had been a Fulbright Scholar in the Canary Islands, and had just finished a master's program in library science.

"You want to work somewhere quiet, how about a library," Ned had told Julia when they heard the news. "Sonia's doing it."

"Hey, Julia," said Brandon. "Tell my dad to get out of the kitchen and come out and celebrate my birthday."

That was like Felix. He was probably the best chef in the entire area code, and didn't trust anyone else to make a better birthday dinner for his son.

"This way, nobody in my family has to wash the dishes," Felix told Julia as he removed his apron, and left the kitchen to join them.

FIVE MINUTES LATER, the last anniversary couple appeared, and waited at the bar while a window seat was cleared. She'd known them for years too. Park Man-hee, who'd been raised with the name Kyle Kowalsky, was here with his husband, Liam. They often came to visit Park's mom, Brenda, and always had dinner and drinks at the Lakeside.

"Hey, my dad's kinda slammed. I can take your order," she told them. "The usual?"

"Yeah, a whiskey neat," Park said. "Sugarbush, if you have it."

"We do," Julia replied. "What about you, Liam? We have Bear Face." That was the hot new brewery, down the road.

With his tattoos, paunch, Dillinger Four T-shirt, and beard, she'd have ordered him a craft beer if he were a stranger. "Yeah, I'll take the Duaine's Choice IPA, thanks."

While she poured the beer, Julia saw her grandma and Brenda, who was her grandma's new home health care aide, push open the door. She yelled out a hello to them.

"Oh, hey, Julia," said Brenda, walking arm in arm with Florence. Florence was angry about this arrangement at first and complained to anyone who would listen, but now she complained on days when Brenda couldn't make it or had to live her own life. Florence wouldn't have ever said it, but she loved Brenda more than most family members, and Brenda enjoyed and knew how to handle Florence, especially in public. No local business slacked off when it saw these two lurching toward the door. They were twice as scary as Yelp and their reviews spread ten times as fast.

"Can you walk your grandma to a table?" Brenda asked. "I've had to pee for an hour."

"I don't need anyone walking me," Florence said, watching Brenda run ahead, before turning to Julia. "It's just nice when someone does it, is all."

Julia took Florence's arm. "How are you doing, Grandma?"

Florence stopped walking, and stood as still as an oak tree, her new eyeglasses picking up the reflection of the Hamm's beer sign behind the bar. "How are *you* doing is what's more important. You're about to leave home, probably for good, I hope."

"I don't know," Julia said. Florence had worked here, too, long ago, and Julia didn't want to be seen as rejecting this place, in case Florence viewed it as rejecting her and her legacy too. But at the time, it was also an honest answer.

"You worried about disappointing your mom?" Florence looked like she was about to laugh. "Stay here and take over this place, that would do it. You want to fulfill your mom's dream for you? Get out of here."

Across the road, over the lake, the sun was washing away in a soup of pink, yellow, orange, and violet. It was so beautiful here in the summer, when she had the time to notice it. "That's news to me. I've only ever heard the opposite."

"When did she ever say that? I don't recall it," Florence replied, and smiled. "This place is in your blood, but not your heart. Go find a place that is."

AS MUCH AS SHE'D looked forward to leaving for Kenyon, Julia had long feared the drive across the Midwest alone with her dad. It had been just the two of them for so long, and now that their life together was almost over, neither could really talk about it. Julia tried to distract them both by alternating who chose the music. Ned liked Dessa's cover of Bruce Springsteen. She liked a song by Paul Simon where he said that lying in bed and thinking of things that might have been was a person having a bad day. And when they crossed into a new state, they tried to see who could name more famous people from that state, and then she would tell him about the state's trees and birds. But in the pauses between songs and the beats between names, she wondered if she was truly breaking both her parents' hearts, and if all that lay ahead would be worth it.

HER DAD HELPED MOVE her things into her dorm room, which took both a long time and not long enough. When Ned said goodbye that evening, out in the parking lot, he seemed tired, and only told Julia the expected "I love you" and "I'll miss you" and "please call," as if he lacked the strength to say any more.

He waved one more time as he backed out of the parking spot. Then, a moment later, Julia was standing on the sidewalk alone.

"Hey," a fellow student said. "It's all right."

"Thanks," Julia said, wiping her face.

"I'm Angelica. And that was me yesterday."

"Hi, Angelica," Julia said. "So what's going on tonight?"

JULIA ADORED KENYON. She loved living in the all-women dorm nicknamed the Norton Nunnery, and quickly became close friends with Angelica Hsu and others there, including her roommate, Erin Grazioso. Erin was brainy, quiet, and considerate, although she seemed unduly agitated upon learning that Julia had never seen *Star Wars.* Any of them.

"This aggression will not stand," Erin said. "I already know what order you'll see them in. *Four, Five, Two, Three, Six.*"

This was both confusing and daunting, but it seemed important to understand a new friend's enthusiasm, even if she didn't share it. "All right," Julia replied. "I'd also like to spend some time outside. I'd like to go back to the BFEC. That place is one of the reasons I wanted to come here."

"Me too," Erin said. "But first, *A New Hope.*"

THE EXPERIENCE OF BEING a college student at Kenyon was even better than she'd imagined. She loved a program called Outdoors Pre-O, where she explored an unfamiliar wilderness with more new friends. And almost every weekend until it snowed, she biked the Gap Trail. The strong trees and early chill reminded her of Minnesota. As her grandmother would have put it, it was her church away from church.

THOSE EARLY MONTHS, she thought often about what her grandmother said, about her mother wanting her to find her own path. Now that she was on it, Julia wondered if this is where she'd finally sense her mother. Even on the quietest mornings in the woods, she couldn't hear her. But maybe that was all too much to ask. She now had favorite places that no member of her family had ever laid eyes upon. They were hers and hers alone, and it felt lonely and real and wonderful.

Campus was equally awesome. Between her dorm and her biology classes, she found her people. Julia actually looked forward to going to parties. She lost her virginity on a rug her dad had bought at Target. Her best friends, Angelica and Erin, were from Tucson and Los Angeles, places she'd never been and couldn't imagine. She'd learned that Angelica was conceived via IVF, just like she was, a piece of knowledge that mattered to Julia, because this was the first fellow IVF baby she'd ever knowingly met.

Angelica and Erin each had goals. They were already planning on grad school, while Julia couldn't envision life after college. Sometimes she'd wake up before dawn on a cold morning and pace back and forth on Middle Path, listening to birds and watching lights come on as she tried not to think about the future. When she did, she'd hope that maybe she could have it both ways, whatever that looked like, and somehow, everybody would be happy.

WHEN THE FUTURE ARRIVED, Julia couldn't have it both ways. She inherited the supper club the final week of her junior year, and when she returned to Bear Jaw for the summer a few days later, she immediately put it up for sale.

Her father had known her plans for years, but she was still afraid of how he would take the news. She waited until she had interested buyers.

"I got an offer above asking, from a woman in the Cities. She's some kind of big deal chef down there."

Her dad had the same resigned expression as he did when the Twins pulled their starter in the first inning. "Well, I suppose that's good," he said.

"Just wanted you to know. And I told her about you, and she even said that you could stay on as the bar manager, if you want."

"Well, it's been losing money," he said, and exhaled. "And it's a different place now, since Felix retired." His tone was kind, but devoid of joy. It seemed like he'd made his peace with Julia's decision but wished he hadn't.

FELIX'S LEAVING HAD BEEN hard on them. But Brandon Peralta was doing well in the NHL, and he'd been eager to make his parents' lives easier as a show of gratitude. It was nice to see, but it also pulled the guts out of the Lakeside, just as much as when

Big Al passed away. At least back then, there was a chef like Felix ready to take charge. Julia didn't have to work in the kitchen to know that Felix was worth a hundred young aspiring chefs today.

The most eager, intelligent, and qualified person her father had interviewed was a kid who'd name-dropped a lot of famous chefs and restaurants as influences. He was full of ideas, which was too bad. Like many young cooks who watch too much TV, he had more opinions than knowledge. He even had an ethos about how food should be plated. Her father would've been more impressed with an ethos about how to manage time or prevent food waste. Ned didn't have the patience to train someone who'd leave for someplace newer and hotter. Now, at least, no one had to worry about that.

"But I thought I'd offer the place to Felix first, before I accept an offer from anyone else," Julia said.

"He'll say no." Ned smiled. "But you can try."

HER DAD WAS RIGHT. Felix laughed and said, "The American dream isn't to own a business. The American dream is to go fishing." And that's what he did.

"Myself, I want to take a summer vacation," her dad told her. "A long one."

"Then what?" Julia asked.

"I might get a bartending job somewhere." Maybe she was projecting, but he seemed okay. "I know one place where I'd love to work, but they don't have a bar."

Every successful restaurant in the area that wasn't fast food had a bar. "Who owns it?"

"You'll never guess. Someone who quit eating restaurant food."

EARLIER THAT SPRING, Mary Sands reclaimed the closed-down Jorby's building in Bear Jaw and set up a new restaurant that served locally sourced Native cuisine, inspired by the work and recipes of an Oglala Lakota chef named Sean Sherman. Mary hired Madeline Roy, the forager and former Lakeside vendor, and Madeline's sisters, Summer and Amelia, to run it, and by that June, Three Sisters, the newest restaurant in Bear Jaw, had become a destination in itself.

When Julia was back from Kenyon for spring break, Ned booked a table, just the two of them. The food was all local, all fresh, all seasonal. Wild greens pesto. Braised rabbit. Ingredients like tamarack, sumac, and hopniss. Some of it Julia had known from her foraging trips with Madeline years ago, and some of it she'd learned from her mom's cookbooks.

The meals were like nothing she'd ever eaten, even from her mother. It wasn't even just a credit to Madeline's talent, or Mary's vision. It was perfectly chosen ingredients, in the hands of people who knew what to do with them.

Julia wondered if she could end the meal with a guilty pleasure, but didn't see what she expected to find on the menu. When Madeline came by to say hello, Julia had to ask. "No fry bread?"

Madeline shook her head. "You want something better, try the blue corn cakes. Or if it's dessert you want, the maple sorbet."

After they finished, Julia watched her father look around at the gutted Jorby's they were sitting in. Certain things, like the rotating pie display case, had been repurposed, but most of it, from the ugly color scheme to the vinyl-coated booths, was gone. The ceiling was ripped apart and the ugly wallpaper had been painted over with murals. Oddly, the sign outside that read JORBY'S had yet to be changed.

"What do you think?" Julia asked, watching her dad's eyes.

He looked around thoughtfully, and she wondered if any part of him was upset or discombobulated, but it didn't seem like it. He had the same expression he always had when a large, satisfying meal was over. "I think it's great," her father said.

She looked around the place herself now. "I don't know, this decor is the only part of this experience I don't like." ·

"Mary Sands told me it was the only vacant restaurant space available. I guess it's just until they build their dream location. Whenever that's going to be."

"Did she tell you what that looked like?"

"You should ask her yourself," her dad said.

MARY AND JULIA MET the next day. It was an early Tuesday afternoon, and it was just the two of them at the quiet Lakeside bar.

"You know who gave me the idea I could open a restaurant?" Mary asked. "Your mom."

"That's nice to hear," Julia said. "I'm glad she inspired somebody to go into the business."

"I have to say thanks for reaching out to me. I wouldn't have thought to ask you. I heard you were going to sell this place to some hipster from Minneapolis."

There was indeed that generous offer from a chef named Eva, and it seemed like she had her heart in the right place, but she had no connection to this area. "I'm glad it's going to a local," Julia said.

"Well, are you worried about getting grief from people for closing a supper club? They're not making more of these places, you know."

"There's still quite a few around," Julia said. "I hope that people appreciate them."

Mary touched the scratch on the bar that had been there longer than Julia had been alive. "You know, my grandpa might have helped build this room."

"That's cool," Julia said, and looked around the place she'd just agreed to sell, the photos and taxidermy on the walls, briefly wondering how it'd all be changed, and not minding either way. It was time for this chapter in the building's life to end. That's all it was.

"That reminds me, there's one more thing," Julia added, picking up an ornate crystal bottle from behind the bar. "If you decide to serve alcohol, my mom loved this gin. It's distilled locally, from local ingredients."

"Sure. Just get me the contact info for that vendor."

"Absolutely," said Julia, and retrieved her mother's red address book from behind the bar. "Here, you can have it."

"Written in her handwriting," Mary marveled, leafing through its pages.

Julia had never thought about it before. Numbers were on the computer, but people were always longhand. That was her mom. "Keep it as long as you need."

"I loved your mother, you know. I hope she wouldn't be mad about all of this."

"Are you kidding? Your idea is pretty much her dream restaurant, and she could never have it. Now she gets to be a part of it."

WALKING INTO THREE SISTERS on the day it opened in the new location, Julia was somehow certain that she'd feel her mother's presence, so much that she'd nearly been afraid to enter. But the former Lakeside building was so heavily refurbished it felt like a different place, in a different time. The enthusiasm and skill of the new owner and chefs had made the building aglow with success again, and Julia was proud that her family had helped enable that in some way. Mary Sands and Madeline Roy made a toast to Julia, and she knew it wasn't just because she'd sold them a building. They knew what this place had meant. "Before you, two women in your family gave their lives to this place," Mary said. "We're going to honor them."

SHORTLY AFTER JULIA ARRIVED, Mary gave her back the red address book, saying that she'd copied the info inside, and Julia should have this piece of her mom.

It didn't hit Julia immediately how thoughtful this simple gesture was. At the time, it just underscored her mother's absence. As Julia looked into the eyes of her mother's friends while holding her valued red address book, Mariel Prager was somehow nowhere to be felt. Her mom had spent decades beneath this roof, but in all the ways that mattered, she was not here anymore.

When only a few people remained, Madeline took Julia aside and asked if she was looking for work.

"I don't think I can work here," Julia said.

"I understand, but this is about something else," Madeline said. "I know someone at the Minnesota State Forest Nursery, over in Akeley, and they might have an opening soon. I'd be happy to put in a word."

For Julia, it would be a dream job. "Thank you," she told Madeline.

HER FATHER ARRIVED LATE. As Julia watched Ned Prager within an unrecognizable version of a place where he'd met his wife, filled with their friends and family, her heart went out to him. He must've found it wildly surreal for any number of reasons.

"Did you take tonight off?" Julia asked him. He'd taken a job as a bartender down at Crappie's, and he loved it, as much as locals complained that the place wasn't as shitty and cheap as it used to be. He didn't mind, because he had no stake in it; for the first time in his life, he was just a man working a job. He wore his work shirt that read I GOT CRAP-FACED AT CRAPPIE'S even when he wasn't there.

"No, I'm going back in a few," Ned said, looking around. Surprisingly, he seemed relieved. "This is real neat, what they did."

Besides the owners, the last people to leave that night were Julia, Brenda, and Florence. Her grandmother asked Julia to escort her out the doors for the last time.

"She's not here," Julia told her grandma.

"Of course she's not," Florence said. "You need to know that it was you, not this place, that changed her. Your mom became the person she was because of you."

JULIA WAS SURPRISED SHE didn't feel her mom's presence at graduation, alone on the stage, or afterward with her father, grandmother, and Brenda. She didn't sense her mother when she found her mementos while packing, or when Julia needed comfort after she hugged her best friends goodbye. They both knew exactly what was next for them, and Julia didn't yet. Angelica and Erin were headed for their grad schools on the coasts, and Julia was just going back to Minnesota, of all places, with no particular goal or direction she could name.

SHE'D USED PART OF the proceeds from the restaurant sale to pay off her college loans, and most of the rest bought her a cabin in the woods near Grand Marais, north and east of Bear Jaw, a few miles from Lake Superior, on the edge of another country. She did some volunteer work for the county soil and water department, and for money she took a job at a restaurant in town. Her father was surprised, but she explained that most jobs were noisy, and she was used to this kind of noise.

The restaurant wage would've been impossible to live on with both college debt and house payments, and she was grateful every day for the freedom her family had given her. Her friends from college reminded her often how lucky she was that she had a legacy to cash out just so she could have normal problems and not existential ones.

.   .   .

A WEEK AFTER SHE moved into her cabin, a kind neighbor gave her a black Lab pup she named Wally. As the days cooled and shortened, Julia and Wally walked the forests within and around her property, and as the snow fell, made pairs of tracks into and out of the woods in a hundred different patterns. She tried to forget the guilt she felt that generations of her family's toil and dreams were now exchanged for this peace. She still didn't know what she was going to do with her life. All she knew was that this is where she wanted to start.

ONE COLD EVENING, while out alone, she admired the snow piled on the tall trees and watched the birds flicker on bare branches, and wondered if there was anywhere else she'd rather be. Then, suddenly, there she was. Her mother was all around her, in the snow, in the air, in the sky, in the silence.

I was looking for you, Julia whispered.

I was waiting, her mom whispered back. Right here.

Julia stood alone in the embrace, and felt the chill and quiet of an old and present home. A cardinal swapped his swish of color between gray trees. Pale cedar smoke climbed from a chimney to soothe the sky. Wally began to bark, and at last, she walked back to the house, through fresh snow, to make their supper.

Acknowledgments

This book would not exist without these people: Brooke Delaney, Pamela Dorman, George Ducker, Ryan Harbage, Lou Mathews, Jeramie Orton, and Jeffrey Stradal.

Immense gratitude is due these dear fellow writers, for their substantial patience and peerless input: Christi Clancy, Beth Dooley, Seth Fischer, Spencer Foxworth, Christopher Hermelin, Meg Howrey, Julia Ingalls, Sarah LaBrie, Sarah Langan, Daniel J. Safarik, Chris L. Terry, and Sarah Tomlinson. You knew what I needed, when I needed it.

A heaping platter of thanks to these hospitality industry professionals and veterans, including the current and former supper club owners and employees, who patiently tolerated my questions before and during a pandemic: Patricia Clark of Patricia Clark Catering, Miami Beach, Florida; Debbie Daanen, formerly of the Out-O-Town

Supper Club, Kaukauna, Wisconsin; Hugh Higgins of Hearth Restaurant, Peoria Heights, Illinois; Connie Karstens of the Lamb Shoppe & Wellness Center, Hutchinson, Minnesota; Rebecca Maier-Frey and Monte Maier of the Dorf Haus, Roxbury, Wisconsin; Mike Rowan and Patrick Rowan, formerly of the Steamboat Inn, Prescott, Wisconsin; Sean Sherman of NĀTIFS, Indigenous Food Lab, and Owamni, Minneapolis, Minnesota; Amy Jo Wieland, former owner of the Bungalow, Emily, Minnesota; and the inimitable JD Fratzke, who needs to write a book himself. Special thanks as well to Jill Hannah Anderson; Mary Bergin, author of the essential *Wisconsin Supper Club Cookbook*; Anne Bramley; Joan Collins of Joan Collins Publicity; and Tracy Opper of Baileys Harbor Library, Baileys Harbor, Wisconsin, who took the time to help facilitate some of these conversations. I'm also extra grateful for bookseller and cocktail maven Nick Petrulakis, who concocted the Betty's Lemonade recipe especially for Betty.

Thank you so much to these brewing industry professionals, whose generosity and support of *The Lager Queen of Minnesota* kept me going as I wrote this book: Scott Johnson and Murphy Johnson of Black-Stack Brewing, St. Paul, Minnesota; Natalie and Vinnie Cilurzo of Russian River Brewing Company, Santa Rosa, California; Deb Loch and Jill Pavlak at Urban Growler Brewing Company, St. Paul, Minnesota; Hollie Slaton at 3 Floyds Brewing, Munster, Indiana; the entire team at Over Town Brewing Company, Monrovia, California; and Duaine Annis-Bercier, who worked with Scott and Murph at Black-Stack to make Blotz lager a reality—a fact that still blows my mind.

Immense thanks for these people and organizations, for their tangible and intangible support: 826LA; Gretchen Anthony; Mike and Malora Guerrero Azbill; Michael Barnard of Rakestraw Books, Danville, California; Angela Barton; Kirstin Bement; Tom Benton; Doris Biel; Ron Block; Summer Block; Jutta Bucher; Stefan Bucher;

Nickolas Butler; Ellen Byron; Crispin Ian Cain of American Craft Whiskey Distillery, Redwood Valley, California; Liz Camfiord; LeBria Casher; Meighan Cavanaugh; Steph Cha; Rebecca and Tim Chamberlain; Carlynn Chironna; Amy Comito; Tricia Conley; Mandy Cox; G. C. Cunningham; Susan Delaney; Andy Duncan; Tess Espinoza; Dr. Michelle Evans; Molly Fessenden; Linda McLoughlin Figel of {pages}: a bookstore, Manhattan Beach, California; Brendan and Gigi Fitzgerald; Susie Fleet; Brandon Foxworth; Ann Friedman; Joan Funk; Rico Gagliano; Kate Gibson; Jason Gobble; Daniel Goldin of Boswell Book Company, Milwaukee, Wisconsin; Chris Good; Kat Good; Nathan W. Gratz; Amelia Gray; Anthony Grazioso; Rich Green; Dennis Gurwell; Tim Hedges; Claire Heins and everyone at SELCO; Robin Herring; Mona Hester; Mary Holden; Karen Holman, Sophie Howlett; Peter Hsu; Carolyn Carr Hutton of Mrs. Dalloway's, Berkeley, California; Gretchen Irvine; Amy and Zach Jones; Jennifer Jubenville of the Bookstore at Fitger's, Duluth, Minnesota; Margot Kahn; Wendy Pearl Karanfilian; Amanda Karkoutly; Matt Kay; Tamar Kaye of Tamar Distillery, Redwood Valley, California; Anne-Marie and Abe Kinney; Pamela Klinger-Horn; Zach and Jody Rosen Knower; Amy and Jay Kovacs; Diana Kowalsky; Sarah Krammen; Sophie Krichevsky; Greg Kunstel; Dr. Melanie Landay; Lorna Landvik; Krista Langeland; Doug Latch; Corrina Lesser; Carole Lieber-Wilkins; Michael Loomis; Ron and Betty Lovejoy; Tim Mantel; Rebecca Marsh; Adam McBroom; Lisa McGivern; Ruth McKee; Dana Menard; Marie Michels; Anthony Miller; Mary Beth Nebel of I Know You Like a Book, Peoria Heights, Illinois; Patrick Nolan; Ken Nicholas; Tony and Ann Norgaard; Mary Webber O'Malley of Skylark Bookshop, Columbia, Missouri; Peggy Palmer; Erin Pinheiro; Taylor Pipes; Thurgood Powell; Mel Preczewski; Lindsay Prevette; Jason Ramirez; Kate Rattenborg of Dragonfly Books, Decorah, Iowa;

Alysyn Reinhardt and everyone at the Penguin Random House Speakers Bureau; Gregory Lee Renz; Brian and Sue Roegge of Chapter2 Books, Hudson, Wisconsin; Frances and Erick Roen; Skye Rohde; Kayleen Rohrer of InkLink Books, East Troy, Wisconsin; Leslie Ruch; Stuart Sandler; Kristen Sandstrom of Apostle Islands Booksellers, Bayfield, Wisconsin; Alex Sarrazin; Jeremy Schmidt; Pat Schultz; Andrea Schulz; Elina Shatkin; Deborah Simmons; Connie Simonson; Kris S; Jen Sincero; Pete and Ashley Slapnicher; Carter and Catherine Cavanaugh Smith; Jill and Aaron Solomon; Kerensa Spencer; Kate Stark; Travis and Jodi Steele; Eric J. Stolze; Roger Stradal; Jacob Strunk; Brian Tart; Mark and Sara Finnerty Turgeon; Alison Turner; Shannon Twomey; Brian K. Vaughan; Katie and Ryan Vincent; Amanda Weier; Gretchen West (of Valley Bookseller, Stillwater, Minnesota); Toni Wheeler of Mendocino Book Company, Ukiah, California; Stephen Witt; the Stradal, Johnson, and Biel families; the entire sales team at Penguin Random House; to my mom's wonderful Vegas crew, Jan Blace, Mary Johnson, and Mary Mikes; and to Abbey Luck and Peter Van Leeuwen, for the kind welcome and the excellent ice cream.

This book is dedicated to my son, Auden, who, after a long and difficult journey to conceive, was born to us shortly after I'd started the first draft. For most of his first year, I shared my office with him, and wrote much of this book while he napped beside me, my heart full and incredulous.

Words cannot express the depth of my gratitude for him, for my partner, Brooke, and my mother, Karen, whose light lives on and shines through my son every day. Thank you, family, for finding your way to me.

The Lager Queen of Minnesota

A Novel

A family is split when the father leaves an inheritance entirely to Helen, his younger daughter, while Edith, the older sister, struggles to make what most people would call a living. With the proceeds from their farm, Helen builds a highly successful brewery. But one day, she will find she needs some help, and she may have a potential savior close to home . . . if it's not too late.

"[A] charmer of a tale. . . . Warm, witty and—like any good craft beer—complex, the saga delivers a subtly feminist and wholly life-affirming message." —*People*

Kitchens of the Great Midwest

A Novel

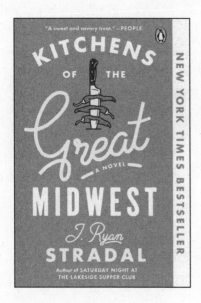

When his wife falls in love with a sommelier, Lars is left to raise their daughter on his own. He is determined to pass on his love of food to Eva, and she learns to find her salvation in the flavors of her native Minnesota as she becomes the star chef behind a legendary, secretive pop-up supper club. By turns quirky, hilarious, and sensory, this is an unexpected story about missed opportunities and joyful surprises.

"An impressive feat of narrative jujitsu . . . that keeps readers turning the pages too fast to realize just how ingenious they are."
—*The New York Times Book Review*, Editor's Pick